Maaijke

Maaijke

A NOVEL

Thomas J. Vander Salm

To

THE LATE MILDRED McCONKEY FROM KALAMAZOO

AND

JESSICA, JAMIE,

AND

ADDIE

Part I

CHAPTER 1

Maaijke

—— 1875 ——

I WILL BE DEAD IN A YEAR—IN 1876, AT THE AGE OF SIXTY-ONE. HOW DO I know? Perhaps this story will explain.

I was born in a Dutch farming village a mile east of Spakenburg in 1815, two years after Napoléon and the French were driven out and replaced by William VI of the House of Orange, thereafter known as King William I.

There were six of us: four brothers whom I adored, and my sister, Antje, who was nine years my elder. That my siblings and I were the offspring of hardworking Jacobus and Johanna De Jongh was evident from our appearance, but I stood out from them all, and not in a way that always pleased my parents. Antje and my brothers were all smart—maybe smarter than I—but even as a baby, I was far more independent, more stubborn, than any of them.

As I grew into a sturdy little girl, my interests were almost exclusively boys' interests, and in boys, with whom I played as an equal. I ran as fast as they did, jumped as far, and in occasional fights, sometimes came out on top. Had I been born into a later century, I would have been labeled a tomboy. I was happy and friendly, and had a mobile, expressive face on which were imprinted deep dimples and a nearly permanent smile; but I was often wistful, notwithstanding my smile. I had no reason to be unhappy; my parents and my brothers and sister all loved me. But something seemed to be missing. While I made friends easily, and almost everyone liked me, later in my life, I realized I never had a deep relationship with anyone. Eventually, I fixed that.

I also had an incredibly vivid imagination and harnessing that gift enabled me to travel to many places, varied both in location and time. For years, my travels were somewhat empty as I could not interact with anyone, these being solely adventures of the mind.

Eventually, that too changed.

CHAPTER 2

Peter

—— 1960 ——

A SHOT, THEN ANOTHER: NOT THE SHARP, FOCUSED CRACK OF A RIFLE but the diffuse, oppressive explosion from a shotgun. It was no surprise to Anna. It had been predicted by Rusty's solid point before the birds flushed and should have been no surprise to me; I had pulled the triggers of the Fox 20-gauge side-by-side. Still, it's always jarring to hear the twin, almost simultaneous detonations so close to my ear.

The day before, I'd stared northwest, along the eastern flank of the Wind River Range foothills, wishing I were up there, where I am today, in the high plains. It was the best time of the year. Fall had just arrived, but the warm days still felt as summer, with September coolness seeping into the nights. Fish were still plentiful, and bird hunting season had started. I thought of the sere landscape with birds lurking in the brush, of the nearly dry streambeds with others, still full and home to golden and cutthroat trout: I had escaped school, at least for the moment as I visualized tracking a grouse's flight. As I stood looking up into the mountains, I felt the motion of raising a gun to a flight path, felt the flow of my arm creating the rhythmic sinuosity of a fly line. As I watched dust devils corkscrew across the playground, Anna jarred me from my reverie, backing against me, twisting her head to look up at me. My arms naturally folded around her.

"Let's go up there," I said, pointing into the foothills. "Bring Rusty. Get a couple birds, maybe some fish, build a fire, you cook dinner."

She leaned harder against me, smiling. "You're crazy. School—remember school? Dad would kill us. And let go of me; I'm going back inside." She continued pushing back, making no attempt to move away. "And besides, what's this 'You cook dinner?' I'm your sister, not your chef."

"Kidding, Anna. I'll cook. How about tomorrow? Saturday? Pack in a lunch. Maybe dinner. Or we could even bring sleeping bags, stay out all night, and come back Sunday," I said, trying to convince her.

"Maybe, Peter…but it's a long ride up into the hills," she said, again twisting to look at me with a smile that said yes.

"No. I'm not talking about riding. We'll take the Ford."

"Sure you will. Dad won't let you take the truck. You're not old enough to drive. You won't be sixteen 'til next year."

"It's only dirt roads. We can do it. Bet you he'll let me."

Dad was a rancher. We lived a bit north of Lander, Wyoming, and very near the south border of the two-million-acre Wind River Reservation, home of the Shoshone and Arapaho. After you crossed the bumps of our cattle guard and drove through the gate WITH "Maasen Ranch" flanked by our brand burned into the large timber lintel above, you'd find the mile-long road to our house where my sister Anna and I lived with our mom and dad—Patsy and Bill—and of course, Rusty. I was the first born, in 1945, and growing up on the ranch, I was shy and timid about new challenges and experiences. Looking back, I guess it would have been fair to say I was skittish from birth. But I forced myself to do what frightened me, even though a lot did. I think my fear spurred me to accomplishment, perhaps because I was also stubborn. If one thought about it, there were dangers to ranch life for a small child. I thought about them excessively.

Up to the age of about five, the ranch machines, the cattle, and the horses entertained me; they were just larger versions of the toys I played with. When I was five—I remember it vividly—Dad sat me on a saddled horse and, holding the reins, led me around the paddock. I was so proud as the horse sedately walked me around, until I fell, sliding off the saddle, striking my head against the split rail of the enclosure. It was off to the small hospital in town, me screaming the entire time. I had no serious injury, but the gash in my head took fourteen stitches to close. To this day, I can still feel the scar beneath my hair.

After that, the huge animals (as cattle and horses seemed to me), the ranch equipment, large machines, and tractors—all frightened me. I compensated by forcing myself to overcome my fears, thereby also avoiding Dad's pointed, only partly good-natured criticism. He wasn't a bad dad, really, but he was uncompromising, and stern. He demanded; he rarely praised. At least, he rarely praised me, and the best I could hope for was the absence of criticism. It seemed that I didn't quite measure up to his standards. I kept trying; his acceptance was what I most wanted.

During those early years, Barnaby, my pet rabbit, followed me wherever I went. I sought solace with him, got advice from him, took him to bed with me. It surprised me that no one else could see him, but Mom at least acknowledged him, and talked to me about him. Barnaby helped a lot when Dad disparaged me. Barnaby was my best friend. Of course, as I got a bit older, I realized that he was imaginary, but that did nothing to diminish the comfort he gave me.

It wasn't his intention, I am sure, but Dad tended to tear down my self-confidence. Mom was the opposite. She had a knack of getting me to try new things by the way she asked. She usually began with, "I don't suppose you are big enough to…" She might then say, "put a new log on the fire," or "get up on that pony by yourself." And whatever it was, it merited a big hug and a smile whether I succeeded or not.

And then there was my great-grandfather, Pieter, with whom Dad compared me, always demeaning me. I grew up with a mixed reverence for my great-grandfather, who had settled in this area in 1871, and at the same time, resentment of my father when he kept comparing me to great-grandpa. So many times, Dad's sentences began with, "If only you had some of Pieter's (fill in the noun of choice—always some indispensable trait necessary for rugged living)." Pieter must have been suited to the rigors of life in Wyoming Territory, almost twenty years before it became a state. I never knew him; Dad did. According to Dad, Pieter bought the ranch for almost nothing and built it up with hard work, frugal saving, and buying out distressed neighbor ranches. Dad said his grandfather Pieter knew Sacagawea, who is buried just north of the ranch on the reservation. I saw her gravestone with a date of 1884. I also found notations from Lewis and Clark journals that she died in 1812, so the whole story may be phony. Anyway, that's what Dad tells me. If I were to believe him as I grew, his grandfather, my great-grandfather Pieter, nearly invented ranching, barbed-wire fences, and maybe even cattle and horses. Of course, I *didn't* completely believe him, even when I was young. I eventually came to believe that despite the tall tales and hurtful comparisons, Pieter probably was a pretty special person, as must have been all those early settlers who prospered in this primitive country.

I subliminally knew that Great-Grandfather Pieter wasn't born here, but in the Netherlands. When extolling Pieter and simultaneously demeaning me, Dad often appended, "…and not only that, but he had to learn English, too." I was and could not think that I was anything other than American, so when I was young, I had little interest in the origins of my family. I was vaguely aware from hearing Mom and Dad talk that Pieter came to America a century earlier and settled first in Michigan before moving to Wyoming, where he transformed himself into a cowboy and rancher.

Although my parents never allowed ranch work to interfere with or prevent us from going to school, ranch chores were continuous and varied by the season, and Dad worked us hard. From the time Anna and I were in first grade, we lived by the chores, first tagging along with the ranch hands and Dad, and later, doing more and heavier work: riding fence and making repairs, delivering hay bales to the cattle in winter, mending more fence, assisting with the calving and with the vaccinations and branding in spring. In the summer, we sprayed weeds, maintained and repaired irrigation, moved cattle from field to field to prevent overgrazing, and later, cut and baled hay; and in the fall, there was more haying and preventive maintenance on the ranch machines. It was all dirty. The wind blew almost continually, and the kicked-up dust coated us, infiltrated us. The weave of our clothing became clogged with dirt so that by the end of work each day, our shirts were almost windproofed. Each night, Mom had to wash everything we wore. The wash water effluent was grey. When in the fields, our teeth became gritty. We spit grey. It must have been healthy dirt; we were never sick.

As a teen, it didn't take long for me to hate barbed wire. Wild game would stretch or break the wire. They pulled out the staples from the posts. And we had to repair it. My hands looked like I had been in a knife fight. Even the leather gloves we wore were of little help. I carried a bag of staples, a claw hammer, and some smooth wire to make splices when the barbed wire was broken. I became a splicing pro. Make a twisted loop in the broken end of the barbed wire, then make another through it with the smooth wire, then another loop in the other end of the break. Then, bring the free end of the smooth wire through the final loop in the second side of the break, twist the wire on the hammer and engage the standing end with the claw and push the handle away from the last loop, thereby tightening the smooth wire before twisting it on itself. That's how I got tight repairs. And that is how I kept cutting my hands. Where the barbed wire had pulled the staples out, I could often find the old staples and reuse them, or just grab a few from my bag of replacements. Stapling I liked better than splicing. So did my hands.

It was a hard life on which we thrived. At early ages, Anna and I were given not only responsibility but independence. Dad taught us to hunt and fish. I shot my first gun, a .22 rifle, when I was six, and was able to cast a fly rod by my eighth birthday. Anna and I were both more at home outside than inside our home. For me, especially, hunting and shooting were among the few accomplishments that I grew naturally to love, at least in part because I was pretty good at them.

Anything I did that hinted of independence pleased Dad, so it took only the briefest of arm-twisting to persuade him to let me take the truck. On Saturday, before sunrise, we loaded up the old Ford, threw in a box of 20-gauge shells and the old side-by-side, a fly rod and flies, a ground blanket and two sleeping bags, plus food. Rusty jumped in to squeeze behind the seats.

"Peter, your friends make fun of you hunting with Rusty. They all say pointers or English setters are better and Irish setters are dumb," Anna said.

"Yeah, but that's only 'til they hunt over Rusty. Then they want one like her."

At the end of the mile-long ranch driveway, I turned west, away from the main road. As we drove, the fences and gates disappeared. The rutted dirt road threw up a dust vortex behind the pickup. Ahead, the center of the road gradually yielded to grass. With the tires following the two tracks, the bridging yellow prairie grasses grew higher and scraped the truck belly, releasing from their seed heads a sweet-pungent smell that overtook us when we stopped. Beyond the mountain brook, even the tire tracks disappeared. We parked the pickup on a ballroom-flat floor of dry, yellowed mountain grasses. In the breeze, waves coursed through them, creating a mesmerizing ocean of ochre.

By ten that morning, we were walking the grassy plain, as Rusty ranged a hundred yards ahead, following hand signals and quartering before us across our path. As if grabbed by a lariat, she skidded into a classic point, tail flagging, her neck contorted almost behind her as the scent grabbed her nose. We walked forward with tense anticipation, knowing the dog never to be wrong. Following her nose, we flushed a covey of chukar from the side. The sudden thunderous wing *thrrrr* was all the more startling because it was expected. The morning sun caromed off their tawny backs, the black wing strips a blur of gray. Instinctively, I shot, getting one bird but missing the second. Rusty had the downed bird retrieved in seconds.

"Ha, smarty! I thought you never missed," said Anna.

"Ha, yourself. Bet I don't miss again."

I didn't. After a ruffed grouse, a blue grouse and another chukar fell, succumbing first to the #7 shot and then to Rusty's soft mouth. I gave the gun over to Anna after lunch, and she got three birds, missing two.

As the sun grew large and molten red in the west, I cut wild asparagus from the stream bank while Anna dug up a few wild onion plants. She diced the lower stems and bulbs, and in an old cast iron pan of Mom's, sautéed them in butter over our small fire.

We dressed two grouse and drew the other birds for Mom to cook later.

Anna dripped the butter and onions on the plucked and drawn birds, adding salt and pepper, roasting them on wet sticks over the open campfire as if they were marshmallows. In the onion pan, Anna added more butter and sautéed the asparagus. Tender, moist, and delicately flavored, the birds were quickly gone, along with the asparagus and onions. Only a small bit of meat was left, which Rusty devoured, then crunched as she ate the bones. As it does in the mountains, dark fell quickly, as if suddenly switched on.

"How come," Anna asked, "people say grouse and chicken bones are bad for dogs?"

"Dad says that's silly. Have you ever seen a coyote or wolf die from eating a grouse? Dogs don't either," I said.

"I don't believe you. First, how would you know what killed a dead coyote? And second, coyotes and wolves don't eat cooked birds. Doesn't cooking make the bones more brittle or something? You're not always right. Dad either."

"Maybe. But maybe not. Never hurt Rusty, did it?"

Anna, with a wincing look, said, "maybe not yet…"

I brewed what Mom called cowboy coffee: loose coffee brought to a boil several times over the fire.

With the sun disappearing, the temperature dropped quickly and we retreated to our sleeping bags. After a minute of silence, Anna said, "I wish I could shoot birds as well as you do. You're a really good wing shot."

"I didn't used to be. I practice a lot. That's what Great-Grandpa did," I said rolling my eyes.

"Yeah, I know. If I had a dime for every time Dad said that, I'd be rich. *So* tiring."

"And for my sister, you're not too bad a shot, either."

Even in the dark, I sensed her face flushing at the compliment she had sought. "So, next year it's high school," she said. "What's after that?"

"Promise not to laugh? I want to go to the Naval Academy."

"Really? A cowboy in the Navy? Isn't Annapolis hard to get in to?" she said, scrunching her face and eyes as she tried to picture me in such a foreign setting.

"Yeah. I'm worried; they seem to like jocks, especially football players, and the state has only three slots. But Senator Crowell hunts with Dad. Maybe he'll recommend me. I think Willis, Willis Hollister, might want to go. It'd kill me if he got accepted over me."

"That's stupid, Peter. You're a ton smarter."

"Yeah, but he's a football player. I hate football."

"You hate him, don't you?" she said.

"Not exactly. He's sort of a bully. Good night, Anna," I said, with a finality meant to end the discussion.

"But you used to play football after school with him and your other friends, before he was old enough to join the football team. Right?"

"Yeah. I liked playing it then, even when I was always the last one to be chosen when we divided up into teams. Probably because I wasn't all that good. Plus, I was one of the smaller kids. And Willis, if he was on the other team, always chose to knock me over. Never anyone else. Only me. So no, he wasn't my best friend."

She was silent for a minute or two, lulling me into relief that we could now sleep. But she used the quiet to segue into another topic.

"Peter, do you think it was like this the night Mom and Dad met?"

"You don't know what 'good night' means? Probably, except it was raining that night, they say."

"Do you think they really fought over who shot that grouse?"

"I guess. Why would they make it up, Anna?"

"Well, I just can't imagine hunting a hundred feet from each other, separated by a hedge row and not even knowing the other was there. Until both shot at the same bird, and each claimed it."

"If it did happen, I bet it was Mom who got the bird," I said, smiling as I imagined the scenario.

"And do you believe that when it started to rain, Dad just *happened* to have a ground cloth and bed roll on his saddle, and he just *happened* to have a tarpaulin there too? And that he built a lean-to they had to spend the night in because it rained so hard? And when they got up in the morning, they were in love? And they managed to cook the grouse in the rain?"

"Well, maybe, miss Anna smarty pants. You know they got married two months later and that I was born seven months after that. So, something might have happened that night."

"Peter, shut up. Mom and Dad would never have done that before they were married."

"Sure. OK, Anna. Time for bed."

"Peter, how come you don't have a girlfriend?"

"Anna, go to sleep."

"No, really. Why not? You're not that ugly. You've gotten to be taller. Not the shrimp you were a couple years ago. Not that skinny anymore. More sort of cowboy lanky. Girls probably like your curly hair. Blue eyes. I wouldn't mind being your girlfriend if you weren't my brother."

"Dunno. Go to sleep."

"What about Katy Paulsen?"

"What about her?"

"I thought you liked her."

"Anna, shut up and go to sleep."

"But I know she liked you."

"Stop, Anna. First, I never know what to say to her, and second, she's Willis's girlfriend. So just stop."

"I thought he was your friend once."

"Guess not. Not anymore. Stop talking and go to sleep."

"Night, Peter."

CHAPTER 3

Maaijke

— 1820 —

WITH MY SISTER ANTJE SO MUCH OLDER—NINE YEARS WAS AN ETERNITY when I was five—while we were together, it was more like she was taking care of me, rather than being my friend. But I loved being with her. She was more an example for me than anyone else. Maybe it was our age separation that kept her from being a confidante and close friend.

It was different with all my brothers; they were closer to my age, so they mostly treated me as just one more child. They were older—not as old as Antje—so they sometimes tried to bully me. Then, I pushed back against them and instead did what I wanted. Eventually, they gave up trying to control me and welcomed me in their games, during which they mostly did not treat me as a little sister but more like one of them, another brother. When they teased me too much, I retaliated by making up taunting, ridiculing poems. But when they all attacked me, I cried, or became very angry and red faced, and ran home, sulking. I always returned to them because I had more fun being with them than I did indoors.

Where I was most different from any of my family was my insatiable curiosity, and imagination. It was this latter trait more than any other that set me apart. That, and a very early fascination with sex, which I thought separated me from all my family. Looking back on it, I'm not so sure such a fascination was all that unusual.

CHAPTER 4

Peter

—— 1960 ——

AT DAWN, WE WALKED SOFTLY DOWN THE STREAM BANK UNTIL WE CAME to a small pool, the water surface glassy black and limpid. I stood on Anna's left, away from her casting arm, and watched the poetic geometry of the fly line as she cast the #16 Adams onto the pool, where it blemished the surface with a little dimple as the gray-and-brown fly drifted with the current. *Nothing.* She cast again and then on the third cast, ringlets suddenly appeared around the fly. She waited a couple minutes, then cast again, and at the first sign of disturbance near the fly, she lifted the rod tip, and the brief fight was on as the small cutthroat trout came to the bank. She caught three more: lovely, graceful fish all. These Snake River cutthroats had less of the red color than some other subspecies, and more and smaller spots. The only red was a faint tinge on the back end of the gill cover, which made the red for which the fish was named more startling. That brilliant red slice of color on the bottom of the jaw on each side looked like the little fish had been injured and was bleeding.

We gutted the fish and then slowly fried them in butter over the open fire in the still-chilly, crisp air, along with more fresh wild asparagus from the stream bank. When they had a thin, amber crust on both sides, Anna filleted three of the fish, which we shared. Rusty ate the entire fourth trout, plus the heads and tails of the other three. Rusty was far more the glutton than the gourmet: a whole trout spent two seconds in her mouth.

We drove back home, where Mom cooked the rest of the birds for dinner.

I grew quickly in that, my eighth-grade year. The following year, I grew up.

CHAPTER 5

Maaijke

— 1820 —

LATE DURING THE SUMMER WHEN I WAS FIVE, I HEARD, NOT FOR THE FIRST time, my mother screaming in my parents' second-floor bedroom after lunch. Worried for her, I went up the stairs, but their bedroom door was locked. So, I climbed the beech tree beneath their window. I was at home there; "monkey," my brothers often called me. The leaves were only beginning to lose their somber green in favor of the rich coppery color of fall, but they were thick enough that the view I had was stuttering as the breeze pushed leaves in and out of my vision, creating the type of animated view I would later see when thumbing through the pages of flip books. Through the open window, I saw my mother held down by my father, who appeared to be battering her. She was screaming and tears were running down her face, but she had the most intensely happy visage I had ever seen. After a bit, they traded places and my mother, sitting, bounced up and down on my father until, with a choked-off scream, she stopped and fell down on top of him. Holding each other, they seemed to go to sleep.

That was boring, so I climbed down, playing over in my mind what I had just seen. Mama was crying out but not in pain. Instead, she seemed to be very happy, even joyous. I could not understand what had happened but whatever it was, I felt a delicious curiosity.

My father was rather stern. I would not consider asking him about it. But when he went to work, and my brothers and sister were out playing, I stayed behind with Mama.

"Mama, was Papa hurting you? I heard you screaming."

"When was that, Maaijke?" Her face turned red.

"After lunch. In your bed."

"No, Maaijke."

"What were you doing?"

"Oh, nothing, Maaijke. It is something married people do."

"I saw you, Mama. I saw you and Papa."

"You certainly did not, Maaijke."

"Yes I did. I climbed the beech tree and watched through the window."

"Maaijke!" She reached out to grab me, but I was too quick for her, and escaped through the door. "Maaijke, you come here right now," she commanded with undisguised anger.

I slunk back.

"Maaijke. Go to your room. Stay in your room. No dinner for you. Tomorrow, we shall see if you are sorry."

I went up to bed, crying, but mostly for show. As punishments go, it was pretty feeble.

Lying there, I tried to make sense of what I had seen, and why my mother seemed so angry. With my hand, I tried to imitate what Papa had done to Mama. It was vaguely pleasant, but not like it seemed for Mama. Perhaps I would try it again sometime.

CHAPTER 6

Peter

—— 1960 ——

S OCIAL SURVIVAL WAS DIFFICULT FOR A TIMID, FRIGHTENED BOY LIKE ME. I was also skinny and small, especially during grade school. I shied away from the cattle and the horses. When I tried to work the cattle, or ride the horses, Dad chided me, repeatedly reminding me of Great-Grandpa Pieter and the indomitable heritage he bequeathed to me. The remarks—partly good natured, partly serious, and always disappointed—stung. With his threatened disapproval as my companion, I drove myself to learn riding and roping and became a passable rider, and a better roper.

When I was eleven, my father's constant pressure led me to try rodeoing. I didn't really want to do it, but I felt he forced me to. While he never told me I had to rodeo, I knew it would please him. I wanted to do barrel riding, but it was only for girls. So, I entered a twelve-and-under calf roping event, although they used goats for kids my age. That day is stained in my memory. When my goat ran out of the chute, I quickly closed in. My lariat loop sailed smoothly and floated down on the goat's neck as my horse braked, jerking the goat to a stop when the lariat tightened. I was out of the stirrups before the rope was taut and ran to its end. Then things fell apart. It took me several seconds to upend the goat into the dirt, as it outweighed me by twenty-five pounds. Whipping the piggin' string out of my mouth, I tied off three legs, and throwing my arms up, stopped the clock. The leg tie held. My time of fourteen seconds was slowed by the five seconds it took to "tackle" the goat to the ground.

Willis Hollister rode two back from me. Although his riding and roping were sloppy, he took the bleating animal down quickly. He beat me by almost three seconds. Willis, from the next ranch north and of my age, was my sometimes friend. In school, my enthusiasm and aptitude carried me above most classmates, especially Willis. But Willis was bigger, physically more mature, and perhaps because he lagged behind me academically, he habitually tried to belittle and best me at after-school activities. He usually succeeded.

After the event, Willis approached me by the corral fence, thrust a Levi-clad hip against me, and said, "You might be the teacher's pet, but y'ur a wimp. Cain't even tip a little goat over."

I said nothing as I turned away, swallowing my anger and humiliation. It was made worse when my father walked up.

"Peter," he said, "you rode and roped well, and I'm proud of you. If only you had brought the goat down better, you'd have beaten Willis. Next time, if you practice, maybe you will come out on top."

He must have seen my crestfallen countenance because he put his arm awkwardly around my shoulders and said, "Don't worry, Peter. Grandpa—Grandpa Pieter—told me a couple times as I grew up on this same ranch that only the tough could survive such rugged country as this. A couple of times was all it took: I got the message, and by the time I was five or six, he never had to tell me again. I know that someday you'll be every bit the man he was."

Somehow, that didn't make me feel much better. However, something else did—but not for very long. That September when I started ninth grade, I thought I had my first real girlfriend—Katy Paulsen. Later, I realized she didn't completely share my feelings. She was fun to talk with, but I lacked confidence and worried that I might be saying stupid things to her. Besides, I think I was in awe of her. And with the fairly recent changes in her body, I was preoccupied and always thinking of what it would be like to kiss her.

Or even more. She made the shirts she wore look very nice, very inviting. But I was too shy. Too afraid of being rebuffed if I asked her out. I sensed that girls, and especially Katy, were from a totally different and mysterious species for whom permission was required to interact. And I was way too embarrassed to ask Mom or Dad for advice about her. I guess I could have asked Anna because, being my sister, she didn't really count as a girl, but she was two years younger, and so wouldn't know much.

When I finally asked Katy to go to our high school football game, I accidentally bit my cheek and got blood all over my teeth. She looked at me and laughed but still agreed to go with me. Willis, also a freshman, was already on the varsity team and from his fullback slot, scored the winning touchdown. At game end, I asked Katy if she wanted to go to our soda fountain for a Coke. But she stood to leave. She apologized and said that Willis had already asked her to go with him. I was embarrassed, and with feelings hurt, said nothing. I tried to block disappointment from showing, and as tears filled my eyes, I wanted to disappear.

Even so, it was better than when I went to the football games with Mom and Dad. My dad almost always had admiring, gushingly complimentary remarks about Willis. *Willis this… Willis that… Willis is so strong and fast, and how it must take a lot of skill to run through the opponents as he did.* I don't think Dad tried to hurt me, and he probably didn't even notice that I took his praise of Willis to be making a direct comparison with me. The worst was when he said Willis reminded him a lot of my great-grandfather, Pieter. It wasn't just once that he said it. As I was growing up, in many situations involving Willis, Dad repeated this opinion. I sometimes wondered if Willis and I had been switched at birth—he was so much more like Great-Grandfather Pieter than I was.

It got worse, much worse a couple months later when I overheard Willis bragging to a group of his school friends about Katy—telling them what her breasts felt like, stuff like that. I grew hot, molten hot with anger and jealousy. Then one of the friends asked, "What else?"

Willis said, "Do you mean, did we go all the way? Let me put it bluntly: fucked her really good. I had her screaming, she loved it so much."

With that, he looked up and saw me. He broke from the group, came over, and said, "Remember when I told you, you couldn't handle a little goat? Well, looks like you don't know how to handle a woman either, baby boy."

Without thinking, I hit him as hard as I could in the belly. He stood there and laughed at me. As did his friends. I had only the satisfaction, then, of believing he was lying about Katy. That satisfaction dwindled several weeks later and turned to confusion when she left school with no explanation. She came back after about two months and was very friendly with me again. She shunned Willis, but she refused to discuss her absence. It was quite some time later before I realized there was truth in his braggadocio.

CHAPTER 7

Maaijke

— 1820 —

Papa came home that same evening after Mama banished me to my bed. After dinner, and after my brothers and sisters had gone back outside to play, I snuck partly down the stairs and listened to my parents discussing what had happened. Mama no longer seemed angry. In fact, she was telling the story with some amusement. I was confused. How could she think what I did was funny after she had punished me for doing it?

"Well, maybe a bit young for that," Papa said.

"She didn't appear upset; only curious," Mama said. "She has more curiosity than any child I have ever known. She insists on knowing everything, and for information we want to keep from her, she is especially insistent."

He started to laugh.

"What is so funny?"

"She reminds me so much of you when you were young. Remember the trouble we were in when our parents discovered us behind your shed when we were six and we had our underpants down?"

"Ah, Jacobus, you certainly led me astray!"

"Me? It was your idea. You did that; I just did what you said to do."

"Well," she laughed. "I guess it worked out okay. I still like you leading me astray. But maybe we should be more careful. Shut the window and curtains, at least, if the kids are up. But knowing Maaijke, we haven't heard the last of this. What should I say to her when she asks about it again?"

"I'm glad it's your problem; she won't ask me. Can you simply tell her something nonspecific about making babies?"

"I'll try. But you know how she is. She doesn't accept simple. She is likely to pursue this until her curiosity is satisfied."

I crept back up the stairs. In the morning, I was allowed to come down for a somber, silent, uncomfortable breakfast. When everyone left, I was again alone with Mama.

"Mama, did I drink milk from your breasts when I was a baby?"

She paused and gave me a puzzled look. I knew she was trying to anticipate my thoughts. "Yes, Maaijke. Like all babies."

"Why didn't Papa eat enough for lunch yesterday?"

"He did, Maaijke."

"Then why was he getting milk from your breasts when I was in the tree?"

She turned red as a bad sunburn and said nothing for a while.

Then, deliberately, and slowly, she said, "Maaijke, he was not drinking. He was kissing me."

"Why, Mama?"

"Because he loves me."

"Does Papa love me?"

"Yes, of course he does."

"But he doesn't kiss me there."

"No. Only married mothers and fathers do that."

"Oh," I said, feeling even more confused. I went outside. I thought about our conversation, and came back in.

"Mama, why were you crying?"

"When, Maaijke?"

"When Papa was doing that to you yesterday. You were crying and screaming, but you didn't look sad."

This time I wasn't quick enough to get away. Mama reached out and grabbed me. She held me very tightly and she jerked up and down. I was not sure if she was laughing or crying, but when I was able to pull away, she was smiling.

"Maaijke, someday I will explain what we were doing. But not yet. It is what married couples do to make babies."

I got that type of non-answer a lot.

CHAPTER 8

Peter

—— 1960 ——

IN THE NINTH GRADE, MY ENGLISH TEACHER, MISS CLARKE, WAS IN HER first year out of college. At fifteen years, I had a large growth spurt and shot up to nearly my full size. At five foot nine, Miss Clarke was almost as tall. She was a serious, enthusiastic instructor. Her love of language burst forth in every class, and she took a special liking to me. Early in the year, she must have seen talent in my writing, and often kept me after school, not for discipline but for extra teaching.

By March, these sessions changed. When she leaned over my desk to point out suggestions for improving my daily essay, her arm or body often brushed against me. I could feel the heat in my face from the blushing. When I sneaked a look at her face with this contact, she was smiling. I guess I was a bit slow socially and didn't fully appreciate the extent of her interest, even when these sessions progressed to Cokes at the soda fountain in town.

One afternoon, she wanted to show me some of her books. In her house, the walls of filled bookcases transported me to a new world. She pulled out a leather-bound book from her Shakespeare collection, and handed me *As You Like It*. I clutched it to my chest, repeating "thank you" effusively.

A week later, after class, I asked if I could trade it for another of Shake-speare's plays.

"Sure. I think you'd like *Twelfth Night.* I have it at home. You remember where I live? I'll be there after school," Miss Clarke said.

She gave me the play as we sat beside each other on the couch, flipping pages together. She leaned toward me, then against me.

"Do you have a girlfriend?" she asked.

I tensed. Nervous sweat. "No. Not now."

"You should, with such cute dimples and blue eyes. But you did, right?" she pressed me. "What about Katy? Katy Paulsen."

"Maybe, sort of," I said, and I could feel the rosy flush spreading into my face. "No, not really."

I wasn't sure if Miss Clarke looked happy or sad when she said, "Too bad. Did I see her with Willis last fall?"

"I dunno. I guess."

She was closer to me now. Her face near mine.

"Have you ever kissed a girl?"

"Only Mom and Anna." The heat, the redness burned my face.

"Anna?"

"Yeah. My sister."

Then she moved to me, softly kissing my lips.

I jumped up.

"Bye, Miss Clarke. I have to go," I stammered, quickly backing out of her house and feeling so stupid. And embarrassed. And intrigued.

The next day, after school let out, I rang her doorbell.

"I forgot the book. *Twelfth Night.*" I couldn't look at her as I shifted from foot to foot.

"Peter, of course you did. Come in and I'll get it."

She walked a step ahead of me, then stopped and abruptly turned. I almost crashed into her, stopping with just inches between us. She reached up with both hands, held my face, turned her head up, and kissed me again. A longer kiss. I felt her hands around my back. Her body pressed against me. I ran from the house, again. Why, I am not sure. I left without the book. Perhaps that was not an accident.

CHAPTER 9

Maaijke

—— 1820-1826 ——

I ENTERED SCHOOL WHEN I WAS FIVE. I THRIVED THERE. ALL MY COURSES delighted me. I had a gift for language and could speak English and French by the time I was ten. My curiosity was fed and nurtured, and I began to see what the world might hold for me.

There was something else that delighted me as well—the sea. I was introduced to sailing and fishing when I was four. Papa had a fisherman friend, Diederik van der Meer. Dirk kept his fishing boat in Spakenburg and fished the Zuiderzee. Papa's sister, my widowed Aunt Jenny, also lived in Spakenburg, but much closer to the harbor than our farm, so we stayed in her house before we sailed with Diederik. Weekends, Papa took me to visit with his friend and sail and fish on his boat, the *Het Houten Paard*. It was like most fishing boats, with sails for pushing them along, very shallow bottoms, and *zwards* or lee boards, one on each side of the boat, that were lowered into the water to prevent the boat from slipping sideways. The shallow-bottomed boats, Dirk told me, were necessary because the Zuiderzee was so shallow. Even though it was part of the North Sea, it was no deeper than three to five meters in most places and near shore, much shallower.

Dirk was a big bear of a man, and very gruff. He scared me a little bit, especially when enfolding me in his big arms, as he frequently did. But I soon learned to love him like an uncle. He smiled almost always. He laughed a lot. He loved being out on the water with the wind tugging at the sails, pushing us so easily as the *botter* dragged its nets. It wasn't long before I became infected with Dirk's love of the water and fishing. His boat was confusing at first, with all the lines and sails and nets, but by the time I was seven, I had become quite good at steering the boat, although not strong enough to wrestle the heavy sails or to hold the sheets controlling them.

Around that time, Papa was so confident in my seamanship that he let me go alone; Dirk became almost a second father. Sometimes, when I did not have school, I was allowed to stay on the boat out on the Zuiderzee for several days and nights as we hauled net after net of fish before returning to Spakenburg. After my tenth birthday, I was able to do most everything on the boat that the men crew could do. Dirk treated me as one of them, except that he never was quite as affectionate with them as with me. Mostly, I was the helmsman, but I could trim sails, raise and lower the sails (with a bit of help on the halyards), and sort the catch when the nets were pulled in.

The cod, with their little beards hanging off their lower jaws, were the easiest to recognize and sort. They had a distinct lateral line that arched up as it went forward toward the gill cover, and skin that was green or brown with dark spots. Their three dorsal fins were also quite distinct. The pollock were not much different but without the beard. We caught plaice and sole from the floor of the Zee, and I had difficulty telling them apart. But both were very different from the other fish. They had continuous fins down the top and bottom of their bodies, and bodies that were tilted so that the fins appeared to be on the right and left. Their eyes were especially strange, with both being on one side of the body or the other. The side toward the sea bottom was pale, and the other side—the one facing up, the side with both eyes—was dark and patterned. Sometimes, we pulled in salmon, or *zalm*. They did not bring in as much money as some of the other fish we caught, like cod, but with their bright silver skin and deep red flesh, they were my favorite.

When the fishing was slow, or we had filled the boat with our catch and were sailing home, I still savored the experience. With little demand for the crew to be working, I delighted to lie on the cockpit floor—sole, they called it—or up on the forward deck and warm myself in the sun, rocked to sleep by the comforting, mesmerizing motion of the boat. Or I would place one ear against the wood planking and listen to the burbling of the small waves against the hull, sounding like multiple dogs lapping up water from their multiple bowls.

After my thirteenth birthday, Mama and Papa told me I could no longer fish and sail. I was too old, they said, to go out on a boat with the fishermen. I argued, but not too hard, and sulked—but deep down, I knew they were correct. I did not want people saying bad things about me. My mom had already worried about that kind of problem with Johannus, one of my brothers' friends, whom I liked, and who did some things—with my encouragement—Mama said were very bad.

I began to wear braids before I was five. The boys liked to pull them. That, of course, was the reason I had them. Pulling them would lead to fights, and wrestling with the braid-pullers was great fun. I sometimes won. I always got held by the boys. That's why I liked the wrestling. When I was seven, one of my brothers' friends, Johannus, wrestled me down and was half sitting, half lying on me. Leaning up, I kissed him on the lips. He jumped up, like he had been struck by lightning, wiping his mouth on his sleeve. But he started to hang around me even more.

Even before that, I had been in trouble with Mom because of Johannus. I remembered when I overheard what my parents did behind a shed when they were six. So Johannus and I went out behind the school, and I persuaded him to slide his pants and underpants down. I tried to be polite, and I was very curious, but I was not very impressed. With my dress up, and my underpants down to compare, our teacher caught us. Her face became so red, I thought she might explode. Verbally, she did, with the result being I was soon at home in the middle of the day, where Mama spanked me with a very hard hairbrush and banished me to my room. From my vantage point across her knees, I couldn't tell if she used the bristle side or the wooden side. It hurt so much it could have been either. Hard as I tried, I could not keep from crying. She spanked me again when I told her that she had done the same thing with Papa when she was my age. That cost me two days in my room. Mama brought me food, but otherwise, I was banished. But not for long; I was learning a trick to get out of my mama's imprisonment, and to escape into another world.

At that age, when I kissed Johannus and we were caught with our pants down behind the school, I had almost no interest in girl games. The girls played with dolls our mothers made. Boys got to play outside, rolling hoops with sticks, hitting balls with sticks, playing tag, chasing each other, and hiding from each other. Dolls were boring; outdoor games were fun and mostly, I escaped from the house and went with the boys. Exasperation more than anger was how Mama reacted when I came home—more often than not—with face and hands dirt covered, and my face totally consumed with happiness. Behind her stern expression shimmered a hint of a smile. It almost seemed as if she were delighted by my boy play. But sometimes, she made me stay home with girls my age and our boring dolls.

That is when I would start to think about being somewhere else. Usually, I thought myself outside to play the boys' games. The more I practiced this, the better I got. I could spend a whole afternoon with dolls and not re-member any of it. Instead, I would remember the imaginary play I had had with the neighborhood boys and my brothers. I often lay in bed at night, imagining being outside, running and wrestling with my brothers and their friends. At dinner, Mama and sometimes Papa would ask about our days. My brothers offered enthusiastic tales of their games and exploits, all of which were exactly as I had imagined. But when I was asked about what I did on days where I was forced to pretend dolls were fun, I could recall none of it. Mama was home all day and loosely watched what I and my girlfriends did. I was concerned by the worry written on her face when I seemed not to remember what I had done during the day.

As I got older, I thought myself into places I had never been. Once, in January when it was very cold, I went all the way to Amsterdam and skated on the canals formed by the slow-moving waters of the Amsterdam-Rijnkanaal. When I joined games of tag on the ice with boys and girls of my age, I was so happy to be included, but at the same time, I was sad because they never knew I was there. When I tried to talk with them, they never heard me. Even so, weaving around the city, and ducking under the low, arched brick bridges exhilarated me. By the time I was ten, I went to England and wandered the dirty, smelly streets of London. But I still loved being there and I practiced my English at free moments so I could understand the London children. But even though I could watch and hear them, they never noticed me. When I spoke, it were as if I did not exist.

And then I went to Paris, the best place of all. The gardens and parks were exquisite during the days, but at night, the city was miraculous. The millions of city lights turned Paris into a fantasy, almost like seeing a living kaleidoscope, almost like being in one. During the day, and especially in the evening, I loved to walk along the Avenue des Champs-Élysées. I started at the newly completed Arc de Triomphe at the Place de l'Étoile (a wonderful structure even though it was begun by that horrible Napoleon we evicted from my country) and finished two kilometers away at the Place de la Concorde, with its recently erected obelisk, which was several thousand years old when Egypt gave it to France. That place, where more than a thousand people had their heads guillotined during the French Revolution, now formed a stark contrast with those times as aristocratic ladies and gentlemen promenaded along the Avenue des Champs-Elysées with me. The fine men's clothing and tall top hats, and the elegant gowns worn by the ladies were unlike anything I ever saw at home.

Even though my lack of interaction made these visits somewhat sterile, my language skills moved forward quickly. When back in school, my ability to speak and read English and French was as good—even better—than my brothers and their friends who were three and four years ahead of me in school.

I don't want to seem to be complaining. I'm not. But these trips were very difficult for me. As much fun as they were, as much as I learned from them, I found that unless I concentrated with my total being, I could not stay in any place. And if, even for a few minutes, my concentration flagged, I was right back where I started when I began to imagine a trip. Still, the almost exhausting concentration was all worth the effort. But it was so tiring. After each of these trips, I felt very hot and often went straight to bed. Mom thought I was sick, but I wasn't. I felt fine—even better than usual. When I awoke from these unavoidable naps, I was contentedly floating with happiness.

CHAPTER 10

Peter

—— 1960–1962 ——

AFTER SHE HAD FIRST KISSED ME, AND EVEN MORE AFTER THE SECOND time, it was difficult to enter into class discussions when Miss Clarke was present. But nothing else happened. A week later, I sheepishly rang her doorbell.

"I forgot the book. Again."

"So you did! I was actually reading it again last night in bed. Come," she said, with a warm smile which should have warned me, perhaps even scared me.

Bad judgment maybe, but I followed her. At her bedroom door, she turned to face me, and began to unbutton her blouse. I watched, riveted, quivering: she wore nothing under it. She took my hand, touched it against her breast. I felt my forehead, then my whole face flush. But I didn't back away. I'd never seen a real breast before, excepting in pictures. I felt as if my brain were detaching from my head. Touching a real breast was much finer than I had imagined.

An entirely new course of study began with Miss Clarke. I was a pliant, eager student, a quick study; she demonstrated teaching skills I had imagined and that awakened me in the night. Through the rest of the school year, on at least one afternoon per week, and occasionally after dinner, we lay in her bed.

Then, when I entered tenth grade—she was gone, fired. No one would discuss it; I was too afraid to ask why, afraid I would be punished. I knew what we did was wrong, knew that in her position, she had violated trust. But besides my guilt, I also felt somehow accomplished, freed. I'd lost some of my shyness and gained enormously in self-confidence. Miss Clarke had been an antidote for my father and for Willis.

Beginning in the tenth grade, my next three English teachers were demanding, appreciative of my talent and work, and spent extra hours with me. But only in school. Now I have difficulty in distinguishing them. Each required and graded a full-page essay every day; I learned and thrived and excelled. In math and sciences, I also drew high grades. The approbation, the success were addictive. I graduated first in my high school class—Katy was second—and knew I was nearly guaranteed a position at the Naval Academy.

I misled myself. Each of our two senators and the single representative from Wyoming nominated other candidates, all of them star football players. One was Willis Hollister. Senator Crowell had let me down. I was forced to go with my backup school.

I sought out my father for support and condolence. That was a mistake.

"Well," he said, "you are still going to a good school. I'm sure you will make me proud. And remember, Willis is a fantastic athlete, and no doubt deserves to go to Annapolis."

I replied, almost inaudibly.

"What, Peter?"

"I said, 'as good as Great-Grandpa.'"

"Well, no, my grandpa never did play football. He was too busy building up the ranch."

Dad hadn't noticed my sarcasm, or maybe he just ignored it.

CHAPTER 11

Maaijke

— 1824-1826 —

THEY WERE *SO* TIRING, THESE TRIPS TO DIFFERENT PLACES AND DIFFER-ent times. I had to focus on being in the different place, and if I faltered, even for a few seconds, I would be back home. The longer I stayed away, the more tiring it was, and no matter how hard I tried to stay, eventually I would be back where I started, which was usually in my bed. It was almost as if no time had passed since I left. It was so, so very hard; the focus and concentration drained all my energy.

When I got to be older, and my older sister, Antje, had her first baby, Mama shooed me from the room, but I peeked through the open window. Antje was sweating, and screaming, and writhing. Her face was as black-red as Mama's hollyhocks. I had the same degree of struggle to get to a different place or time, but I had it after every trip, time and again. Although it didn't hurt like it did for Antje having her baby, it was still a struggle.

I knew enough not to tell my parents about these trips, these imaginary trips I took, but they became longer and longer. Even at dinner, I would sometimes be somewhere else until, as if through a fog, I heard Papa asking if I was in another world (I could hardly tell him I was) and would I please pass the potatoes, or sit up straight, or keep my fingers out of my food.

The year when I was nine, my sister Antje got married. I was allowed to attend the party after the wedding. Antje left the reception soon after it started to go to her new husband's house, and everyone started singing and laughing and asking them why they were leaving so early. Antje blushed. When I asked Mama about the questions, and why Antje blushed, she gave me her usual answer that she would explain when I was older.

When I was eleven years old, and studying history in school, I asked the teacher why we didn't have books about what happened in the future and not just in the past. She stared at me for a long time before she continued on with the class. At the end of the day, she asked me to stay after school.

"Maaijke," she said, "why do you think that someone could write a history book about the future? The future hasn't happened, so how could anyone know what *will* happen? History is about what already happened."

Miss den Bleyker was always nice to me. She seemed to understand that I was a little different.

"I know all that, but don't you ever imagine things? Like what is happening someplace else? And sometimes, what you imagine is what actually happens? So, why couldn't someone imagine what was happening in the future?"

"Well, Maaijke, if you can do that, you would be very special. Lots of people predict what will happen in the future, and by chance, they are occasionally correct. But predictions are just predictions, and usually wrong."

"No, no, Miss den Bleyker! I don't mean predict. I mean imagine the future really hard and maybe you can see what happens."

She laughed, and put her arms around me, hugging me. Then she looked at me very seriously and said, "If you can do that, come tell me about it right away."

I wasn't sure if she thought I was kidding her, or not.

CHAPTER 12

Peter

—— 1962-1966 ——

COLLEGE WAS MORE COMPETITIVE THAN MY HIGH SCHOOL. EVEN SO, MY classroom success continued at Harvard. I'd gained social confidence in high school (thank you, Miss Clarke), but I was still a bit shy, especially around my much more sophisticated classmates, which included all of them. But I think my shyness was interpreted as aloofness, and maybe a bit of arrogance. Both seemed to be valued commodities in abundant supply in Cambridge, Massachusetts. For me, I knew better; it was just shyness.

At the end of that first September, I met Sarah Moorland. I was waiting for a Rumanian pastrami sandwich at Elsie's deli, and she was in front of me, waiting for her thin-sliced roast beef with Russian dressing, which I'd had the last time I was there. Standing behind her, wondering if the front view looked as nice, I hoped her sandwich would never arrive. But it did, and she was out the door, giving me a brief glimpse that confirmed front and back views were equally pleasing. When my sandwich arrived, I quickly left and saw her ahead of me on Mt. Auburn Street. As I started to catch up to her, she turned on Holyoke toward the river. Convenient, since I was on the way back to my dormitory, Winthrop House, anyway. Just short of it, she turned off into the little park, so I followed. She sat against an old maple to eat, and I, pretending not to notice her, walked by. I could sense her eyes on me.

"Since you've been following me ever since Elsie's, you might as well sit," she said, as I blushed from being caught stalking.

"Well…," was all I got out, and, as invited, sat.

"You got my favorite," she said. "Wanna trade half of yours for half of mine?"

"Sure." I gave her half of my cut sandwich, as she gave me half of hers.

"Think that'll last you through to dinner?" she asked.

I nodded, yes.

"And what time would that be?"

"I dunno. Six, seven?"

"Have you been to Casablanca? Under the Brattle?"

"Nope."

"Good. I'll take you. You look pretty safe. Meet you there at seven."

So that was the start. Although I was an Engineering Sciences major, it was her English major that gave us a lot in common interests.

She was slim, with a rosy-cheeked outdoor look of sleek good health. She came by her athletic appearance honestly, playing soccer and field hockey in boarding school. Neither of us liked or could understand the radical Vietnam war protesters. There weren't many who thought the way we did—at least, not at that school—and so we became good friends. She had a way of looking at me, a "come-hither look," and we quickly became better than good friends: in two days, we were lovers and companions. That continued for the entire four years in Cambridge. She came from a very different world of country clubs, yacht clubs, entrenched old East Coast money, and considerable privilege.

Sarah introduced me to skiing, and to sailing on her father's Concordia yawl (complete with a little pot-bellied, coal-burning stove for cold weather, and with her father's concertina for sea chanty accompaniment), which was kept in front of her home in Osterville on the bottom side of Cape Cod. Although intimate and nearly constant confidants, our interaction was more that of best friends. We even jokingly referred to ourselves as friendly lovers, but neither of us had any inclination to seek out other partners. Our level of interdependence can best be illustrated by how happy I was to see her again in the fall, but how little I missed seeing her during the summer vacations. Later, after the Navy, I realized how much was missing between us. "Platonic" and "lovers" shouldn't ever be in the same sentence, but they were with me and Sarah. Maybe I was deficient…missing something. Or maybe she was.

CHAPTER 13

Maaijke

—— 1826 ——

So, I started to work more on going into the future. Papa always kept secret what he would get for Mama on her birthday, which next fell about two weeks after my talk with Miss den Bleyker. When in bed every night, I tried to imagine what he might give her. I thought of a scarf. I thought of a new plate for the kitchen. I thought of a new bonnet. None of these seemed right. One night, I imagined following my father. He went into the millinery store, and I watched through the window as he bought some lace. The lady in the store carefully wrapped the lace in paper and tied some string around it and then a red ribbon.

A week later, on her birthday, we finished breakfast and Papa gave Mama a package. It had paper wrapping and a red ribbon exactly as I remembered. Mama opened it while I held my breath. It was the same lace I saw with my imagining. She hugged Papa and thanked him. I hugged them both and thanked them. I was so happy. They looked at me and at each other, puzzled.

"Maaijke," Mama said. "The present is for me. Why are you so happy?"

"Mama, it is so pretty. That is why I am happy. I am happy for you."

"Oh, Liefje. Thank you. This makes my birthday even nicer."

I dared not tell them why I was so happy. I didn't even think I could tell

Miss den Bleyker that I had gone into the future, even though she had asked me to tell her if I did. I liked that she thought me cute; I didn't want her to tell people that I was crazy or bewitched.

Every night, if I was not too tired, I lay in bed and began the struggle to concentrate so fiercely that I could go into the future. Sometimes it worked, mostly it didn't. I kept practicing and by the time I was thirteen, I was able to go forward most of the times I tried. But whenever I tried to go backward, nothing ever happened. It wasn't until much later that I reasoned why I couldn't. Maybe if I could go back in time, I could change what happened then, which would in turn change everything subsequent to that moment. So that might mean that all events that already had happened would be changed—that the present would no longer be the same. History would no longer be the same. But how could something that happened before, and was written about in books, be made to unhappen?

CHAPTER 14

Peter

— 1967 —

Summers during college, I was back on the ranch working. Rusty was getting on, and she and I helped train Red, a new Irish setter puppy from the same kennel. By the time I entered my senior year, Red was better than Rusty had been at her peak: better nose, steadier on point, and a never-miss retriever.

I graduated near the top of my class and was accepted to Navy officer candidate school (OCS). I think they packed four years at the Naval Academy into the twelve weeks in OCS in Newport. I must have done well; I got accepted to flight school. Still feeling the sting from my Annapolis rejection, I was further impelled to succeed. Flying fascinated me, even as I sometimes feared it. I needed to surpass those who (it seemed to me) had taken my position at the Naval Academy. I turned out to be a pretty good pilot. Visualizing the link between what I did at the controls and what the plane did seemed completely natural.

I excelled in flight school, where flight training began in a T-28 Trojan, then progressed to the F-4 Phantom in fighter school. Willis Hollister was in my class, giving me more incentive to succeed and best him, and vindictive satisfaction when I did. At the same time, I had to grudgingly admit that he was a pretty good, although sometimes dangerously aggressive, pilot. In idle moments, I would conflate Willis with my great-grandpa, Pieter, and experience a silent, mirthless laugh.

CHAPTER 15

Maaijke

—— 1828-1829 ——

I WAS THIRTEEN WHEN I NOTICED CHANGES IN MY BODY. MY BREASTS GREW. My hips got wider. I wasn't as skinny as before. The monthly bleeding began. Mama did explain that to me and disgusting as the bloody mess was, it helped a little bit to know that it meant I was a woman and would be able to have children someday.

The boys I played with started to treat me differently. They used to try to beat me in games, and when we fought and wrestled, they fought really hard. Now, they seemed shy around me. They stared at me, and I was embarrassed about my body. And even though they had difficulty talking with me, they wanted to be around me even more.

For my fourteenth birthday, Mama and Papa—both of them together, which was very unusual—sat me down and told me that I could no longer play with the boys. I was becoming a woman and people, they said, would say bad things about me if I was too friendly with the boys. I was angry and sulked, but I was not surprised. It was the same as the year before when they banned me from fishing with Dirk unless Papa was also there. I knew exactly what Mama and Papa were worried about; I noticed that when Johannus wrestled with me, his hands would often touch my new breasts. And I was a little frightened that I liked it when he touched them.

Most of my best friends had been neighbor boys and my brothers, but amongst girls, Gerta was my best friend. I told her what Johannus did to me, and she giggled and blushed. Her breasts were also growing, and she insisted that I tell her what it felt like when he moved his fingers over one of mine. Gerta and I pledged to keep this secret. I felt as if no one else had ever had such an experience; I was the first.

Some nights, before going to sleep, I imagined doing much more with Johannus. I would put my fingers down between my legs and rub, like I had seen Papa do to Mama many years earlier when I climbed the tree outside their bedroom. Now when I did it, I could feel the moisture begin and after a while, my whole body began to shake, and I could do nothing to stop it until I felt I was erupting with warmth, and a wonderful feeling came to me. I slept well those nights. Those nights I made no attempt to go traveling.

Yet when I did travel, I was getting better at it. I could go farther, do it more often, and move further into the future. The future was fun. Not being able to go into the past didn't worry me because I could read about the past, but everything was new in the future. Of these travels, I could tell no one. Not my parents, not my teachers, and not even Gerta.

The things I saw! The furthest I traveled in time was to 1970 in Amsterdam. There were no horses pulling carriages. None. The carriages moved without horses. Autos, they were called. One almost killed me. So fast they went, I could scarcely believe it. And lots of bicycles, which we did not have back home. The costumes were very strange, and I was quite self-conscious about mine, but I realized after a time that no one could see me. That changed later, when I went even further ahead.

My favorite place in Amsterdam was the library. They had books in many languages, but I could read best the ones in French, English, and Dutch. I found one book called *De Breugde van Seks*, written by someone from America named Dr. Comfort. I wondered if that was some kind of joke, but I think it really was his name. I learned a lot. It also made me start to get damp between my legs when I saw his drawings of how to do sex. I learned that orgasm was the word for the wonderful warm feeling I sometimes gave myself lying in bed.

At home, Gerta and I talked, in private of course, about sex and what we imagined it was like.

"How do you think it is done, Gerta?" I would ask.

"Well, maybe...," and she would describe what she imagined it would be like.

"Do you think a man would ever...," and I would describe what I saw in the book, but I could never tell her about the book or my travels. She would have thought me crazy.

Mostly she would blush when I suggested different positions, but she liked talking about it. We both started to look forward to when we would get married so we could do sex.

CHAPTER 16

Peter

— 1971 —

I LEFT THE SECOND DINNER SEATING, THE MORE FORMAL OF THE TWO in the officers' mess, and climbed up three decks to immediately below the flight deck and out one of the several doors to the catwalk edging the aircraft carrier flight deck. I leaned outboard against the rail, and forward into one of the speakers. As the USS *Ranger* pushed through the oily water, consuming its bow wave, I looked at the empty horizon toward the Philippines. Perhaps it was a vanity, but I was proud of my accomplishments and my Lieutenant rank. I was an ace, with five and a half kills tallied over the skies of North Vietnam. Dad had never even served; it was one sphere, at least, in which I stood over him.

Standing in the catwalk, my head level with the flight deck, I looked up at the Phantom F-4 fighters—one of which was mine—and the A-7A Corsair II and A-6A Intruder attack planes of the air wing. The warm, thick, humid breeze combed furrows in my hair. In the absence of true wind, the South China Sea barely undulated and had a greasy, black, dead appearance. The apparent wind came solely from the aircraft carrier pushing through the water at 17 knots. Aft, the phosphorescent wake stretched out to the western horizon before being swallowed by the curve of the earth. Flight operations had been shut down because we were steaming away from combat. Other than the deep diesel thrum, and the half-hourly ship's bell marking the time, we were quiet, and combat was now far behind us as we headed east.

In combat, we often used infra-red, heat-seeking Sidewinder missiles, which automated the killing process and thus minimized the piloting skills needed to succeed. They had what might be considered a victim's advantage in that the Sidewinders usually exploded in the tail of the bandit plane, thus often allowing the opposing pilot to eject with little injury. There were Sparrows, too, which I hated: they required that we stay in radar lock with the target until the missile struck, thus leaving us in predictable and unprotected flight while the Sparrow flew. Every time I fired one, I thought I would foul my flight suit during the wait. We also had 20 mm Vulcan cannons, which had far more pilot appeal.

I thought back to childhood Wyoming with hours of fishing and bird hunting on our ranch. Dad's lessons in bird shooting in the high plains and eastern foothills of the Wind River Range, although sometimes painful and contentious, had turned me into an exceptional wing shot. The intuitive trigonometry required to guide a shotgun along a grouse's flight path so that lead shot and bird intersect had given me a massive advantage in dog fights. Turning an F-4 Phantom and using the Vulcan to shoot where the enemy was going to be—deflection shooting—seemed much the same as wing shooting in Wyoming. I thought of opposing planes as birds and hunted them with little thought of the opposing pilot. Even so, before each mission, I chewed on fear and the possibility of being killed. Only airborne was I able to strangle and forget the fear.

I had been given one leave during my tour, which I used for seven days in Oahu. Most of the unmarried guys went to Bangkok, which mandated that their first stop back was with one of the flight surgeons to treat what they caught from the Thai pay-for-service women. That didn't much appeal to me. Many of the married guys went to Hawaii, so I tagged along with one of my buddies where he rendezvoused his wife. Alone on the island, I tried and failed to learn surfing. I was a bit surprised by the many nurses crowding the bars and the ease with which I met them. A few were from the Navy, and the much larger number came from Tripler Army Medical. Must have been our summer whites and my Navy wings that were so seductive. Too soon my time was up, and I was on the airlift back to Vietnam and then out to the *Ranger* and my Phantom.

As I reminisced, I looked down at the bow wave cascading off the ship and conducted a silent debate with myself as to whether my missions above Viet Nam—the dog fights, the corkscrew rolling away from missiles, the bandits knocked from the sky—was for my own satisfaction and sense of accomplishment, or whether it was to prove my value to my father, and to live up to great-grandpa's standards. Maybe it didn't matter.

CHAPTER 17

Maaijke

—— 1830 and 1888, 1901, 1915 ——

I WASN'T ONLY INTERESTED IN SEX; I WAS INTERESTED IN EVERYTHING.
I went to Paris in the France of 1888, where I met Gustave Eiffel. Well, he did not meet me; no one could meet me, of course, because I was invisible to everyone. But I met him. He was an engineer who a few years earlier had built the frame supporting a large statue of a lady with a torch that stood on an island in New York in America. He was so forceful, so charismatic—not to mention so handsome, with dark wavy hair—that I followed him around Paris. He and his factory were building a tall, tall tower—which, when I first saw it, was already almost sixty meters high to the first platform, where they planned to build restaurants.

Several days later, when I came back one year in the future, in 1889, to see my first World Fair, the tower looked like fine filigree, extending over 300 meters into the sky, and appearing so delicate that I was sure it would fall over in a wind. I also discovered, on the third level high above the city, a secret apartment Monsieur Eiffel kept. He stayed up there some nights, but I am not sure why. He had a lovely wife, Marie, and five lively children. Maybe he needed to get away from them to think about his next project.

I often attempted to go back in time, but finally quit trying; it never worked. I revisited my reasoning that if I could go back in time, and interact, everything that ever happened after that time would be different. Since the present is already happening, it can't be changed by doing something in the past, but since doing something in the past *would* change the present, there was obviously no possibility of going back. Going into the past would end the present. At least that is what I thought. But this seemed wrong, also. Because when I went into the future, I did not interact. No one saw me. Why wouldn't that happen if I went into the past? Still, I was never able to go there. It didn't worry me; the future was more fun. Everything in the past was already written down someplace.

As my visits with M. Eiffel show, my time appeared to pass at a very different pace from the time I visited. It didn't, really. But because I could skip ahead days or years in just a few minutes, the brief time that passed with me could span years of time in the future.

One day in Amsterdam in the library, I read about the Great War. I decided to go there. It was more difficult and took more straining and forced concentration to get there, but I finally succeeded in going to Lille, a town about thirty kilometers east of Antwerp, in 1915. The Deûle Canal cuts through the elegant city and, with its two limbs, forms an island right in the middle of the town. There were German soldiers everywhere, their sinister countenance negating the beauty of the city. There, I met a truly great woman.

When I say "met," I mean that I observed her. She could not see me. No one could. Her name was Louise de Bettignies. She was apparently from a very old, distinguished family. She was one of the prettiest ladies I ever saw and paradoxically, one of frail appearance. The paradox was that she was in an extraordinarily difficult, dangerous job, and one that eventually led to her death. She also went by another name, the pseudonym Alice Dubois. Alice was a spy. In fact, she led a spy ring and was so successful that she was reputed to have saved the lives of more than a thousand downed British pilots. She rode the back of remarkable success and would have been even more successful if her superiors had believed her impeccable intelligence. She pinpointed, in advance, the location and time of the Kaiser's train: the British did not believe her, and he escaped. She warned of the attack on Verdun: the

French did not believe her, with tragic results for both armies. In October of 1915, as my concentration weakened, I was back home and back to 1833. Alice was caught shortly after I left and sentenced to life in prison. There, she developed an infection in her chest (empyema, I later learned it was named), and because it was treated poorly, she died. She was an incredibly heroic lady. I wanted to be like her; but only if I didn't have to die.

Once I traveled to the England of 1901, which was so different from when I was there fifty years earlier. Sewers had since been built, and the noxious, stifling smells were gone, and in their absence, I could enjoy the lovely underlying city odors: the wafting scent of park flowers ranging from bitter, through sour, and onto sweet; the delectable, yeasty smell of bakeries; wood smoke permeating clothes; coal smoke—which in small doses was quite pleasant—from the blacksmiths' forges; and of course the smell left behind by horses that reminded me of the farms back home. There I encountered a woman with an expression that looked like she was trying to solve a puzzle. I followed her home from a bakery and watched as her shoulders began to jerk in a convulsive manner. She wasn't very old but walked hunched over, as if an old lady, and when I got ahead of her, I saw how depressed, how hopeless she appeared, and I realized that she was crying. She had rivulets of tears on her dusty cheeks. At her apartment—I assumed it was hers—she went in while I looked at the mailboxes. She had gone into the door marked 5C. The mailbox with that number had the name of Potter, Beatrix. When I thought myself into her house, she was talking to a friend.

"No publisher likes my book," she said. "No one will ever get to read it."

"Beatrix, why don't you publish it yourself?"

They talked about that for a while, and thankfully she stopped sobbing and stood up straighter.

While they talked, I went into a little study and found pages from a book named Peter Rabbit. I leafed through it and the illustrations of the funny bunny. He had apparently got caught stealing and eating vegetables from the garden of a farmer who chased him out. The poor rabbit, in his haste to escape, caught a button of his coat on the fence and lost the button. When he finally got home, his mom scolded him and sent him to bed with chamomile tea, which had a soporific effect on Peter, the rabbit. That word, "soporific," stayed with me. I had never heard it before, so I had to find a dictionary. But I never forgot that word. I also never forgot the name of that rabbit, Peter, because of what happened to me later.

CHAPTER 18

Peter

— 1971 —

D ESPITE THE THRILL OF FLYING THESE FANTASTIC PLANES, AND MY EN-joyment and expertise, I knew it was time to be leaving it behind. I had conquered that challenge and had been accepted at medical school for the class of 1975; my obligation to the Navy was nearly over. The USS *Ranger* was headed for Subic Bay and I for civilian life.

Now, standing in the catwalk around the carrier flight deck, I was nearly done. I thought fondly of Sarah, with whom I had exchanged letters with decreasing frequency during my time on the *Ranger*. Her last note told me of her forthcoming marriage to an old Osterville neighbor and friend. I felt neither hurt nor jealousy from this news but did try to imagine myself in the position of being Sarah's husband. It didn't fit. My reveries continued a bit longer before I ducked down to my stateroom, a decidedly un-stately room of five by eight feet. Everything was built-in and of gray-painted steel. The room consisted of a small clothes locker, a small bunk bed (with restraining straps for rough seas), a fold-down metal desk, and a small safe where, like most other officers, I kept an illegal bottle. In my case, it was Remy Martin, whose graceful, frosted-green bottle appealed to me more than the taste, something I would never have admitted to my cigar-smoking pilot buddies.

Every one of our pilots, myself included, had a kind of insouciant swagger. We broadcast a feeling of supreme confidence derived of flying a really hot, deadly plane. And for almost all of us, a varying amount of this was facade without which we probably would not have survived our missions. That night, I had no taste for maintaining that image or for the macho flight officer badinage, so I skipped the wardroom movie.

For the hundredth time, I thought of Willis and how he died. I felt guilty for resenting, even despising him. But there was no one with whom I could discuss it. Beneath nearly all my thoughts lurked the gnawing realization of what I had done. It was too late to apologize to Willis; I wasn't even sure I'd want to, anyway. Just thinking about it, I could already feel my service khakis starting to soak as I sweated my way through reliving the event.

I felt my way along the catwalk, one hand on the outboard railing, until I came to a door down to the deck below. As I walked to my stateroom, an image came to me of my great-grandfather in his ranch clothes—but instead of riding a horse, he was piloting his own Phantom while wearing spurs. The realization crystallized that he probably, even born into my century, could not have done what I did. "Dad, I bested your idol," I thought as I fell asleep.

I awoke with the four bells of 2:00 am. I lay in bed, comforted by the deep rumble of the diesel engines driving the ship on to Subic, where I would leave active duty. I had no plans for the five months between my discharge and the start of medical school back in Boston, but as I lay there, one took shape: I could visit the Netherlands to learn more about my heritage, and perhaps even track down some family history, of which I knew almost nothing. Could I learn more about my all-star great-grandfather? I knew only that my forebears immigrated to the US in the mid 1800s, and that they might have come from Spakenburg. It would be wonderful to come back home and be able to teach Dad about Pieter, his hero and grandfather, and the person against whom he measured me.

CHAPTER 19

Maaijke

—— 1830–1832 ——

WHEN I WAS FIFTEEN, MAMA AND PAPA STARTED TO DISCUSS FINDING A husband for me. That's mostly the way it was done where I lived in the nineteenth century. At church, where we went twice every Sunday, I noticed Mr. Maasen looking at me in a way that made me feel squirmy and dirty. At supper that afternoon, Papa said to Mama, "That Bertus Maasen is a very fine man. Maybe he would make a good husband for Maaijke." As if I were not present for the conversation—as if I were just a chair sitting in the corner.

"No, Papa, no," I said. "He is an old man."

"Maaijke," he said, "Bertus is kind and generous. He gives to the church every Sunday. I know he likes you. And he is not old; he is only forty."

I was too big to spank, but had I not been, that is what would have happened to me when I stood up, shattered my plate when I threw it into the sink, and ran sobbing to my room. I slunk down later that evening, and no one mentioned it again. A week later, Mama asked Papa—I was standing next to her—if he had ever noticed the beautiful farmhouse and fields Bertus had. "Ja. He has done well. He works very hard."

Thus began a campaign that grew in intensity over the next year until I knew that I would have no choice in the matter. In all of these doings, it was almost as if I didn't exist and was merely an object, not a real person.

"Good morning, Jacobus," Bertus would say when we met him on the street or before going into church.

"And a very fine morning, Bertus," Papa would answer. "How are the crops this year?"

"Very good, Jacobus. And how is your lovely family? Johanna is well?"

"Oh, yes, very well. And I believe you know my daughter, Maaijke?"

So then, amid this stupid talk—Papa normally did not do small talk—I had to curtsy to Mister Maasen, who smiled down upon me. I felt like I did when leeches would attach to our legs in the summer while we swam and waded, and we would pour salt on them and they would writhe, and curl into a ball, and fall off.

"Bertus," Papa would say, "would you do us the honor of sitting in our pew this Sunday?" *Pour more salt* was all I could think.

"I would be delighted, Jacobus, but it would be my honor."

That went on for several weeks, until, "Bertus, perhaps you would like to sit next to Maaijke this Sunday. I am sure Maaijke would be honored."

I knew I should have been but could not think about him with any fondness. I admit he was very polite, and quite handsome. Papa had given a push to a big rock at the top of a hill, and it was picking up speed. Slowly, I realized that I could not avoid being run over.

But he was so old. It was hard to imagine doing sex with Mr. Maasen. Slowly I convinced myself that with his age, and far greater experience, at least he could teach me about such things. Stupid me.

Amid this build-up, Gerta asked me why Bertus Maasen was sitting next to me in church. At first I evaded her question but once I saw the inevitability of my parents' campaign, I confided in my friend. Her normally rosy face turned white, starting at her forehead and moving in a line that descended to her neck as I watched. I couldn't interpret her strange expression.

"Oh, Maaijke! Are you serious? Are you sure you want this?"

"No, Gerta, I'm not, but I don't seem to have any choice. Papa and Mama have decided. Besides, with his older age, I'm sure he can teach me how to do sex. Like we always talked about."

"Maybe it's not true, but I have heard weird things about him."

"Such as?" I said.

"It's probably rumors, Maaijke. I shouldn't have mentioned it, especially since I don't really know. Just things I heard." But she avoided looking at me when she said it and refused to talk about it anymore.

So, I pushed it to the back of my thinking. I had too much more to worry about than some rumor.

The inevitable arrived. I was seventeen. I wore Mama's wedding dress. She had earlier helped me prepare clothes for my new marriage, including what to wear the night of my wedding. She gave me a nightgown. It was sheer, and although it covered me from wrists to neck to ankles, it was flattering, and quite revealing. That single act changed the way Mama and I interacted. From then on, I was a woman and an equal, and she was my confidant. Although I had read about sex, I really had no experience. Mama told me what to expect the wedding night, and although I was apprehensive, with her help and calm explanations, I came to look forward to it, even though it was with Bertus Maasen. He would surely be able to show me the things I had seen in Dr. Comfort's book.

I was a lovely bride, and felt quite proud, walking arm in arm with my new husband, Bertus, down the aisle after the wedding. Everyone seemed so happy for me at the reception and I came to believe I was a very lucky young woman to have married such an upstanding man.

Gaily colored ribbons decorated Bertus's wagon. The two horses had flowers in their manes, and as we drove away to my first night as a wife, my parents and brothers and sister, and many village friends stood on the side of the road cheering. I felt sorry for Johannus. Standing in the happy crowd, he stared at me and looked so sad. His eyes were moist, and he glanced away when I waved at him. But my feelings quickly passed; I was on my way to my wedding night!

I was a little apprehensive, I admit. But mostly I was excited and eager. I tried hard to remember what I had learned from Dr. Comfort's book. I was right to be apprehensive, but not for the right reasons.

We came up to his big house, and a servant helped us down from the wagon. Bertus solemnly took my arm, and into the house we went. He showed me the sitting room, and the kitchen. He had a dining room. Upstairs, there were three bedrooms and he lived there all alone, at least until this day.

"This is my bedroom, Maaijke. And this is yours. Do you like it?"

"It is lovely, Bertus." And it was. But why, I wondered, did we have separate bedrooms? My parents shared the same one. Maybe this was what wealthy people did.

CHAPTER 20

Peter

— 1971 —

TWO DAYS LATER, THE SHIP PULLED INTO SUBIC BAY IN THE PHILIPPINES in full dress. The flight deck perimeter was lined by enlisted sailors in their summer dress whites: black, square-knotted neckerchiefs streamed downwind from the collared jumpers, and bell-bottoms billowed in the breeze above black shoes on the non-skid flight deck. I watched, moist-eyed, and thought for a few moments that perhaps I should stay in. I was nostalgic even before I mustered out but realized that the melancholy-producing pageantry was ephemeral and misleading. I had been offered an instructor's billet in Navy Fighter Weapons School at Naval Air Station Miramar (more well known as TOPGUN School), accompanied by a promotion. Because of Willis and what had happened, I also felt I didn't measure up. I could not think of Willis without guilty shame, and with the certainty that I did not deserve to teach at TOPGUN. My superior officers thought I did; I disagreed. But they didn't know. They assumed that his death was an act of mercy, for which I deserved praise or at least solid understanding. Perhaps they were correct. I am not sure their sentiments would have been exactly the same had they known the backstory.

The next day, discharge papers were in my hand. Our Chief Petty Officer got me a Military Airlift Command flight for Ramstein AFB. Two days later, I was on a train to Amsterdam, where I rented a car and headed east on the A1, then north for about four kilometers on the Amersfoortseweg to the Spakenburg harbor on the Eemmeer. A couple blocks south, I found the only hotel in town, the small three-story brick, Hotel Sint Nicolaas on Dorpsstraat. I checked into a comfortable but hardly elegant room with double bed, en suite bathroom, and two windows looking north toward the harbor. The walls were adorned with a couple prints, one by the Dutch Renaissance master, H. Bosch, and one by Rembrandt, a self-portrait. The art and quality of the Bosch were difficult to appreciate, so ominously, eerily frightening was the subject, Hell. I considered asking for a change of rooms, so off-putting did I find it. Later, I came to cherish the room, but not for reasons of art. I left my rental car behind the hotel and walked down to the harbor.

It was too late to start looking for Great-Grandpa Pieter's records, so it was dinner and I sacked out, waiting to begin the next day.

CHAPTER 21

Maaijke

—— 1832 and 1971 ——

IT WAS AFTER TEN O'CLOCK, AND BERTUS WENT INTO HIS BEDROOM AND shut the door behind him. I thought that this was intended to give me privacy so that I could change out of my wedding gown and into my negligee. In the candlelight, I brushed my hair until it gleamed in the mirror. I stood and looked at myself. Even with the flickering light, I was happy with my appearance. Although my nightgown covered me, its gossamer silk showcased my body, concealing nothing.

I blew out the candle and crossed the hall to Bertus's bedroom. I knocked, and at the same time opened the door. The candle on his bedside table was lit and he was in bed, reading from the Bible. Startled by my entrance, he looked at me, and his face tightened and turned red. When he tried to talk, spit came out of his mouth, and he could articulate nothing. Eventually, he talked to me. No, he snarled at me.

"You look like a whore. I thought you were a good Christian woman. I did not think I was marrying a slut! Get out," he said. "Do not ever dress like that in my house. Burn that shameful thing. Jezebel, leave me."

I slunk back to my room and cried myself to sleep.

In the morning, with trepidation, I went downstairs to the kitchen. I was very modestly dressed.

"Good morning, my beautiful new wife. How did you sleep?" As if nothing last night happened. I was confused, and as I sat down for breakfast began crying.

"What is wrong?"

"Last night. You said bad things to me."

"This is a Christian home, and I expect you to be the God-fearing wife your parents said you would be."

"But I am your wife."

"Yes," he said.

"My mama and papa sleep in the same bed."

"I will have no sinners living in this house."

"Aren't we going to have children?"

"God willing," he said. "Speak no more of such matters."

"How can we if we do not become man and wife?"

"Maaijke. You are my wife."

"But we can't make babies in different bedrooms."

"You will end these disgusting thoughts. When God wants us to have children, he will give them to us."

"Bertus, you have horses and cows. How do they have babies? How do they get them?"

He screamed at me. His face was purple, his veins stuck out, his eyes bulged. He snarled at me as if I were Lucifer. "Maaijke," he said, "we have souls and are God's children. Animals don't. They know no better." With each word, a fine spittle spray spewed out. "When I was growing up, my mother warned me of wicked women and the depravity they wanted to visit upon men. You shall not do that. Do you understand? You shall not; I will ban you from my house."

Never had I been so frightened. He seemed more monster than man. I spent most of the day in my room, crying. But when I came down for dinner, Bertus was very kind to me, and told me how beautiful I looked. Dinner with him was nice, and maybe, I thought, the previous night had been an aberration. Maybe he simply needed some time to adjust to becoming a husband.

That night, dressed in a heavy cotton nightdress and a bathrobe, I knocked on his door and when he did not answer, I timidly pushed the door open. As he screamed at me to get out, I noticed the tenting of his sheets at the middle of his bed.

"We are not cattle. We are not dogs. We are better. We fear God. We worship him. Leave me. Go pray."

I did leave. I cried myself to sleep again. But in the morning, he was kind and solicitous of me.

The next night, I crossed the hall and listened quietly at his door. I heard what sounded like sheets thrashing about and then a loud sigh and no more sounds. I crept back to my bedroom and cried again.

My marriage went on like that for days. When I saw friends, they all told me how wonderful I looked and how marriage clearly agreed with me. After church the next Sunday, Gerta pulled me aside, and as we walked, she wanted to know all about being married.

"Tell me about the first night. Everything. Did it hurt? Was he gentle? Was he good?"

"Oh, Gerta. I just got married; I would feel disloyal telling you exactly what we do in bed." I couldn't very well say, "It was hideous."

"Can I tell you a secret, Maaijke?" She rushed on without waiting for my answer. "I have a boyfriend."

"Wonderful, Gerta. Tell me about him."

"Do you remember Johannus?"

I began to sweat. I felt my face flush. I was jealous. I also realized how much happier he would have made me than Bertus did.

"Sure. I thought he moved away to become a fisherman."

"He is still here, fishing out of the harbor. He is at sea fishing for two months, and then comes home. When he is here, and my parents are not around, he keeps trying to touch me where he is not supposed to. I don't let him, of course. But I really want to.

"Please, Maaijke—tell me a little about you and Bertus," she pleaded.

"Did it feel as good as when we touch ourselves down there?"

"Well, I can say that it felt every bit as good."

Gerta sighed. I was telling the truth because when I was not allowed in Bertus's bedroom, that is exactly what I did back in my own bed.

Bertus and I had fallen into a routine, a depressing routine. He was always polite and considerate but after dinner, he became distant. He erected a wall around himself. Never did he invite me into his bedroom; never did he come into mine. I was able to maintain a pleasant, even happy facade around him, but inside, I was becoming desperate and miserable. I had no way out. I began to hope he would die, and soon. Widowhood would be far sweeter than to be shunned in my own home. I even thought of poisoning him, and then at night, I would pray God to forgive me for such thoughts.

He was so hard to figure out. He often told me how nice I looked. He complimented me, at least once a day on what a good cook I was, and how clean I kept the house. But physical closeness, never.

After two weeks, I went back to my parents' house after breakfast. Once Papa went out to the fields to work, Mama asked me how the new bride was. I couldn't hold back my tears and she folded me into her arms. As I soaked her shoulder, she said, "Maaijke, does he hurt you in bed?"

I cried harder. Finally, I blurted out my problem. "No, Mama, no, no, no! It is like we are not married. He won't let me get in bed with him. He won't get in bed with me. When he saw me in my wedding nightgown, the one you gave me, he called me a whore. What can I do? Antje already has three children. Why? Why not me?"

Mama was quiet for a long time. She held me tighter. I cried even harder.

Finally, she said, "Give it time, Maaijke. Maybe with time, he will come to your bed and give you a child."

I knew better; I think she did too. But I returned to Bertus's house.

Nothing changed. After making breakfast, I went back to bed every morning and cried.

Two months later, Gerta, without trying, made me feel worse. She came by to see me. After her parents gave permission, I was the first she told that the day before she had become engaged to Johannus and was to be married in less than a month. She was so happy. I wanted to tell her about me and Bertus but didn't want to intrude on her joy.

My wedding had been bigger and more splendid than hers. But I was so envious of Gerta. Johannus was very handsome. Gerta looked wonderful. She filled out the bodice of her mother's wedding dress more than I expected. Her cheeks were rosy red. Her normally thin face was a bit fuller. She was beautiful. After the ceremony, the bride and groom came down the aisle looking so content, ecstatic—and six months later, she delivered a big baby boy.

The joy in her household provided such a stark contrast to mine. Every day after I finished my morning cry, I splashed cold water on my face to take the red away from my eyes and went to visit Gerta. She let me hold her baby, little Johannus, named after his father. Her expression of absolute contentment as the baby suckled dragged me down with envy. I am sure that she was being kind to me by not asking why I was not pregnant, but the question lay unasked, albeit obvious, between us. I felt worse.

On my eighteenth birthday, after breakfast, and after Bertus left for work in his fields, I began my travels again, now because I had to escape. I had planned to stop these trips when I married Bertus so that I would devote all my time to our new lives. In fact, I did stop for a while, but for a totally different reason. I was so sad, so depressed during the nights that I was at first incapable of the concentration needed to travel through either time or space.

When I started again, I visited many places, but mostly where they spoke English and French because I was now fluent in those. I made some exceptions, including to a corrida de toros in Sevilla, Espagne, where I was both revulsed and fascinated. It was less of a bull fight and more of a morbid ballet—a pas de deux with the death of one partner as the sword plunged through the bull's neck and sliced through his aorta. I went to London many times, and to Edinburgh, where at first I thought I was hearing a totally new language, so different was the Scots accent. Mostly, I traveled to France where the sound of the language was so musical and pretty.

In all these visits, I stayed longer each time, but I found that it didn't matter whether I was gone for a few minutes or even longer than a day: when I came back to Bertus's house, hardly any time had elapsed. Since Bertus was always at work in the fields when I left, or in his own bedroom, he never knew about my travels. As when I was younger, I was never noticed when I went to a different time or place. I could pick up a library book or newspaper and read it, but when people were around, I was invisible to them. One constant was that the longer I stayed away, the more difficult it was to remain there. The concentration to stay someplace took more and more effort as time passed. While with practice, going someplace new got easier and easier, such as the time I went to Howth, Ireland, in 1914, where I saw a beautiful sailing vessel, the *Asgard*, owned by a man who I later learned was a famous author who wrote a spy novel, *The Riddle of the Sands*. Curiously, he—his name was Childers—was delivering a cargo of rifles to an unruly band of men when I was there. Several years later, and I am not sure if it had anything to do with these rifles, he was tried and executed by the British military.

I traveled almost every day and as easy as it became to go someplace, lengthening my stay required fierce concentration until I got sweaty and could no longer sustain my visit. It was like running so fast and so far that I had to collapse to the ground—except when I traveled, I collapsed back to my own time and my own house. These voyages of my imagination were very much similar to dreams I had at night. The dreams occurred in just a few minutes of sleep, but the dream time was much more prolonged, long enough to have complete adventures. My imaginary trips could also transpire over hours or even days, but upon returning, only a few minutes had passed. The only difference between the two was that after my imaginary travels, I was exhausted and sweaty. After my dreams, I felt refreshed.

Still, I kept at it and one day, I decided to go to Spakenburg, where Johannus worked as a fisherman. That was not a reckless act; I went to the year 1971 long, long after Johannus worked there and long after I had helped

Dirk fish. The fishing industry had disappeared because there was no longer access to the sea since the big dijk had been built. I imagined myself in Aunt Jenny's house. She died when I was fourteen, and her house was still empty. When I got there, it was as if she had gone to buy groceries or had left for church just minutes ago. Nothing had changed since she had lived there. The table was set for one person with a clean white tablecloth.

I walked from her door down toward the harbor and arrived at a building near the water and the quays, where I saw a group of older ladies dressed in the type of clothing I wore, except that their dresses were all brighter and of cheerful colors compared to my tired-looking brown dress. But like mine, they went from the tops of their shoes to their necks, then down to their hands, with no skin open to the sun except hands and faces. The skirts of the dresses were cinched tightly at the waist with belts, then billowed out below. The blouses were loose except on their forearms, and they all had white aprons tied around the waist that extended nearly to the bottoms of the dresses. Their hats were quite varied. Some were cylindrical and looked like a birthday cake sitting on their heads. Others were like mine: simple white cotton or wool snugly covering most of my hair, with little starched wings sticking out on the sides. Still others were made of two pieces of cloth sewn together with a seam in the middle of the head so that a sharp prow was formed in the front and back, with each side cut so that lazy wings came to a point hanging down over the ears.

There, in 1971, everything about my travels suddenly changed. One of the ladies—she told me her name was Anneke—came up to me and asked when I was giving my tour. I was no longer invisible. I had no idea what she was talking about; at first, I thought she might have been talking to another woman, but none were around. When I seemed perplexed, she told me that she and other people who were dressed like me were acting as tour guides in what she called "period costume" to tell tourists about the history of the city and of the fishing industry there before the dijk had been constructed. She complimented me on my "costume" and told me how authentic it looked. They were, she told me, looking for more guides. Would I like to be one?

I told her I didn't know anything about being a guide, but it didn't matter to her. She would teach me. She gave me a small book about the local history and said that after I read it, I should come back tomorrow and be a guide. Anneke said we would get a free lunch when we guided tours and a small payment. I had seen their money. It looked nothing like our money so I would not be able to use it when I went home, even though the denominations had the same names. But I couldn't tell Anneke that!

As I left her, I walked back toward Aunt Jenny's house. I looked around furtively and then removed my wedding ring and put it in my pocket. I knew I did not want to appear married here; at the time, I was not sure why. But when I looked back, I had unconsciously made a decision.

On the way to Jenny's, I came upon a bookstore and went inside, immediately finding a section with children's books. I saw one with a familiar drawing on the front cover. How wonderful to see: it was the book I saw Beatrix Potter trying to get published about the little rabbit named Peter. She was successful after all, with her book still in demand almost seventy years later. What a happy discovery!

When I returned to the docent building by the quays the next day, Anneke said I needed to do one more thing before I could teach about the sailing and fishing history of the village. She took me down to the harbor and there, introduced me to an old sailor on an old boat. Botters, they were called. On a botter named *Het Houten Paard*, she introduced me to the captain, Jacob van der Meer, as a new docent. I was startled: he had the same surname, and the same boat name as Dirk, who taught me to sail when I was a young girl. I started laughing.

"Young lady, what are you laughing about?" he asked. "Do you find my name amusing?"

"No, sir. I like your name. I think I have heard it before. I like your boat, too. Please tell me about it."

"Well, Maaijke," he said with a big grin, nearly a laugh, "if you stop laughing, we may become friends. This boat is more than a hundred years old, and it was made by my grandfather as a copy of a nearly identical fishing boat made by *his* grandfather, Diederik. My grandfather kept the same boat name but added a "II" at the end. I got lazy and dropped the "II" off the name. These botters are almost the same as their boat ancestors, except now, with the dijk, we can no longer go out to the Zuiderzee to fish, so we use them for tourists and for racing."

I tried really hard not to laugh, but Jacob could have traded places with Dirk, his great-great-grandfather, who taught me to sail and fish. It was so confusing to be seeing the same kind of boat with the same name and the same (almost) captain but 150 years later. With such a long background with Dirk, and so much fun with him, I immediately took to Jacob. We shook hands and I made the mistake of laughing again, but this time he only laughed back.

"I suppose you want to learn to sail, Maaijke."

"Yes sir. Yes I do."

"Well, you can't go in clothes like that."

"But this is all I have." And, I thought, I sailed in a dress for many years, thank you very much.

"Then go get something more suitable."

"Where?" I said.

"Do I look like a ladies clothes expert?" He laughed. "Anneke can help you."

So, off we went, Anneke and I. It was the first time I had ever been in a ladies' clothing store, at least the first time in 1971. It was enchanting. The fabrics were so seductive. The colors, amazing, dazzling. An eye feast.

"But, Anneke, I do not have any money for these."

"Don't worry, Maaijke. I will buy them and take the money out of your earnings as a tourist guide. But what about your normal clothes? Some of those might work."

"But these are…." I started to say these were my normal clothes but managed to stop in time. I must have had a bemused look.

"What, Maaijke, what?" she asked in puzzlement.

I searched frantically for an answer that would make sense to her. "Well, I am visiting my aunt for a short time, and brought no clothes other than dresses, and I found what I am wearing in a closet she had filled with old clothes. She told me about the tour guides wearing costumes like the old dresses in the closet from her great-grandmother's time, so I put one on. But I have nothing for sailing." I suddenly felt weak with the relief that came from inventing such a good answer.

I got some heavy cotton trousers, a shirt, and a heavy, navy wool sweater. But Anneke encouraged me to get more. I had seen bras in pictures, but we had nothing like that in my time. Nor did we have panties; instead, we wore what might be called pantaloons under our dresses, pants-like garments that came down to our ankles. I bought each and thought that with what they covered, I might as well be wearing nothing under my clothes. I had no trouble getting into the tiny sliver of silk they called panties, but the bra seemed to be some kind of a puzzle. I tried hard to solve it. The two miniature triangles of mostly transparent cloth seemed situated so that each might be a receptacle for a portion of one breast but then the skinny straps sticking out were all tangled together, and I couldn't figure it out.

I went back outside the fitting room and found a mannequin wearing one. The wider straps went around and fastened in back with the little clips, and the smaller straps went over the shoulders. Back in the fitting room, I managed to get it on properly, but fastening the clips where I couldn't see was such a struggle that I gave up. So, I put it on backward where I could see the clips, and then twisted it around so that the bottoms of my breasts lay in the little triangles, and then I was able to stick my hands and arms through the openings created under the skinny straps so that I could put them over my shoulders. When I studied my image in the mirror, I was grinning after my success with the bra puzzle, and wearing only the bra and panties, I was quite pleased with what I saw. Too bad for Bertus, who would never get to see me, and I smiled even more at the thought. I also bought a skirt and a sweater. The one was of fine wool, cream colored, and fit across my waist and hips in a way that was not what Mama would have thought modest. The other was the softest thing I ever felt. Light yellow, high necked and short sleeved, it too left no doubt about what lay beneath it.

When I went back, dressed in my heavy pants, shirt, and sweater, Jacob had gone out with his boat, and I watched the botters with their brown sails dance amid the sun sparkles on the rolling water.

The next day, I went down to the harbor again and met Jacob and his crew of three others, and off we went. Even in my baggy sailing clothes, the crew watched me, and when I appeared not to be looking at them, they watched with covetous eyes. The harbor was chock-a-block with boats, and there was barely room to get the boats out to the open water of the Isselmeer. One crew member on either side of the *Het Houten Paard* wielded a long pole, pushing as needed to keep from ramming other botters. It was hard not to laugh at the syncopated "phut, phut, phut" of the one-cylinder engine.

It was also hard to pretend to be learning what I already knew from my childhood experience on the mothership to this boat.

"So now, Maaijke, these lines are called 'sheets.' They pull the sails in and let them out to catch the wind at the proper angle," said Jacob. "And these are called 'halyards.' They pull the sails and the gaff up."

And with a fake look of confusion, I said, "A gaff? What's a gaff, Jacob?"

"Well, it is the curvy piece of wood that separates the top part of the mainsail from the bottom part."

"Why?"

"Maaijke, if not for the gaff, the sail would be much smaller, and triangular rather than four sided. So, it is more powerful. It allows the sail to be much wider at the top than if it were triangular. If we tried for the same size with one sail, it would be too big to move around."

"Oh, I think I understand, but it seems so complicated," I said, as I thought what a good job I did not to laugh, and not tell him I already knew everything he said.

In the open water, sails up, on starboard tack with the port zward down, we zipped along. Jacob let me steer a bit, with my hand on the tiller and his as well, to be sure we tracked along nicely. As soon as he let go, I started to move the tiller to and fro to create a serpentine wake. I knew I shouldn't let him know I could do it as well as he could.

"No, Maaijke. Hold it steady. Like this. Very light pressure. Feel the wind through the boat. When the wind picks up, feel the pressure on the tiller and give in to it; let the boat head up a bit."

"What is 'head up' Jacob?" I think I was quite convincingly the novice.

"It means when the bow, or front, tends to move closer to the wind," said Jacob.

"Oh, let me try again."

He slowly removed his hand, and I steered a straighter line, forcing myself to continue to sail a little erratically. After about ten minutes, I allowed my hand to do what it did naturally, and we started to gain distance on the other boats following us.

"Maaijke! You are a natural at this. I have never seen anyone learn so quickly. You must come out with us more," he said.

I smiled, pretending to be pleased with the compliment; I struggled hard not to giggle about my "natural" sailing ability that I had learned at the patient hands of Jacob's great-great-grandfather. I don't think Jacob would have understood.

We spent the early afternoon racing other boats. We did well. Especially well, Jacob said, considering that I was at the helm for much of the time and such a neophyte. I almost laughed again but smiled as if receiving a compliment.

Back at the quay, with the boat put away and made shipshape, and the crew leaving, Jacob grabbed me in his bear-like arms and gave me a big hug. It was avuncular, I think—at least mostly, and I liked him even better then. He was so much like his forebear who taught me how to sail.

The next day, dressed in my usual clothes—what the guides called period clothes—I met Anneke, and for a week she showed me how to be a guide. She gave me some books so I could learn the history of the town and the surrounding area. It seemed strange and familiar to be reading as history what I had experienced firsthand.

The next Monday, I had my first tour group. It was kind of fun. I noticed that the men in the group were really attentive and very good students. Their wives were less so. They kept staring at their husbands staring at me. At the end of that week, I was so tired from concentrating on being there that I knew I would shortly be back in the previous century. I told Anneke that I could not work regularly but would try to come back soon. I tried to continue my concentration so I could stay, but the harder I tried, the less it seemed that I could maintain it. I began to get sweaty. I could feel my concentration flagging. I knew that I could stay no longer, and then, I was back in Bertus's house, minutes after I had left it.

I continued to go to different places, but I was always invisible wherever I went. A few times, I returned to the docents' house by the harbor, and as was the case everywhere else, no one could see me; I could not interact. But when, instead, I imagined going to Aunt Jenny's house and walked from there to the harbor, I could be seen, I could talk to others. I was a real person again. But only when I visited through my aunt's home did it work that way. When I skipped her house, I was invisible. I began to realize that something about her house allowed me to shed my non-being to become actualized. So Spakenburg is where I went most of the time and always through the gateway of Jenny's house.

One of the other places I imagined myself to was Belfast, Ireland, in the early twentieth century. It was notable because of a young lad I saw who overflowed with curiosity, whose head seemed barely large enough to contain all his thoughts, and who was a connection to the Peter Rabbit lady. His name, I heard his tutor say, was Clive Lewis, but everyone called him Jacksie or Jack. Jack loved Beatrix Potter stories. Although, as was always the case, with the singular exception of visiting Spakenburg through the portal of Aunt Jenny's house, he couldn't see me. But I loved watching him read the storybooks of Miss Potter because he was so enchanted by them, and so enthusiastic about them. Their influence on him must have been profound because in the library in Amsterdam, I later found that he was a teacher at an old university in Oxford, England, where he too wrote children's books about a family of four children who enter into a fantasyland called Narnia when they go through the back of an old wardrobe.

CHAPTER 22

Peter

—— 1971 ——

S PAKENBURG ONCE SAT ON THE BANKS OF THE ZUIDERZEE, A GATEWAY to the ocean for generations of fishermen. Then, in the 1920s, the Dutch built the Afsluitdijk (we would spell it "dike"). The fishermen were robbed of ocean access, land was reclaimed from the sea, and the water gradually converted from salt to fresh, creating lakes. There were two large ones, the IJsselmeer and the Markermeer, with some smaller interconnected lakes, one of them being the Eemmeer. That's where Spakenburg sat. With the fishing economy only a memory, the town was regaining prosperity through boating and tourism.

In support of this, some Spakenburg women served as docents and dressed in brightly colored period costumes from a century earlier. In the small history museum, a pleasant woman—middle aged, with apple-red cheeks, and enough on the portly side to have jumped from a Rubens painting—told me her costume marked her as an historical guide for the town. She jumped up and pirouetted one turn to show me. She wore a blue top with long sleeves pushed up on her forearms, and with a cutout at mid-chest front and back that was filled in with a draped white scarf. The voluminous skirt was covered with a waist-to-floor apron and her white bonnet had pointed ends turned up on either side. I thanked her for her offer of a tour but instead went to look for a restaurant for lunch.

I wandered up Spuistraat, going away from the water, and approached another of the docents. She had her back to me and was speaking with another visitor in Dutch. I understood only a rare word but was taken in by her confident, rich contralto voice. Blond hair fell astray from under her bonnet. She had nicely tanned ankles and neck, and pretty forearms. All else was covered. I waited until she finished her conversation.

CHAPTER 23

Maaijke

— 1833 and 1971 —

Bertus was still out in the fields when I returned from Spakenburg of 1971. It was still the same day I had left in 1833. At lunchtime, Bertus came into the house without a word about my being gone. He was almost kind.

"Maaijke, you make wonderful potatoes," he said, beaming.

"Thank you, Bertus." What I didn't say was I thought there must be more to life and marriage than potatoes.

That night, nothing changed. After dinner, he grew distant and went into his bedroom. It had a lock now, and I could hear the bolt click closed. I was as miserable as ever. A month had passed. Nothing changed. I thought of asking for a divorce but knew I would be branded as an unstable or even an immoral woman, and would be shunned. Papa and Mama would be disgraced.

I grew increasingly confused and despondent. All day long, Bertus was kind and solicitous, but distant. He never touched me. His demeanor commanded that I not touch him. As soon as dinner ended, he spoke no more until breakfast and, of course, continued to isolate himself in his bedroom. I grew to hate him for my deprivation. I also felt that his coldness must in part be my fault, so I felt guilty for hating him.

At least I had an escape: my travels. I found that lying in bed at night, without the distractions of the daytime, I could focus better on being someplace else, and could visit more sites, more easily. I went to a lot of places, and to a lot of different times, but only in Spakenburg could the people see me. So, that's where I traveled more and more. Also, I was able to stay in Aunt Jenny's house. It had been empty since she died in 1829, but when I visited four years later, when I was eighteen, there was no suggestion that she was gone. Even the bed sheets were clean and pressed. In the mornings, when in this Spakenburg of 1971, I awakened and after breakfast, walked down to the water and met Anneke and her friends. I gave tours about half the time, mostly in Dutch but occasionally in English or French depending on the group.

The other days, I usually went sailing with Jacob and his crew. By now, I had been with them enough that I no longer needed to pretend to be a novice. We won our fair share of races, and all the sailors celebrated after the races in De Schip restaurant. I was introduced to alcohol; it made the evenings more fun. I was the only girl in the group, and the attention I got was a wonderful relief after what went on (or didn't) with Bertus. Many of the sailors tried to get me to go outside with them and sometimes, I did. Occasionally, I even let them kiss me, but none of them were interested in stopping with a kiss. Their roving hands wandered over my breasts and even other parts, and although I didn't completely dislike it, I resisted. It didn't feel right to me. I think I felt that I would be disappointing Jacob, whom by this time I was calling Uncle Jacob. Still, I loved the attention.

CHAPTER 24

Peter

—— 1971 ——

"EXCUSE ME. DO YOU SPEAK ENGLISH?" I ASKED THE LOVELY DOCENT. She turned to me. "Yes, h…" She stumbled, then regained composure, asking, "How may I help you?"

I stared at her, my speech faltering. "I… I…"

I was paralyzed; both verbal and mental paralysis clutched me. I could only stare at her. Words backed up in my throat, clogging my speech. I had wanted to ask for restaurant advice; now I searched desperately to say anything, everything, and couldn't get a sound out. My lips moved; my vocal cords didn't. I could feel the redness creeping into my face. She was the loveliest girl I had ever seen. She must have been about eighteen or twenty, perhaps five or six years younger than me. She was almost my height. Her blond hair was curled at the ends, away from her neck, and ended midway between her ears and her shoulders. I expected blue eyes, but they were a dark brown. Her nose was straight and prominent, as were her high cheekbones. She had very white, somewhat crooked teeth, but her smile nearly felled me, it was so inviting. Her period costume was clean and starched but more worn and less colorful than those of the other docents. It also somehow appeared less a costume than a piece of everyday clothing. She wore it effortlessly, unselfconsciously.

There was something more about her that drew me in. She was clearly young, but her face…her expressions seemed old, wise, kind. It was if she exuded great inner substance and strength.

"Poor boy," she said, her lovely Dutch accent inflecting understandable English. She giggled, then laughed. A solid, gay laugh. "You are red turning."

"I… I…"

"You what? You can say it," she said.

But she was wrong; I couldn't. Like a mute, I finally pantomimed, pointing to my mouth indicating my desire for a restaurant.

"You want to kiss me? I don't even know you!" she responded, delighted in my embarrassment and awkwardness.

"No, no," I shook my head, thinking, *Oh God, yes, yes.* "Restaurant," I finally managed to stumble out, feeling foolish, thinking I must appear mentally challenged.

"Why you not say so? Come, I show you."

Off we went. First, I followed her by a step, but she slowed and put her arm through mine as if we'd been friends forever.

A block off the Spuistraat, we arrived at a restaurant, an *eethuys,* she called it. I got to where I could almost think and act normally. I started to thank her, but instead of leaving, she shushed me, placing her index finger against my lips as she drew me inside.

"My-yick-a," she said, pointing at her chest by way of introduction.

"What?"

"M, A, A, I, J, K, E. *Maaijke.* Me. Like you Maaijke?"

I tried not to smile at her awkward phrasing. I didn't know if the two meanings of the question were deliberate or accidental, so I chose only to answer the less personal one.

"Yes. I like your name," I said, answering the second question in the affirmative but silently. And then I pointed at my chest, saying, "Peter."

We were seated in a booth. Dark wood. Dim lighting. She glowed. The waitress asked if we would like something to drink.

I ordered a Grolsch, one of the only two Dutch beers I knew.

"No, no," Maaijke said. "I order for you. Local beer."

Two rich dark drafts came, but I was intoxicated without a sip. Maaijke also ordered the lunch for us. The promise of what might come next made it difficult to breathe normally. Was I misreading the signs?

CHAPTER 25

Maaijke

—— 1833 and 1971 ——

ONE DAY, THERE WAS A CHANGE, A BIG CHANGE. IT WAS MY DAY TO GIVE tours. I had a Dutch group, and they seemed to like me so much that they—at least the men—all gave me tips afterward. As I said goodbye and was putting the coins in my pocket, a man came up to me on the Spuistraat.

"Do you speak English?"

I turned and looked at him. Stared at him.

"Ja. I mean, yes." Giggling I could not stop. I felt the way I did when I drank too much beer. "May I help you?"

He was about six feet tall, a little bit thin, and had fair but tanned and blushing skin, and hair not brown but not blond either. Sort of halfway in between. He seemed not to be able to speak but only stare, as I stared back. He looked at my face with gorgeous blue eyes, as if he had never seen a girl before. I'd never seen him before but even so, he looked familiar. Maybe it was the strong chin and high cheekbones, much like mine. Finally, he point-ed to his mouth. I didn't know what he meant, nor do I know what made me say, "Do you want to kiss me?" I hoped he did.

He blushed crimson and shook his head. Finally, he said one word, "Restaurant."

"Why didn't you say so? Come, I will take you."

Off we went. He started by following, so I slowed for a moment, linked my arm in his, and he sped up to my pace. We spoke no more until we reached the restaurant. At least we spoke nothing verbally. But he kept looking at me, and I at him. I squeezed his arm a bit tighter; he blushed. I felt so comfortable with him. As if we had known each other forever. As we reached the restaurant, a plan emerged in my mind, a plan I realized had been subconsciously drawn up long before and was part of the reason for my travels.

At the door, he started to go in and thanked me, but instead of leaving as he expected, I walked in with him and shushed him when he started feebly to object.

I told him my name, which seemed difficult for him, and he told me his was Pieter, but he told me it was spelled without an "i."

We sat in a booth. The restaurant was quite dark, and I could not see him well. But not for lack of trying. I stared at him. I tried to invade his thoughts. Everything was strange. He was much older than me (but still much younger than Bertus), and probably much more experienced. When he spoke, he did so slowly, deliberately, and very clearly. But he seemed shy. At first, he had difficulty talking with me and only gradually was he more at ease. I asked him questions. When he asked me to tell him something about me, I deflected him by asking another question. He told me about a place called Viet Nam; about flying a "jet fighter plane"; about his dog, Red; about his sister and his mother and his father; about hunting and fishing in the west of his country. He told me so much about which I knew nothing. But I pretended to know, nodding my head as if I did, and later, I went to the library and looked up everything he mentioned. I, of course, told him little or nothing about me. How could I? I couldn't tell him I traveled from a previous century; I did not want him to think me insane.

And clearly, he did not. Keeping our gazes locked, we spoke. I could not escape his eyes and face, nor could he escape mine. "I love you," I read from his expression. I felt the same. So quickly it happened.

During lunch, we held hands. Remarkable hands, he had—tanned, strong looking, but very graceful. I thought he must be a piano player. I imagined what they would feel like touching me. He made me giggle and laugh, and sometimes he made me very serious. He was enchanting. I tried to be so, too.

He asked my full name, and I started to tell him but stopped and told him my maiden name rather than my married name. It was good that I did so because then he told me his name was Maasen! I shivered and felt sick. I ran to the bathroom and stayed there for many minutes, washing my face with cold water. How could he have my last name? Could we be related? No, that was silly; he came from more than a century later. Gradually, I dismissed the coincidence and went back into the circle of his warmth.

From my travels in England, I had become quite fluent in English, but he still laughed at my grammar. The word order can be quite different, and I made him promise to teach me better English. But for us, the English was superfluous; we had an immediate, more basic level of communicating.

CHAPTER 26

Peter

—— 1971 ——

W E ENTERED THE RESTAURANT JUST AFTER NOON AND LEFT AT FOUR. It was my longest lunch ever, and it seemed to last about sixty seconds. Gradually, my ability to speak returned. Everything I said seemed to delight her. She was alternately solemn and gay. She tried to teach me a few Dutch words and sentences and laughed at my troubles with the language. I tried not to laugh at her sometimes-strange word order.

She made fun of me. She was sympathetic. She bounced from wise to puppyish. She clung to every word I uttered, and by her demeanor, I was the most important person ever to exist. I told her about my parents, my sister, growing up in Wyoming, hunting, and fishing. I told her about being a Navy pilot and about some of my experiences in Viet Nam. I did not mention Willis Hollister.

She told me almost nothing about herself, but I didn't care. I was too absorbed in her aura. Her smile was everything. It invaded me, beckoned me. It joined us into one, walling others out. She smiled with her eyes alone, her lips alone, her cheeks and forehead alone, and often with every part of her face. She had limitless gradations of smile; all drew me in.

I felt isolated, as if we floated in a pool containing only the two of us.

Later, I could recall almost nothing of the restaurant but everything about her. And still, I never realized at the time that she told me nothing about herself.

After a salad, we waited for the main course, a wait I hoped would last forever.

"Put your hands on the table," she said.

What a strange request. I obeyed. I placed my tanned outdoorsman's hands palms down.

"I like them," she said.

Then, she picked up each of my fingers, dropping them with a thunk back on the wood. Each time, it felt like a caress. She asked if I were a pianist. I laughingly confessed to having no musical talent.

I was charmed, maybe too much so. I watched her face, her exquisite face, and she returned my gaze with intimacy, an enigmatic smile, and an expression of sorrow-tinged happiness.

"My turn," I said. "Put your hands on the table." She did. I picked one up and placed it on my left hand, palm to palm, and sandwiched it with my right.

"Don't let go," she said, almost visibly melting. "Tell me your whole name."

"Peter Maasen."

She shuddered and withdrew her hand, staring at me with an expression of horror-tinged shock.

"I must visit toilet," she said, abruptly leaving the table, nearly running and holding her dress up to avoid tripping.

After about ten minutes, she returned to the table more composed. At first, she was subdued but gradually regained her previous state of infectious happiness.

"So, tell me your name. Your whole name," I asked. "Maaijke what?"

She paused, as if thinking. As if it were not an automatic answer. How could anyone not know their name?

"Maaijke De Jongh," she said, smiling shyly, warmly. "And with your name, you are Dutch, too?"

"Well, not exactly, but my family did come from somewhere around Spakenburg. Did my name scare you? You ran away looking frightened."

"I was startled; I used a family to know with the same name. Many, many years ago…Why you smile when I talk?"

"Because I like your voice, and because sometimes your English is not quite right. We would say, 'I used to know a family with the same name.' But you can't be more than twenty years old. How could you know someone so many years ago?" I was confused.

"I am eighteen."

"Then how could you know a family with my name many, *many* years ago?"

"It doesn't matter. Age is not everything. I think maybe it is family memory."

She placed her hand on the table, palm up, as I had done before she left.

"Come," she said. Her smile erased any inconsistency she had introduced.

I covered her palm with mine, and she placed her other hand on top.

"What if I want to take my hand back?" I asked.

"I am strong for a girl," she said. "You may be forever between."

And with her solemn look that elided into a warm smile, we returned to a private world where only we existed, until the food came, way too soon.

It was a cod dish finished with a frothy butter sauce and saffron. I wished the best meal in my life would last forever. But too quickly, the check came and Maaijke helped me with the various denominations of coins and bills. Guilders, I knew. But stuivers, dubbeltjes, and kwartjes bewildered me, which delighted her to an equal degree.

Still laughing at me, with me, she pulled me out of the restaurant. I offered no resistance. I wondered if I misinterpreted her intentions. She was so young, so innocent seeming, yet so knowing. So…*well*…so seductive.

CHAPTER 27

Maaijke

—— 1833 and 1971 ——

THE PLAN. IT WAS COMING INTO SHARPER FOCUS. I WANTED A BABY like Gerta had. I also wanted to know how it felt to be a woman. Back home, Bertus would never give me either. It would be unthinkable to have a baby with another man. I would be shunned and would have to leave the village, and never see my family again.

But if I got pregnant in 1971, what could Bertus do? Or say? Since no one knew I traveled—I was only gone a few minutes each time I left—and I was never out of our home except with Bertus, he could never say publicly that I had lain with another man. He couldn't very well tell people that he never had sex with me! Everyone would think him strange or a pervert—as I already thought him—and he would become an outcast. The only recourse he would have would be to accept the congratulations about his manliness and my fecundity, and help to raise his baby, *our* baby. I was not even sure he knew what was done to make babies, but he probably did and was unable to do it.

So, I decided Peter was going to father my child. If I could get him to do so. I wasn't exactly sure how to go about that, but I had a feeling it would happen quite naturally. I didn't even feel as if I were manipulating him or deceiving him, because from the minute I saw him when I was guiding my tourist group, I felt an immediate attraction for him. But more than that, I even knew I wanted to be with him the rest of my life. As content as I was, as happy as I was to be with him, I was also sad because I realized I would have to go back to my time and to Bertus. Only if I were able to sustain my concentration on being in 1971 could I remain with Peter. But I knew I was not capable of that.

The lunch was over very quickly, it seemed. The clock on the wall said "No, it has been four hours."

We finished lunch, and I laughed at him trying to understand our money. Then, we left, and holding hands, I took him to Aunt Jenny's home. We cut through the dense hedge using the old tunnel, crossed the yard, and climbed the steps into the house. Whenever I arrived there, I was moved back into the time when she lived. Whenever I left it, I was back in 1971. I could not explain this, but Peter immediately asked about the ancient nature of the building. No running water, no electricity, no sewer system, no phone. An old wood- or coal-burning cast-iron stove, and on the opposite wall, an old bake oven as part of the fireplace, an old kettle hanging in the fireplace. They seemed perfectly normal to me when I thought of where I came from, but it was certainly different from the time I was in. He didn't notice the outhouse.

He asked about all this, and I could only change the subject; I didn't know exactly how to explain this transformation. But mostly, he was willing to dismiss the house. I was his entire focus. As he was mine.

CHAPTER 28

Peter

— 1971 —

MAAIJKE STOOD FROM THE LUNCH TABLE IN THE EETHUYS. "Where are you going?"

"Come. I show you. I think you like," she said, briefly grazing my shoulder with her forehead.

Out we went. Again, she linked my arm with hers but then switched to holding my hand. We turned corner after corner until I was lost, but from the sun, I knew we were going southwest. South a block, west a block, and then again. She led me to a corner with dense tall boxwoods on the intersecting streets. Walking west along one of them, she released my arm, and suddenly seemed to disappear.

"Follow me," she said.

"I don't see you."

"Come straight ahead," she instructed.

I did and found that I seemed to be in a tunnel through the boxwood. It went in diagonally, then turned and suddenly emptied into a yard facing a small brick house with a gambrel roof and stone foundation walls. She placed my hand in hers, and led me up the walk, and up the three granite front steps. She opened the door, and we were in a brick-walled, white-washed room with a very old fireplace. Soot crept up over the lintel, and within the darkened opening was an iron rod with hooks from which hung a large, old, black pot, and some other smaller ones. A grill-like shelf came out of the back wall. Above the lintel was a square recess with an iron door on heavy hinges: an oven door. On the other side of the room stood an old, cast-iron stove. The adjacent wall had a freestanding soapstone sink on supports, and behind it was a pump handle for a well with a spout hanging out over the sink. Nonexistent were the usual chrome handles for hot and cold water; in fact, there seemed to be no hot water. The sink drained through a hole into a pan to which was connected a half-tubular sluiceway that led through a hole in the wall to the outside. In the center of the room were a crude table and chairs sitting on a smooth, worn, and unvarnished wood floor.

She led me through a door into what might be a living room, but there were no electric lights, only candles and lanterns. Along the base of the walls, there were no electric outlets.

Upstairs, she led me to a bedroom with a small double bed, neatly made up. The covers were turned down a bit on the near corner, showing coarsely woven white cotton sheets. The west-facing room with a single window was bathed in the afternoon yellow sunlight bouncing off white plastered walls.

Nothing made sense. It was if I had stepped back into another century, consistent with the period of her clothes. Was I imagining this? Was it an historical facsimile? Something like Old Sturbridge Village?

"You wait, please," she said, and stepped behind a screen in the room corner. After some rustling, her dress was thrown over the screen top, and I heard cloth sliding on cloth, after which she reappeared, rendering me nearly mute again. She wore an off-white straight wool skirt; stylish, tailored tan shoes; and a pale yellow, short-sleeved, high-neck sweater. The knee-length skirt fit perfectly, but modestly. The sweater appeared to be of the softest wool, showing her to be small in the waist and lusciously bulged out above. Only with effort was I able to keep my hands from reaching out to feel the sweater.

"You like? The old dress very smodgy."

"Smodgy?"

"Yes, like old lady dress from long ago."

"Oh, do you mean stodgy?"

"*Ja, ja.* Stodgy," she said, accompanied with musical laughter.

"Do you live here? It seems so old. Do you cook here?"

"Of course. I think I make you dinner. You will like."

"Now? It's too early for dinner. We finished lunch only minutes ago," I said.

"No, silly. Later for dinner. Afterward."

"After what?" I felt unaccountably and unusually nervous. I could feel the heat in my face and ears.

She giggled. "Are you afraid of me?"

"No. Well, maybe a little. It's just that...."

"What?"

"Well, I have never been with a woman as beautiful as you."

"Dank u." She blushed and laughed again.

"So, now," she said. "I have question. Did you ever have favorite teacher? One you remember?"

I laughed, remembering Miss Clarke. "Oh, yes. Oh, yes, very much."

"Good. Are you good teacher?"

"I don't know," I said, wondering where we were headed.

"I have more question. Maybe it is not proper to ask."

"No, ask anything."

"Are you furgin?"

"What?"

"Furgin. You know. You never have sex with lady."

Laughing hard, I collapsed onto the bed. "You mean virgin," I was finally able to say.

"Yes, yes," she said, beaming.

Why could it be so hard and yet also so easy to talk to her, I thought.

"So tell me. Are you?" she said.

"No, I am definitely not a 'furgin,'" I said nervously.

"Okay," she said, suddenly serious. "Now you have two things to teach me. English, you promised. Besides, I am virgin. I want you to teach me not to be virgin." Totally unselfconsciously, uninhibited, unembarrassed: like she might say, teach me to tie my shoes.

"I can't do that."

"Do you have problem? Unable to do fuck?" As if saying, "You can't put your shoes on?"

"No, of course not," I said. I felt as if she were accusing me—but of what? I began to feel that I was the inexperienced one. I laughed uneasily, uncomfortably. "It's that you are...so young." I wondered if I had crossed into insanity. Never had I met any woman I would more like to "do fuck" with. I was almost afraid to go forward for fear I would suddenly be thrown from this fantasy.

"Look at me. Do I look too young? Do I have a little girl's body? I am virgin, but I have talked to friends, and I have read. I know a lot about how to do sex."

More and more, I felt like the virginal and inexperienced one.

Then she stood before me, felt behind her waist, and unbuttoned the skirt, which whispered to the floor. She kicked out of her shoes. She crossed her hands in front of her, held the sweater hem, and lifted it slowly over her head, as barely covered breasts popped free of the soft yellow wool.

I stared, mesmerized. She had decidedly modern underwear, with small bikini panties of a sheer fabric that revealed the blond hair beneath. The skin of her belly looked almost out of focus with the sun reflecting off the barely visible blond fuzz that also enhanced her face. The flimsy bra seemed to have no function other than to showcase her breasts, much of which lay inviting and bare above the bra, as her nipples jutted out against the lacy, tissue-thin material.

She moved to me; I trembled. I had by now completely lost my reluctance, my reservations. I unhooked her bra strap. She stepped away from me, the bra fell silently to the floor. And then she laughed in deep, rollicking, joyful tones.

"You do that so quick. You have much experience, I can tell. I am now sure you are not virgin. You will be good teacher."

Her panties were off. I had begun to shed my clothes when she bent to complete the task.

"And you would appear to be a very good student."

She was both young and mature, athletic appearing and softly curvy, innocent, and lusty. From the neck up, and wrists down, she was tan, but her skin was otherwise creamy. Her nipples were a nulliparous, rosy pink. She was splendidly, harmoniously proportionate. She wore no makeup, no nail polish.

She unselfconsciously returned my appraisal. "You are even nicer with no clothes," she said, giggling as she looked down, staring. "I see why your underpants are so hard to come down!" I was unaccustomed to such frankness from women. I could feel the heat in my cheeks as I blushed, again feeling suddenly inexperienced.

She knelt and picked up my hand. "Remember at restaurant? I had your hand between mine. I said you may be forever between. I want you forever between. *Now.*"

CHAPTER 29

Maaijke

—— 1833 and 1971 ——

"Now. I want you forever between. Hurry."

And we were in bed.

It all happened as if we had been picked up by a maelstrom, spinning together.

Lying next to him, I wrapped my hand around him. I wanted to move my hand, but before that, his body suddenly stiffened, and he spurted all over my hand. He blushed again and tried to speak but seemed dumbstruck. I think he was embarrassed to be so quick. He told me that had never happened before, but maybe he only said that to make me feel very sexy.

I took his hand and moved it down to between my legs and had him do what I did to myself in bed at home. It felt very nice. Even wonderful. And every time I was ready to be orgasmed, he stopped and waited a few minutes before starting again. It was almost like torture, torture to be led so close to the pinnacle only to slide back until I looked down and saw he was ready again.

CHAPTER 30

Peter

— 1971 —

T HE SUN RAN ITS RAYS ACROSS HER, CARESSING HER SKIN AS SHE LAY on the bed. My fingers barely brushed along the softness of her cheeks, her neck, her breasts, and down onto her legs. I had never been so tense or aroused. And there was something else I wasn't sure I understood, but I was sure I had never felt it before.

She led me into her, entwining me with her legs, her hips undulating with increasing pace. Her pink chest developed a sheen of perspiration, and she came, squeezing me rhythmically, as she continued to thrust up. She smiled at me and said, "Now. Now you do. Inside me, hurry."

And shuddering, I did, as she with arms and legs pulled me into her. "I am happy," she said. "I am no longer a virgin. That was better than anything in my life."

She was totally limp, totally relaxed, and offered that we-are-one smile.

And then, she said, "Mama, now I understand," and started laughing. Her belly and breasts shook with the mirth. Dislodged, beads of sweat formed rivulets down the slopes of her body.

"Maaijke, I thought you liked that," I said, disappointed. "Why are you laughing? What did you mean, 'Mama, now I understand?'"

Maaijke laughed harder. Tears flowed. But she had a painting-worthy smile, almost saintly.

"Peter, because I am so happy. Because I have been waiting so long for this. It was wonderful. Better than Mama said. Better than I imagined. Much better."

"Better than anything I ever imagined, too," I said. "Almost as if you knew how to do that better than I. You taught me, I am thinking."

"Thank you. It is my first time, but I have thought about it a lot, I have read about it, and talked to my friends, and I have watched it done. I have wanted to do this for a long time."

"Did you watch it in the movies?"

"No, I did not see…*movies*. I watched through the bedroom window, watched my parents. When I was five."

"You did what?"

As she described her adventures in the beech tree outside her parents' bedroom window, I could not contain my own mirth.

"Ever since then, I have been wishing to know what made Mama so happy, to have such an ecstatic look on her face. That is why I said that."

When I could finally stop laughing enough to talk, I said, "You made me so excited, I forgot about… What if you get pregnant?"

"Don't worry."

In a very far distant corner of my brain, I suppressed the question of why this lovely virgin would be on the pill.

"I have never been so excited," I said. "It felt like the first time for me."

"I am very glad. I love the way you touch me, the way you brush my hair with your fingers, the way you kiss, everything. Tell me what you are thinking now."

I paused for nearly a minute before I realized what the unfamiliar feeling was, and gravely said, "I am thinking…I…I love you."

"Do you say that to all ladies after you do sex?"

"No, Maaijke, I have never said that to anyone. Ever."

"Peter, I love you too. Always." And she started crying.

"Don't cry." I wiped the wet from her cheeks. "Why are you crying?"

"Because I am so happy, and so sad."

"Why are you sad, Maaijke?"

"I can't tell you. Maybe someday you will understand. Not now, though."

She slept. Still between her legs, I pushed into a kneeling position and watched her. The sinking sun coated her in gold. Her breasts flattened slightly against her chest. The sun carried the silhouette of the left breast to the base of the wall, and I watched as her nipple shadow moved slowly up the wall from the floor until it disappeared, swallowed in the shadow of trees as the sun fell below them and sucked all the light away. Then, lying next to her, holding her, I too slept until she awakened.

CHAPTER 31

Maaijke

—— 1833 and 1971 ——

I HAD BECOME A FULL WOMAN. WHAT I HAD BEEN ANTICIPATING FOR YEARS was really happening. My back arched in spasms, pushing me up against him. It was better than I expected, and in just a few minutes, my whole insides got warm, then hot. The bottoms of my feet were hot, and the heat went up my entire body in a wave, into my head. I could feel myself squeezing him, but I wasn't doing it myself; something had invaded my body and was squeezing him until the wave collapsed on itself, and my entire being turned to formless honey. Again, his whole body stiffened and when I looked at him, his eyes were closed, and he almost seemed to be in pain. But they opened, and he smiled. A smile warm and sweet like Mama's, a smile that seemed to come from deep within him and a sum of everything good and joyous, but also a smile of solemnity.

No longer was I thinking about my plan. I could only think of him inside me, and the look on his face.

He became soft and then he bent his head and kissed me on a nipple. I wondered if that is what nursing a baby would feel like.

His face became serious. He said he was so excited that he forgot about contraception, and thus reminded me of my plan. I knew I loved him; I did not want to lie, but how could I tell him about me? Because I would be forced to return home, I said he didn't need to worry about me getting pregnant. I know he thought that I meant I was on birth control of some kind and not what I was thinking: that any baby would be born in 1834. With each hour spent with Peter, I knew more that I wanted always to be with him. But with each of those hours, it became more and more difficult to maintain enough concentration to stay in his time. Maybe it was merely hope, but I thought I could tell that it was happening—that the earliest beginnings of a baby were there. And then I cried. I wanted so to be with him to have our baby.

But that was impossible.

Before I drifted off to sleep, my last view was of his reassuring face, and my tears evaporated; my emotional distress was pushed aside by my contented happiness at being part of Peter.

CHAPTER 32

Peter

— 1971 —

AFTER LYING WITH ME FOR AN HOUR, SHE GOT UP IN THE FADING LIGHT, picked up her panties, and—stepping from one tiptoe to the other— slowly and theatrically raised them into place while staring at me as a taunt. Just before we slept, she was crying. Her persona changed with the quickness of a trout's tail flip. Now, the seductive Maaijke was back. Next, she fastened her bra, then pulled it up onto her breasts, cupping them with her hands as she nestled them into place within the scant fabric, first one and then the other, all the while with a devilish look. She tantalized very deliberately.

"You torture me," I said. She smiled. I jumped from bed, trying to pull her back in, but she dodged my grasp.

"Maybe later," she said. "No, not maybe. For sure. But first, dinner." She stepped into her skirt and tugged the sweater over her head and breasts in a reverse strip tease. She grabbed my hands and held them against her breasts. "So you don't forget," she said.

"As if I could."

I lay back in bed, trying to understand what had happened. All of it was confusing, both my never-experienced feeling and the strange nature of the house. Soon, pungent cooking aromas rose from the kitchen below, infiltrating my thoughts and awakening my hunger. Downstairs, the table was set. White wine filled two tumblers. The smell of cooking meat emanated from the frying pan on the stove, from which wafted the odor of burning wood, both scents mingling deliciously. I looked around and, not finding it, asked, "Where is the bathroom?"

She pointed to the window at a small building behind the house.

I was incredulous. *No indoor plumbing?* "You have an outhouse? Why?"

Rather than giving a direct answer, she said, "Have you taken a hotel room?"

"Yes. I checked in to the Hotel Sint Nicolaas."

"Do you have a bathroom?"

"Yes, of course." Until a few minutes earlier, I thought everyone did.

"Good. After dinner, we can stay in your hotel. Then we don't need to go to the outhouse." She had a self-satisfied look.

I nodded.

Dinner was simple, consisting of buttered potatoes with parsley, and veal cooked in lemon, butter, and white wine. It was unclear whether the remarkable taste was a product of the food and its preparation or the joy of being with Maaijke. I asked her questions about her family, and she told me their names but not a lot about them. I didn't really care, especially when she told me that we had better, more fun things to do.

When we finished eating, she pumped well water into a heavy black iron kettle, boiled it on the wood-burning stove, and used it to wash the dishes and frying pan.

Upstairs again, she packed clothes and toiletries into a leather valise that seemed old enough to me to have come from an earlier century.

"Don't you need that dress?" I said, pointing to the period dress she had worn when I first saw her in the late morning.

"No, I do not have to work tomorrow. I have things for us to do."

I carried her valise as we walked downtown to my hotel. Streetlights shone brightly. Was it okay to walk into a hotel room with a single woman? Yes. The hotel clerk looked both curious and envious.

CHAPTER 33

Maaijke

—— 1833 and 1971 ——

AS WE SAT AT DINNER, WE DID NOT TALK MUCH, BUT WE LOOKED AT EACH other a lot. Peter asked more about me. I thought it safe to tell him about my actual family without revealing that they lived in the previous century. I told him about my parents, their names, and the names of my sister and brothers. When he asked what they did, I could tell Peter, with honesty, that Antje lived at home with her husband and was the mother of three children, and that my brothers were all farmers. Then Peter started to ask questions I didn't want to or didn't think I could safely answer, such as: did they go to college, where did they go to school, did I have any photographs of them (it was not long ago that I even saw my first photograph), where did they all live, and could he meet them? All things that might reveal too much about me.

I got out of the predicament by giving a sexy, loving smile, which I wanted to do anyway, walking around the table, winding my arms around his neck, rubbing my sweater and its contents against his shoulder, and saying, "You ask too many questions, and I have ideas for better things to do than talk."

He knew precisely what I had in mind. I read in him the same thoughts, and he was thus easily diverted from his questions.

CHAPTER 34

Peter

—— 1971 ——

WE GOT OUT OF THE ELEVATOR ON THE THIRD FLOOR AND WALKED TO my room, which looked out over the lights of Spakenburg Harbor to the north. I placed the valise against the wall, and as I turned, she was already down to bra and panties. I eagerly helped her complete the process. We spent the night making love and sleeping. She insisted on trying different positions and told me that she liked it best on top so I could watch her as she went up and down, and she could watch me watching her. After one of several rounds, as I lay in dreamy peace, she asked me what I was humming.

"The Beatles," I told her, with surprise she didn't recognize the song.

She lifted up on her elbows with a puzzled look. "I hate them."

"Really? You must be the first. Why?"

"I hate the sound they make when I step on them. 'Splat, crunch.' Then it's hard to get the stain off the floor," she said, with an angry pout across her face.

I started to laugh. "I love you. And I love your sense of humor. I know my humming isn't great, but even so, you must like 'Hey Jude.'"

"Of course I do. I was only kidding. I like your humming." She playfully stuck her tongue out at me.

In the morning, we showered and dressed. She chose my clothes; she wore slacks, a thick, navy wool sweater, and rubber-bottomed shoes. Off we went for breakfast in a café, where, thinking more rationally, I again asked about birth control.

"Peter, you asked me yesterday. Didn't you believe me?"

"Well, sure, but still...if you were a 'furgin' before yesterday, why were you on birth control pills?"

"Peter, stop. That is for women to talk about. Mama told me about all of this, and about getting pregnant. That is why you don't need to worry. I'm beginning to think you don't trust me. How can you love me—you said you did—if you don't trust me?"

"Maaijke, of course I do. Until you, I didn't even know what it meant to love someone. I do trust you. I do." I was trying to convince myself as much as her.

Even with my first glimpse of her, there was something more, far more than her attractiveness that appealed to me. It was if she had some luminosity inside of her that spoke to me. That, and some degree of mystery I couldn't fully understand—yet it increased her allure. In less than one day, my whole life had changed because of her. I felt welded to her. Now, I worried that if I kept quizzing her, she might change her opinion of me.

After that, she led me down to the harbor, seemingly undeterred in her determination to love me.

On the way, a Ford Mustang, going far too fast, almost brushed us as we were about to cross the street. I brought Maaijke to a quick stop by knocking her back with my arm.

"Damn Mustang," I said.

"What?" she said. "What are you talking about? There are none here, but I have read about these American horses. You must have had a lot of them where you grew up."

"Yeah. Dad has one."

"Only one? Did he catch it? Tame it?"

"No, he bought it. From the dealer." And then it dawned on me. "A car, silly. Not a horse."

And she smiled to let me know she was kidding. I could only smile back at her. Invested in her smile was her entire personality. She did have an odd sense of humor.

Lining the quay were about thirty fat sailing vessels. They looked heavy, unwieldy. I guessed them to be about thirty-five feet long, quite old, and to my eye, sort of messy and homely. There were ropes and sails scattered about. The boats—*botters*, Maaijke called them—were all made of wood. Many of the sails lashed onto the wooden booms were brownish red. Boatmen swarmed over the old craft. Engines were sporadically starting with their strange single cylinder syncopation, where each detonation could be distinctly heard. So closely packed were the boats that I thought they could never become untangled to get out to the free water of the Eemmeer.

The boatmen all appeared to know Maaijke, bantering with her as she walked down the pier holding my hand. "Sail with me, Maaijke." "No, don't. My boat is faster. Come with me." "Maaijke, I thought you were saving yourself for me!" "Maaijke, your face is red. What have you been up to?" "Who is your new boyfriend?"

In response, she held my hand more tightly, smiled at the various crew, and kept walking with a somewhat exaggerated sway of her hips until we had passed by most of the boats. At one, with "Het Houten Paard" painted on the bow, she stopped, and an older grizzled man with bent back, short white hair, and a three-day beard of the same color held out his hand, which she took and stepped aboard. She pulled me behind her.

"Jacob, this is my friend Peter."

Jacob squinted, carefully assessing me, and circled me on the broad flat foredeck of the botter.

"I guess he will do. How good a friend, Maaijke?"

She leaned over to Jacob and whispered in his ear.

I thought Jacob might be blushing, but with his deep tan it was hard to be sure.

He turned to me, grabbed my hand with both of his, and gave it a vigorous shake.

"Well, then we will need to take very good care of you," he said, laughing.

My face grew hot as I tried to imagine what Maaijke had whispered to Jacob. Taking me aft in the boat, Maaijke introduced the three other crewmen, all of whom were wielding long poles to push the boat out of her space and into the cramped channel between the two rows of boats. The one-cylinder engine spoke a metronomic, "phhhup, phhhup, phhhup," as we crept out toward the Eemmeer.

Maaijke and Jacob showed me around the boat. On each side was a large, paddle-like structure on a pivot. These *zwards*, or lee boards, were rotated down into the water as a fin on the side away from the wind to reduce sideslip in these wide, flat-bottomed boats. It was necessary, Jacob said, to have shallow draft boats in the shallow coastal water. The rudder hung off the low stern of the boat rather than being under it and was controlled with a rather crude muscular tiller. There were ropes—"lines," Maaijke said—strewn about chaotically. The boom and brown sail filled much of the cockpit. I knew little of sailing, but had seen fleet, graceful sailing vessels before—including Sarah's family yacht in Osterville, on which we occasionally sailed—and knew that a boat this fat and ungainly would be slow. These botters were originally designed for fishing, but since the ocean had been closed off to them, they were now used for pleasure sailing, racing, and to carry tourists, Maaijke explained.

Once out in the open water, Jacob and his crew raised the sails. As Maaijke explained in a running commentary, first came the mainsail. The uneven quadrilateral of the sail was gaff-rigged with a curvy, wishbone-shaped gaff, above which was a smaller triangular sail. The jib, also three-sided, was then raised, and the engine turned off. The bowsprit was pushed forward, and another high-cut jib was raised from it. There was a modest breeze of about ten knots, in which the boat showed immense power and sped off at over seven knots. I was sure wrong about the fat boat being slow.

Maaijke took the tiller. Her steering seemed to be the established practice on the boat. Her windblown hair, streaming out behind, was a perfect accompaniment to the joy the swift craft brought to her face. She was apparently a born helmswoman, and both Jacob and his crew seemed comfortable with her controlling the boat. They sailed up the Eemmeer, tacking back and forth on either side of the northwest wind.

"Jacob," said Maaijke, "Peter is in the US Navy. Can he sail your boat?"

"No, no," I remonstrated, as Maaijke pulled me back to the tiller, placed my hand on it, and removed hers.

It took only seconds to realize that Sarah's tutelage on her Concordia had been dismally ineffective. The straight wake behind us began to look serpentine. Then the boat was suddenly swinging as the wind caught the jibs on their back side—shifting the boat quickly around and putting the wind almost behind us—as the crew jumped to tack the jibs to the other side. Jacob and Maaijke laughed as he wrapped a bear-like arm around her and she reclaimed the tiller, bringing the vessel back toward the wind, now on the opposite tack.

"US Navy?" Jacob said. "I thought they knew what they were doing. With sailors like Peter, no wonder Viet Nam was so screwed up!" But he was laughing.

"No," I said. "I don't sail. I flew airplanes. I did not drive boats and ships. We have a really good navy."

My defensiveness brought more laughter from both Jacob and Maaijke, who, with her free arm, pulled me into her, salving my pride with a pro-tracted kiss.

When I felt the redness leach from my cheeks, Maaijke forced me to take the tiller once more, and keeping one of her hands on top of mine, taught me to sail. I slowly gained a feel for the interaction of wind and sails, and when they dropped the sails and motored in past the breakwater, I was surprised that it was already after noon and disappointed to be leaving the water. When the dock lines had been secured, I shook hands with each of the crew, thanking them.

When I came to Jacob, he said, "Ja, Peter. You come again. We make you a fine sailor. Your navy will be proud of you." Maaijke's arm-squeeze around my waist told me the same thing.

CHAPTER 35

Maaijke

—— 1833 and 1971 ——

I CAN REMEMBER EACH INSTANT OF THE NEXT FEW DAYS, BUT I CAN'T remember the order in which those instants occurred. I do know that I had very little sleep because we made love so much, and that rather than being tired the next day, I felt more awake than ever in my life. During the few times Peter was out of my sight and I was alone, I hugged myself because I felt so good, so content.

Talking with him was so easy emotionally. But it strained my mental capacity because I always had to act as if I knew what he was talking about, even if I had never experienced it.

Take airplanes, for example. I had seen them when I visited Alice Dubois, the WW I spy, but they were flimsy things, mostly with double wings and a propellor. And I saw them again in Berlin during what was called the "Airlift" in 1948, but the ones I remember still had propellors, although more of them, and the newer airplanes were far bigger than ones from WW I. So when Peter told me about flying jet planes, I had no conception of what he was telling me. I pretended I did—trying to wear a knowing expression and not ask questions that would reveal my ignorance—then later read about whatever I did not understand when I went forward in time to

111

the Amsterdam library. But I still betrayed myself, as I did with the singing group and the bugs and the horses.

The first day after that first wonderful night, I put on my sailing clothes and, without revealing my plan, chose Peter's for him. We went down to the quay, and Jacob greeted us as we boarded the *Het Houten Paard*. He looked Peter up and down, suspiciously. I whispered in Jacob's ear, "Would Peter make good babies?" For someone with the experience Jacob had, I was surprised that I made him blush.

Jacob turned around, I think so I would not see him blushing, and started the tiny engine. With our push poles, we threaded our way out of the harbor and with sails hoisted, escaped into the wind. Jacob put me in my usual position as skipper and soon, I grabbed Peter's hand and put it on the tiller, my hand over his to show him how to sail. He wasn't a good sailor, but I tried not to embarrass him by pointing out his errors. By the end of the day, he enjoyed it—or maybe it was me he enjoyed. I didn't care if he was good or not; looking at him was enough to make me happy and fulfilled. It was wonderful, except that in the back of my mind, I knew I would have to return home soon. I tried to ignore how dreadful it would be to leave Peter.

CHAPTER 36

Peter

—— 1971 ——

WE WALKED OFF THE QUAY AND UP THE SPUISTRAAT AGAIN. THE WOMEN in period costume all greeted Maaijke. "We see you tomorrow," a number of them said.

We ended up at the same restaurant as the day before, and had another leisurely, intimate lunch. It seemed so easy to talk with Maaijke; she was engrossed in everything I said.

"Tell me about the first time you had sex," she said.

"Why do you want to know that?"

"I want to know everything about you. Everything. Before we finish lunch," she said, giggling.

"It is kind of embarrassing."

"Even better! Tell me."

"Remember when you asked about my best teacher?"

"Oh! She taught you sex, too? How old was she?"

"She was twenty-one years old."

"And how old were you, Peter?"

"Fifteen."

"Fifteen? Were you old enough? Were you big enough?"

"She thought I was." I felt myself blush.

"Tell me what she taught you. Tell me everything. And then after lunch, show me."

Maaijke seemed enchanted by stories of Miss Clarke, asking many detailed, uninhibited questions.

After lunch, after the walk back to her house, after the transit through the boxwood hedge, we repeated the previous afternoon's session on her bed, as again the sun cast long shadows across our bodies. Maaijke was unfettered by any embarrassment and eagerly tried new variations in our intimacies.

After the sun set, we dressed. Maaijke folded the old historic dress over her arm, and we walked back to the hotel. After changing out of our sailing clothes, she left her dress on the hotel bed, and we went out to find a restaurant.

"I will take you to your restaurant, Peter," she said.

"My restaurant?"

"I will show."

And off we walked at a very rapid clip.

"You walk fast," I said.

"Sure. We walk almost everywhere. I must keep up with my father. So, sure, fast."

"You must take a car sometimes?" I said. "What about when you go to church?"

"No, we walk."

"How far away is it?"

"About a mile. Why?"

"It seems so far, especially when you are dressed up for church."

She paused, a puzzled look on her face. Then she broke into her private smile for me.

"But Peter, it's so much healthier to walk."

Then, near the boat basin, we arrived at the Visrestaurant de Pieterman, and she changed the subject, as she so often did.

"See, Peter? Here, your name would be Pieter—P-I-E-T-E-R."

After a long dinner, during which I again felt as if we were in total isolation, only Maaijke and me, we wandered down to the boats, and with a chilly dew settling into the village, our collars turned up in a futile attempt to fend off the damp cold, we went back to the hotel, where we again slept in the interludes until dawn. Maaijke showered and went through the somewhat complex act of dressing in the docent costume as I watched, entranced, smiling at her. Together, we had breakfast at the café, and with a kiss, I sent her off to work.

An hour later, I went to the museum and waited until she guided a tour, which I joined. I understood very little of her explanations in the Dutch language, and she didn't translate into English for me, but when unobserved by the other tourists, she made funny faces or licked her lips seductively. After lunch together, she went back to her docent duties until I picked her up for dinner. This time, back in her house, she changed out of her dress and cooked dinner wearing an enticingly revealing bra and panties under one of my dress shirts, left unbuttoned. Focusing on the meal was difficult. We cleaned up, and it was back to the hotel for another night of sleep deprivation.

Finishing breakfast the next morning, Maaijke rounded up two fat-tire bikes with handlebar bells to shoo pedestrians out of our path. We rode south of town to the Nijkerkerweg and east to Nijkerk, then north back to the Eemmeer along the Arkervaart canal—a ride of about ten miles—where we saw three of the iconic Dutch canal houseboats, which were long and very slim to facilitate navigating the narrow waterways, and each was surmounted with a small cavalry of bicycles. All the boats were connected to the shore opposite the small island in the Arkervaart by ropes tied to sturdy posts a few feet from the water. Maaijke insisted on stopping and talking with each of the sailors, who could have been identical triplets with their grizzled white whiskers, weathered and creased tan faces, baggy dark trousers held up by red suspenders, and faded denim shirts. With each successive boat, Maaijke enacted greater affection for me with her arms wrapped around my waist as she conducted her animated conversations, none of which I understood, but she left each sailor beaming with pleasure. We ate lunch at the little Clubhuis de Zuidwal, where we sat on the banks of the jachthaven and Maaijke entertained me by offering critiques of boats land-ing and departing from the docks.

"Too fast, too fast, you're going to crash." She was proved correct. "Oh, oh, correct for the crosswind or else. See Peter, I could do better. I always do better. Dirk taught me."

"Dirk? Who is Dirk?"

After a pause and a bemused expression, she said, "Jacob. I mean Jacob. We sometimes call Jacob "Dirk" because one of his relatives with that name many years before had a boat with the same name, the *Het Houten Paard.*"

We pedaled back to Spakenburg, which, after the mostly fried meal, seemed much more distant than the ten miles we had ridden to get to lunch.

Back at the hotel, tired from both the exertion and lack of sustained sleep, we fell into bed and simply held each other, all our senses dead to disturbance. We awoke refreshed, and after athletic sex, went out for dinner. That night, for the first time together, we slept well, awakening only once.

Then, I said yet again, "You told me there was no worry about you get-ting pregnant. Are you on birth control pills?"

"No, there is not any worry," she said, and drifted off. I should have pur-sued my questions. She was skillful in evading them. But knowing that we planned to be together forever, maybe it didn't matter all that much.

In the morning, we sailed again on the *Het Houten Paard.* This time, Jacob brought lunch for all of us, and he stopped the boat with a maneuver that amazed me. With all sails up, the boat was turned so that the wind came onto the wrong side of the jib, exactly as I had done by accident yes-terday. But this time, Maaijke lashed the tiller down to the side of the boat away from the wind, and despite the vigorous breeze, the boat came to a stop. Everything was immediately quiet and serene. "Heaving to," she said it was called. We ate lunch accompanied by a dark beer. Afterward, we raced against about twenty other botters, finishing in second place.

Back in town, the entire crew met for dinner, joining those who raced against us. A lot of beer fueled a raucous evening. Maaijke received a lot of kidding from the sailors, it seemed to me, although I could understand little of it. Finally, Jacob yelled something to Maaijke, causing everyone in the restaurant to laugh and Maaijke to blush. She stood up, took my hand, and gaily waving, led me out to the street.

"What happened? Why did we leave so suddenly?"

"Jacob said he thought you and I might have more fun back in the hotel," she said.

And we did.

In the early morning, I awoke and, running my fingers down her elegant back, awakened her too.

"Maaijke. You know almost everything about me. I know you better than anyone but I know almost nothing *about* you. I only know you are the first girl I have loved and I want to be with you always, want you to have my children. You would love coming to America, but we could come back here a lot. You can meet my family. I want to meet yours. Okay?"

Holding me tightly, she began to cry. "Oh, that sounds perfect. I love you so much. I want to have your children."

"So why are you crying?"

"Someday, you will understand. Someday, I will explain. For now, please hold me."

CHAPTER 37

Maaijke

— 1833 and 1971 —

IN THE MORNING, I HAD TO WORK AGAIN, SO IN MY OLD DRESS, I HAD breakfast with Peter, then went to join the other tourist guides. We met again for lunch, but I was despondent because of what I had to do later. My concentration eroded at the edges; I became sweaty—I now clearly recognized my time would soon expire. When we left to go our separate ways, Peter told me of another restaurant he wanted to take me to for dinner, and I had a hard time not crying. When we split apart, I did cry. I was too cowardly to tell him directly that I had to leave, so I did it by letter. But even then, I was not able to explain what was happening to me. I slipped the letter under the door of his room and ran away, all the way back to my aunt's house.

And then I was back home in my time, and with Bertus, who was still out in the field. Nothing had changed; Bertus never knew I had been gone. My sweat-damp clothes had dried by the time he returned from his farm duties.

CHAPTER 38

Peter

—— 1971 ——

I WANDERED THROUGH SPAKENBURG AND MADE OUR DINNER RESERVATIONS. Back at the hotel, I found an envelope that had been slipped under the door. Inside, the letter, written with a fountain pen, was smudged as if by water drops.

Peter my love,

I am unable here any longer to stay. I could not you bear to tell you to your face because I love you so much it hurts. I must go and I may never be able here to return. I know I shall never anyone meet as wonderful as you. I came here for you looking. No, not looking specifically for you, but as soon as I first saw you, I knew it was for you I looked. More than anything, I wish I could spend the rest of my life with you.

I am also crying because I deceived you. You asked if I could become pregnant and I assured you that you had nothing to worry. That was true because I knew I would have to leave. But I was desperately hoping your child to have, and although it might be too early to be sure, I think I may have your baby inside me. If so, grateful I will be forever. Then I have a baby to help remember you—as if I could ever forget. Every day he (of course it will be a boy, just like you) will remind me of you and I smile. And he will have your name.

I pray that you remember me with your love. Perhaps you think I am being cruel, but if you understood, you would not. I am not able how I got here to explain and why I must leave.

Please forgive my tears I have on this letter spilled. Please forgive me for leaving when we love each other so much. It is not my choice. I love you through all time.

Maaijke

At first, I thought the letter was a joke. I knew she wanted to be with me as much as I wanted to be with her…forever. How could she leave? No, she could not. And thinking of our few days together, I became angry, and then slowly transitioned to sad. I cried myself to sleep and missed dinner. I awoke multiple times that night, looking for Maaijke next to me. She wasn't there.

Exhausted by the time dawn showed, I dressed, walked down to the lobby, and asked the hotel clerk if he knew where she was. He had no information about her. I walked down to the quay, past the many botters, and came to Jacob's.

"Jacob, have you seen Maaijke?"

"You look horrible, Peter. Don't you sleep anymore?"

"Have you seen her?"

"No," Jacob said. "I have not seen her since we sailed together two days ago."

"Where would she be?"

"Peter, I do not know.

"How well did you know her? How often did she sail with you?"

"She was the type of girl you know well as soon as you meet her. Every once in a while, she shows up and goes sailing with us. She seems to have been born a sailor, so we are happy to have her with us."

"So where does she come from?"

"I do not know," Jacob said. "When I have asked her, she smiles. She has been different this past week."

"Different how?"

"Happier, I guess. She used to have a sadness to her face that was gone this week."

"Remember," I said, "when I first met you and you asked Maaijke how good a friend I was?"

"*Ja.*"

"What did she whisper to you?"

"Oh, that. She asked if I thought you would make good babies."

"What?"

"I did not know her very long, but she was so uninhibited that I felt— everyone felt—she was our best friend. She often said surprising things."

"Like what?"

"When I first met her, many of the sailors here asked her for a date. She always said no. When I asked her why, she told me she came here to find a perfect father for a baby. Very first time I met her!"

"I have to find her, Jacob. How can I find her?"

"Maybe you should ask some of the women in the old dresses—the ones from the museum."

"I will. Before that, who is Dirk? She mentioned 'Dirk.'"

"Don't know anyone by that name. My great-great-grandfather's name was Dirk, but Maaijke wouldn't know that."

I jumped from the boat and ran to the museum. The women guides all knew and remembered her. Several commented that she must have been poor because her costume seemed so old and worn out. Others said she spoke differently. None had any idea where she lived. One said she'd always thought her name—her first name—was old fashioned.

I walked up along the little canal where I had first met her. Not there. I went to the restaurant where we first had lunch. No one there knew her, but the waitress remembered us. They had not seen her except with me.

At the police station, there was no record of her or her address. The same was true in the town hall, where they made their records available to me. At the church, going back twenty years, there was nothing about her in their archives of deaths, births, and marriages.

I walked in the direction of her house. I could not find it. I walked around for two hours and still did not find the house. As the sun peaked and started to fall off to the west, I finally saw a house that looked like the one across the street from Maaijke's, but it was bigger than I remembered. Looking across to where Maaijke's house would have been, should have been, there were no boxwood shrubs, no tunnel into the shrub, and no house. Only a vacant lot.

I crossed over to that vacant lot and in the center found a square depression surrounded by a few irregularly spaced large rocks. They had the appearance of an old stone foundation in an advanced state of disintegration, but there was nothing else. The spot where I had seen the outhouse was nothing but a small depression in the weeds.

I knocked on doors of surrounding houses and finally found an older woman at home. No, she did not know if there had been a house there. Certainly not in her lifetime. In all of her seventy-five years, there never had been any kind of building that she remembered.

I wandered around for a week, returning to the hotel every night. I talked to restaurant staff where we had eaten. Several remembered her. None knew where she was; none knew where she lived.

I went back to the quay and the botters.

"Please, Jacob. I have to find her. Help me."

"Peter, I want to, believe me. I miss her too. I came to think of her as my daughter, even though I did not know her very long. And if I weren't old, I would think of her differently—like you do. But I don't know where to look. I never saw where she lived. She said she came from here—but I'd have known her if she did. She was always a mystery to me. She sounded almost foreign at times. I first saw her last year, but she was here only a week. During that time, all of us seemed to fall in love with her. She was a natural, so we liked her sailing with us."

"But, you must know something more about her."

"I don't. She asked questions about everything, and about everyone she met. But when we asked her questions, she mostly giggled and did not tell us much. She was always so charming and delightful; I think none of us wanted to pry. We all miss her when she is not around."

Forlorn, I returned to the hotel to reread Maaijke's letter. As I turned the key in the door to my room, my heart skipped several beats—would she somehow be here, waiting for me? But the room was filled with only the crushing silence of a deserted room. I looked to the bureau, where I had left the letter…but it was gone. I rushed to the lobby. The desk clerk knew nothing of a letter. He found the maid who had cleaned my room; she had seen no letter either.

I spent the next two weeks in Spakenburg retracing my steps multiple times and made no progress in finding Maaijke. Gradually, the sharp-edged pain dulled. I was too depressed to pursue my family history, which was why I came in the first place. But I tried. At the genealogy center in Bunschoten-Spakenburg, the archivist was most helpful. But as soon as I sat down with a volume of marriage records to look for ancestors, I gave up. It was too much. I was unable to initiate any sort of study and wanted only to sleep to deaden the pain.

Insidiously, the thought crept into my brain that I had imagined the entire episode. I tried to push it away, into deep recesses, for Maaijke was too real to have been imaginary.

Maaijke

— 1833 —

And then, as always happens, I was back home in Bertus's fine but spartan house. It was a few minutes after I had left for 1971, shortly before noon, and I could see my husband coming in from our fields, dressed as always in a pressed white but dusty shirt and matching brown wool pants and coat. Objectively, he was rather handsome. But how could I be objective? I was in love. I wrapped my arms around my chest, squeezed my eyes shut and danced with myself, twirling around and running into tables and the kitchen counter as I remembered those enfolding arms as Peter's, not my own. On one mighty pirouette, I fell and was forced to open my eyes to see Bertus coming through the door.

"Maaijke, Maaijke, what's wrong? Are you hurt?" and he bent to help me up.

"I tripped. I am fine."

"But you're bleeding. You hit your forehead!"

I must have done. Blood was clouding my vision in my right eye, turning all I saw a dark pink, and when I tried to wipe it off, blood soaked into my blouse. It ran down onto my lips, where I licked it off, enjoying the salty metallic flavor because all the time, I was thinking of Peter.

Bertus was almost kind, handing me a clean towel to mop up the mess. I approached him more closely.

"Is it a deep cut? Do I need to see the doctor?"

As I got nearer to him, he jumped away from me.

"Maaijke! Do not get that stuff on me and my white shirt," he barked in a high-pitched, frightened voice.

And as suddenly as a hint of kindness had flared, it died down and Bertus was back to his usual cold demeanor.

"Maaijke, I don't think it is serious. You know, it is very hot out in the fields. Please get me a cup of cold water from the well."

Had I not been thinking more of Peter than of Bertus, I might not have uttered what I did.

"Bertus. Get your own water. And your own lunch." And I ran up the stairs to my room, crying, while Bertus screamed at me, his spit spewing across the room.

In my room, my crying stopped immediately as I hugged my bed pillow, imagining the ecstasy of it being Peter. Then, reproaching myself for having been disrespectful of my husband, and for disobeying him, I slunk back to the kitchen and dutifully made lunch for him. Bertus acted as if the incident had never occurred.

Our insular existences continued, but I was sustained by the hidden happiness of Peter, and perhaps of having his baby inside me.

CHAPTER 40

Peter

— 1971 —

RETURNING THE CAR AT AMSTERDAM SCHIPHOL, I FLEW BACK HOME VIA New York, Denver, and then Riverton, Wyoming. Dad picked me up in his truck for the short drive back to Lander.

Well, Peter, two months before you start medical school. Excited?"

"Yeah, sure, I guess."

After a pause, Dad said, "You don't seem very sure. Are you changing your mind about being a doctor?"

"No, Dad. It's… Of course, I want to go. But, please, I don't want to talk about it now. Maybe tomorrow."

For a minute or more, the only sounds came from the wind wrapping around the windows, the tires thumping on the road, and the deep growl of the engine.

Finally, I broke the awkward silence.

"How're Mom, Anna, Red?"

"Well, Mom's fine and right now is baking for you with Anna's help. Anna accelerated and graduates in December. She pretty much worships you and has also applied to medical school. Red reminds me of Rusty. She's buried out behind the house. Red is five, and in her prime. Fine dog. Like you always said, every bit as good as Rusty. Better even."

We drove down the mile-long, two-track road to the ranch house, our arrival announced by a billowing plume of yellow dust behind the truck.

Mom, Anna, and Red rushed out to greet us. I hugged Mom. Anna—dressed in a snap-front cowboy shirt, Levi's, and boots—jumped up, throwing her arms and legs around me, and kissed me.

"Anna," Mom said. "That's no proper way to act."

"It sure is," Anna said, "with a war hero." But she slid down to standing, looking up at me as Red pushed between us, trying to jump up as Anna had done.

"Well, I guess nobody forgot me."

Inside, dinner was already on the table. As we ate, I had to fend off questions about medical school. I could think of little other than Maaijke. Anna, as usual, dominated the conversation. She quizzed me all during dinner about experiences over the skies of Viet Nam, my adventures, if I was ever frightened, and were there any cute men in our squadron I could introduce her to. Red spent the entire dinner with her head on my shoes, probably less out of love than hope that careless eating might deliver a few morsels.

Anna asked, "What are you going to do before you start school? You have more than two months."

"Well, I thought I could help out around the ranch. Maybe fish some."

"Hey! I got a great idea," Anna said, with exuberance written across her face. "Let's go up into the foothills tomorrow, like we used to do. We can take Red, some fly rods, and a gun. Get some fish and birds."

"Anna, since when was hunting season open in June?"

"But no one will be around. We can shoot only what we will eat up there. Please, please. I can put the camping stuff in the truck. Okay?"

I looked over to Dad, who nodded yes.

"Okay, Anna, I'll go. What a saleswoman! Maybe you should go work for the Ford dealer rather than going to medical school." She gave me a fake pout, then grinned.

Before sunrise, Anna had loaded most of the equipment into the pickup.

By nine, the sun already high above the tree line, I felt nearly as I did when back in college. Red, suddenly jerked around by the tether of a scent, landed dead still and quivering, her tail feathers streaming in the breeze. As always, the tension rose as we walked in the direction of Red's nose, knowing exactly what to expect: an explosion of wings. And still, as always, the sudden rush of "*ttthhhhrrr*" startled us as the birds broke in different directions. One was down, two; a double. Red, waiting for the command, burst out to retrieve the birds, one then the other delivered to hand.

"Nice shooting, Anna. Now let me try for one."

Three grouse, spit roasted. After dinner, Red, rewarded with some grouse bones, gratefully crushed them into meal and swallowed them.

As we sat against the rolled-up sleeping bags, finishing coffee, I said, "Like old times, huh?"

"Yup. But you're not," Anna said. "What's wrong? You were so quiet at dinner last night, and you don't seem the same. What's up?"

"Dad asked me the same thing. I couldn't tell him."

"Can you tell me?"

"Dad is worried that I am not excited about medical school, even though it starts in only a couple months."

"*And?*"

"Well…I'm not thinking much about it."

"And that's because…"

"Well, you know I went to Spakenburg to see if I could find out something about our ancestors there."

"And?"

"And I made no progress at all."

"Why? Another girlfriend, I suppose, threw herself all over you."

"Well, pretty close. But this was different. I fell in love. A Dutch girl."

"Peter, that is fantastic! So why are you so subdued? Doesn't she love you back? That would be a first!"

"Oh, no. She loves me. Really loves me. And I think she is pregnant."

"Well, so what? Get married. Lots of people are married in medical school."

"I can't. She left."

"What do you mean, 'She left?'"

I told Anna the whole story of my week with Maaijke. About the happiness we had together. About how we discussed getting married, having children. It seemed so idyllic and then, the note. I told her about it.

"Show me."

"I can't. I don't have it."

"You would't throw that away. Show me."

I explained the missing letter. Anna looked at me curiously.

"You didn't make this up, did you?"

"Anna, stop it. Why would I do that?"

"Well, when you were little, you had an imaginary friend. Your rabbit."

"I'm not little. I didn't imagine it." I spoke forcefully to convince her, as well as myself. But I wondered if maybe the whole thing was an illusion.

"Well," Anna said, "just go find her."

"I tried, I tried. For two weeks, I tried to find her. Everyone seemed to know her; no one knew anything *about* her. She's gone. No idea where. It's like she never existed. If this is in my imagination, how could so many others know her?"

Anna reached over and hugged me. We spread out the sleeping bags, and I fell off to troubled sleep, worried that Anna might hear me sobbing.

She wasn't done with the interrogation. As soon as it was light enough to see the condensed clouds of my breath in the frigid mountain air, Anna was back at it. "Is that it? Anything else?" she badgered me.

I tried to divert her from Maaijke. "No, not really. But I can tell you fighting in a war is not as glamorous as you might think. Even when fighting from a plane far above everything. You cannot imagine the horror of our bombs. Mostly, it's like playing arcade games, but when we fly low, it's not just buildings and rocket launchers that we see destroyed, but people too."

"But they are trying to kill you. Doesn't that justify it?" Anna asked.

"It's not so simple. Bodies blown apart. Afterward, I wanted to cry. And not all of them are trying to kill me. Sometimes I wished I could retract bombs. Undo the damage, the death."

"I suppose, though, the fact that you don't know any of them makes it a little bit easier."

"I wish. I truly do wish it were so. 'What passing-bells for these who die as cattle?'"

"Passing bells? Where did that come from?" Anna said.

"Some poem we learned in high school. It describes what I felt about those bombs." I could go no further. I couldn't explain Willis to her.

In the crisply clear dawn, we caught cutthroat trout and fried them in butter for breakfast.

Predictably, Anna came back to Maaijke. "Are you sure about all this?" she asked. "I remember you used to say you were shy. But in high school, you seemed to be a girl magnet, whether or not you were shy. Maybe this is not different. This Maaijke Dutch girl."

"I wish. It is. Very different. I really wanted to spend the rest of my life with Maaijke."

"So, what can you do?"

"Nothing, I guess. I'll go to medical school and hope I can leave it behind. But to think that Maaijke may have a baby coming almost kills me. But she frustrates me, angers me, too. I poured out my entire history to her. Everything. And what did she tell me about herself? Only the names of her brothers and sister. Nothing else. Every time I asked her about herself, we were suddenly talking about something else. She was so good at not answering, I sometimes thought she should be a politician. Still, I loved her. *Love* her. If you saw her smile, you would know. Would feel the same way."

"Are you going to tell Mom and Dad?"

"No, they'll just worry. I can't do anything about the situation. Neither can they. It'd be unfair to upset them. I'm even sorry I told you."

CHAPTER 41

Maaijke

—— 1833-1834 ——

TWO MONTHS LATER, I TOLD BERTUS WHAT WAS NOW OBVIOUS TO ME, although it did not yet show in my belly. But my breasts were becoming fuller and they hurt a little. He did not believe me. At about four months, I was clearly bigger, but my clothes hid the swelling. At five months, I again told Bertus, who could now see the truth of my pregnancy. He screamed and yelled at me; I thought he might strike me, but he didn't.

"It is not possible," he said.

"Well, you can see it is."

"No, I knew you were a whore. Who is the father?"

"Since I never leave the home except with you or my family, who could be the father but you?"

His countenance softened. I realized that he did not even know how babies came to be. I also knew that he could not tolerate the thought that my baby could have come from another man. I could see him thinking, "our baby."

He walked away, and we discussed it no more that day.

But in the evening, after dinner, he spoke as he never did…warmly.

"So, Maaijke, we need a name. For our new baby."

"Do you have any ideas?"

He gave me several, including, of course, Bertus. None of them would be acceptable; in fact, only one name was.

"Well, Bertus, I am not sure of any of those. But your father's father was named Pieter. It would be a great honor for you and your family if we chose that name."

And that was it. Suddenly, Bertus walked around with the pride that only comes with fathering a child. Except that he hadn't, of course. At night, he still kept me away. Which was now more than okay with me.

I told Mama the day after I told Bertus.

"But I thought…I mean, weren't you… Wasn't Bertus…?"

"Well, Mama, I am having a baby, and we already have a name: Pieter."

"But maybe it will be a girl."

"Then I will name it after you." But I knew it would be a boy. I felt it.

All the while, she had a curious expression. *She knew.* She wasn't sure what she knew, but she knew there was a disconnect between my relationship with Bertus and my being pregnant. She never said anything, and thus blessed my pregnancy.

Gerta was delighted. A join-the-club delight.

"I was worried about you, Maaijke. When you married Bertus, I wondered if he knew how to please you. You never talked about how it was in bed. But now that you are pregnant, I see I need not have worried. It's so wonderful!" She hugged me. Hard.

"And I can feel your breasts so full and big. You are going to have such a wonderful time. I can't wait until you are feeding your baby. I can help if you have any questions."

The next few months went quickly. I felt wonderful. I was so proud of my new plump body. When the labor began, I went to Mama's house. After a few hours, the crampy feeling had turned to real pain. Then, water gushed out between my legs. But I knew all about these things from what I had read, and from Mama's careful teaching.

She shooed Papa and my little brothers out of the kitchen. Antje was there to help, as were some of the neighbor women. I had never thought about how hard her kitchen table was. But I found out, lying on my back. The pains were coming quickly and were worse. One of Mama's friends held one of my feet near the edge of the table and another held the other one while my bottom was at the edge of the table. Antje was pushing on my belly and telling me to push, and Mama was sitting between my legs. Mama had given me a little brandy, and then a whole lot more, but the agony was still much worse than I ever thought it could be. It reached a crescendo, and I heard a baby cry. *My baby.* I had done it. Relief came. Relief from the hurt, relief from the fear of never having a baby. I felt wonderful. Wonderful and sleepy. Mama put Pieter—oh, it was definitely a boy—still bloody, on my chest and sponged him off but not before my gown was dirtied. But what a wonderful way to dirty my gown. My baby boy. My loud, screaming baby boy. He wailed angrily, as if to say, "Put me back." I closed my eyes and laughed. I could only think of Peter and of Pieter.

Mama tied some twine around the cord coming out of his belly button, then cut it off. My contractions continued until a big bloody mess came out, and I felt better.

Bertus came in after everything was cleaned up and I had a clean gown. He was beaming. Proud father. *Idiot.*

With the front of my gown open, I put Pieter to my breast where he sucked mightily. But nothing came; his dissatisfied cries were insistent and persistent. Hard to listen to. I started to cry, then couldn't stop. My sobs almost drowned out Pieter's complaints.

"What's wrong, Maaijke?" Mama asked.

"My breasts are broken. They don't work. No milk comes for Pieter. He might starve."

Mama started laughing. A soothing laugh.

"No, baby, they don't work right now, but wait a day or two and they will. You are normal. It takes a bit of time. He won't starve. I promise."

I felt better then, and especially two days later when, exactly as Mama said, the milk came. Pieter loved it and was so strong and so aggressive, I was very thankful he had no teeth yet.

I squeezed a few drops on the back of my hand to taste it. I guess that

Pieter had little else to compare it to, so he liked it. To me, it tasted too sweet, too heavy.

When Gerta came to see me and Pieter, I told her about tasting it and she laughed. She had done the same thing when her baby came, and also did not like it much. Her baby, named after his father, Johannus, was more than a year old now, and running around. But when I fed Pieter, Johannus climbed in her lap, pulled open her shirt, and also started to drink. Dueling breasts.

After she first married Johannus, our friendship became strained. A barrier rose between us, not because of a conflict, but because our lives were suddenly so different. With the birth of her baby, the barrier became even more pronounced. And when I married Bertus, the barrier grew even higher, partly because he was wealthier, and partly because I was envious of her and Johannus although I tried not to let it show. That envy was inevitable, considering our relationships with our husbands, both in and out of bed. Now, with my baby, we were back to the way we were before. Best friends. And as before, Gerta had no inhibitions about discussing anything with me. She had been afraid that I was not receiving the type of "marital attention" (she winked when she said this) that I needed, that made her so happy. She wanted to know all about what Bertus and I did, and how it felt, and she confided the same information about her intimacy with Johannus. She told me in exquisite detail; I was able to do the same for her—but of course, I lied by using Bertus's name but telling her what Peter and I did. I was very happy that we were close again.

But I still felt separation from her even though she did not from me. She had her husband Johannus to love and hold her; I had no one except a memory. My joy with Pieter was offset by my loneliness for Peter. I went back to Spakenburg often but never found him. I didn't know how to inquire about him; any information I requested could not come back to me: I needed news from 1971, but I lived in 1834. There was no way to get news from the future sent back to me where I was, nor was there a method for me to contact Peter in 1971 when I was living in 1834. I had no 1971 address where I could pick up reports from that time. So, the only recourse open to me was to revisit Spakenburg as often as I could, hoping that Peter would also be there.

So, that is what I did. I did not find Peter. I saw Jacob a lot and sailed with him whenever I could. I loved the water and even more, loved the feeling of the *botter* heeling under the wind as my hair sailed out behind me, fluttering like a flag. My friendship with Jacob became very strong; I thought of him as my best friend and as an uncle. I was not totally convinced that all his feelings were avuncular: when we hugged, he held me a bit longer than I expected and with one arm around my waist, pulled my entire body against him. But I really did not mind, and nothing developed from his hugs, so maybe I was only imagining. I went back home after each sail, my face flushed with happiness and with the sun.

CHAPTER 42

Peter

— 1971-1976 —

THE DAYS AMBLED ON TOWARD MY DEPARTURE FOR MEDICAL SCHOOL, about which I had neither enthusiasm nor excitement. When the day came to begin the journey east, both my parents and Anna buzzed around, vicariously going on the adventure with me. I did my best to share in their anticipation, kissing them goodbye and climbing into the used Ford Mustang Dad had given me, and thinking back to Maaijke's strange comment when one almost ran over her. At the end the mile drive to the road, a wet lick in my ear brought me to laughter as Red's soft nose nuzzled my face. I turned around and drove back to the house, letting out the stowaway, who struggled to stay with me and whined as I pulled her out of the car.

I left for the second time on my three-day journey to Boston, this time without passengers. And on the long drive east, I thought about what Anna had said. She had raised some doubts in my mind, but I was mostly sure Maaijke had been real.

Checking in to the student dormitory on Longwood Avenue, only a few blocks from the Museum of Fine Arts, I felt a moment of discomfort, seeing how young my classmates looked. Nonetheless, they were all older than Maaijke. As I studied the women, there were none with the level of uninhibited joy or the beauty of Maaijke. But all these freshmen med students wore anxious, sometimes frightened faces, so I discounted appearances to some extent. Their obvious worry and concern, coupled with their excited anticipation, relieved me of any unease I had about my age. As I studied the women, and the men as well, a number returned my undisguised stare and then came up to me with self-introductions. Several were forward enough to stare and then ask about my large belt buckle and boots. My dress and speech made me a curiosity among these Easterners, and as a result, the gap between us was bridged. Even so, the next day I drove to the river and crossed the Anderson bridge into Cambridge and visited J. Press, where I bought shoes, a belt, shirts, and pants that were more conforming. I had often looked in the windows when in college, but with my tight budget, I had been afraid to enter. Now, with the savings from my Navy time, I splurged. But for comfort and a sense of where I belonged, I still mostly wore my boots.

Within a couple days of registration, the frenzied pace of classes began. My fear that I would be unable to think about anything other than Maaijke proved unwarranted. Several of the subjects fascinated me; actually, all of them did. The intensity of study served as an anodyne for my deep sorrow about Maaijke and a possible lost son. It took almost no time before I realized how committed I was to this new direction. I also realized how vitally exciting was this new chapter.

Two courses during freshman year steered me. Gross anatomy was joked about by my classmates. Most hated it. The overpowering stench of formaldehyde seeped into our clothes and hair. It was almost impossible to remove, except by the scouring effect of time. As upper-level students knew, a freshman taking the anatomy course could be recognized by smell alone, and from several yards away. But to me, the intricacies and miracle—for so it seemed—of the human body, even on the shriveled cadaver four of us shared, completely blotted out the eye-stinging formaldehyde. And with this anatomic immersion, my career direction was thrust on me: I would become a surgeon. Then, molecular biology, a relatively new field, and its clinical counterpart of transplantation totally snared me; I wanted to be a transplant surgeon. I don't think I had ever been so directed, focused on goals before. Now, I was. Reinforcing this choice was the opportunity to work in the lab of Dr. Joseph Murray, the surgeon with several firsts in kidney transplantation. I worked on rejection biology with Murray for the next three summers.

As was the case in earlier schooling, I received A grades effortlessly. It wasn't that I didn't study; rather, it was that the excitement of each new subject rendered that study effortless. It was identical to the exhilaration of the new world opened to me in the first grade when I learned to read.

Even better, the total immersion allowed the sharp edges of my memories of Maaijke to dull. I thought of her with less pain. At times, I caught myself believing she might not even have existed. I began to date occasionally. During the summer before entering senior year, I met a student two years behind me who also worked with Dr. Murray. Lisa was tall, with dark silky hair, a thin face, vivid blue eyes, a straight patrician nose, and high cheek bones. Her life was well planned: she attended medical school to give her more credibility as a researcher and was headed toward a career in the prevention of the transplant rejection phenomenon. She had a captivating smile but a serious demeanor: the smile emerged infrequently. But from the time I met her, she smiled for me a lot. She had been a ballerina during college and professionally in New York for the two years before medical school, and she retained the lithe, powerful body of a dancer, and a dancer's walk: every step appeared as if she might next ascend in some balletic leap.

Within weeks, we became lovers; for me, the first since Maaijke. And then, I thought, we fell in love, although it did not have the same feel as with Maaijke. It was neither as fiery nor as consuming; it was more comfortable. Over time, we tacitly assumed that we would marry. When we first discussed it, midway through my last year of study, we decided we should wait until after she finished school, two years after me. Looking back, I was fooling myself. I was in love with her more in the way I was in love with Red. But I think Red was more committed to me.

My senior year passed in a blink, and excitement and anticipation slowly built as the class looked forward to being placed in internships. On that momentous day in March when the senior class of all the medical students across the country received the results of the national matching program, I learned I would intern at Boston's prestigious Peter Brent Brigham hospital beginning in July 1975. Concurrently, Dr. Murray had continued to mentor me, and by graduation had helped me obtain a fellowship in Brussels at the Cliniques Universitaires Saint-Luc with Professor G.P.J. Alexandre, the prominent Belgian transplant surgeon who had spent a year with Dr. Murray back in the sixties. My fellowship would begin after the internship year, with residency to resume thereafter. The timing was perfect for both Lisa and me. When my fellowship in Brussels finished, I would rejoin my residency in Boston, Lisa and I would marry, and she would begin working back in the lab with Dr. Murray.

But before we started wedding planning, there was my internship to get through. We interns worked every day except for every other Saturday and Sunday, and worked every other night at a wage far below the poverty level. The schedule provided scant time for sleep in a 120 to 130-hour work week. A typical schedule began at 5 a.m., continued throughout that day, that night, and the next day, ending at 9 or 10 p.m., only to start all over at 5 a.m. I functioned on caffeine, adrenaline, and a lot of free saltines with peanut butter from the surgeons' lounge near the operating rooms. Adding generous sugar to the peanut-buttered cracker made a poor man's instant peanut butter cookie.

The enormous exposure to surgery and sick patients, and the immense responsibility were constantly frightening and stimulating. I survived it; almost all of us did. Only two dropped out, one to pursue other interests in medicine, and one was pursuing his lusts sequentially with a string of nurses when he was supposed to be caring for intensive care unit patients. A senior surgeon burst into his on-call room where my fellow intern was mid-tryst, and in less than a day, he was gone, summarily fired.

Each day's schedule was relentlessly unchanging. We rarely had time for breakfast. We were either in the operating room assisting, or caring for the patients. Drawing blood, performing urinalyses, looking for infection in the gram stains we prepared of possibly purulent drainage from incisions, writing progress notes, trying—often in vain—to learn enough about our patients to present them on morning rounds, trying to stay awake in conferences, the quick breaks for peanut butter and crackers, or a soggy sandwich left over from the free 10 p.m. dinner: all these were the script for every day's short story.

At the intern level, "assisting" was a distinguished and misleading name for an exhausting task. We called it "leaning on a hook," or sometimes, "sleeping on a hook." We stood for hours, pulling on a device that looked like a miniaturized version, in stainless steel, of a garden hoe. It was curled around some part of the body that was in the surgeon's way, which he wanted out of the way. But the body wanted it back where it belonged. "Pull harder, son." "Don't move so much." Hours on end. The worst part was that we could see nothing of what was happening. The first assistant, a more senior resident, standing opposite the surgeon had a great view, and often did parts or most of the operation. As interns, we could but hope for that role in the future. Leaning on a hook all night long, that future seemed very distant.

While the days were indistinguishable, one from the next, what differed were the types of diseases, the types of operations, the frightening emergencies that seemed to dominate our time. We saw operations as minor (to us, not to the patients, I am sure) as hernias and appendectomies, to major vascular procedures lasting twelve hours and more. We saw heart rending (literally and figuratively) trauma, the tragedies of what humans do to others and to themselves. Bodies shredded by a gang hit with a BAR (Browning Automatic Rifle). Internal organs gelatinized by the liquid drain cleaner used in a suicide. But we also saw magnificent saves. The child born with a fatal heart abnormality transformed to a normal life expectancy after a reparative operation. The patient with cured lung cancer. The torrential bleeding of a stomach ulcer extinguished by deft surgical hands. In balance, surgery was a specialty of hope.

The amount of work at night multiplied as we were left on call alone with the need to memorize and record the course of each patient so that we could present them on rounds the next day. Never was I sufficiently prepared, never were any of us. Always I prayed that I would be called to assist in the operating room at night for some urgent case that would exonerate my lack of preparation when I was called on during morning rounds.

Never sufficiently prepared: what better excuse than to have been forced to stand all night pulling on retractors. As we all struggled through, a battlefield-like camaraderie developed among our intern class. Then, a year later on July 1, we all popped out as residents to elevate our learning. My class was moving on to the residency. I was sad not to be continuing with our cohesive band, but I was eager to begin work in Belgium. And I would rejoin them, but a year out of phase.

CHAPTER 43

Maaijke

— 1834–1835 and 1945 —

BERTUS NEVER KNEW I WAS GONE, SO SHORT WERE MY ABSENCES IN HIS time, regardless of how long I stayed in the future. Once, he told me not to go out in the sun so much when he was out working our fields. I smiled inwardly, promising to obey him, and thinking that he would have me branded as crazy if I told him where I got the rosy face. He continued to be polite to me but was always distant. In truth, I did not mind as much because I had the memory of Peter to sustain me, and baby Pieter to nurture and love.

Pieter shot up, first on my milk, then on mashed-up food, and by the time he was three, he was eating as we did, but more ravenously. His best friend became Johannus, Gerta's one-year-older son. But now, Gerta had a little daughter toddling along as she learned to walk. I was delighted and honored that she named her Maaijke, after me.

Pieter was fun. Each day, he seemed to learn more. He talked a lot; I could even understand a few of his words. He almost never stopped smiling. Bertus was very proud but distant with my son; Pieter seemed strangely distant with Bertus, too, even though he was beyond friendly and affectionate with others. Whenever someone came into the house, he ran to them and, encircling their legs with his arms, hugged them, his face at thigh level. But never did he do that with Bertus.

I found it easy to travel when Pieter took his nap each afternoon. I was always back before he awoke. I finally concluded that I would always be back before he awoke because his restlessness upon awakening broke my concentration, and thus I would be back in my time. During one of these trips, I went to Paris. I remember thinking when I first saw it that the tower Monsieur Eiffel built was too flimsy to stay standing. I was wrong. When I visited in 1954, It stood defiantly filigreed in the sky, much higher than any other building in Paris.

I also found in a bibliothèque a book about world wars and about the Great War where I had met Louise de Bettignies—known as the spy Alice Dubois. Because there had been an even worse war about ten years before my most recent trip to Paris, the Great War had been renamed World War I, and the more recent, more horrendous was called World War II.

CHAPTER 44

Peter

—— 1976 ——

HELPED BY THE HOSPITAL STAFF IN BRUSSELS, I FOUND AN APARTMENT for the year, a third-floor walk-up efficiency, close to the #1 Metro line and a few stops from the Alma station—an easy walk through the park to Professor Alexandre's office and laboratory. Fortunately, nearly all the Belgians could speak English. But I was constantly buffeted by the French in one ear and the Flemish in the other. Gradually, I became more at ease with the two, especially with the Flemish, which sounded so much like the Dutch I had heard five years earlier.

Autumn brought a carpet of oak and beech leaves onto the green of the hospital grounds. I shuffled through them with the shhhhhhsh-shhhhhhsh sound bringing me back to October walks with Lisa in Cambridge. As the fall eased into winter, the weather turned colder and damp, and I was happily submerged in research with Professor Alexandre. I was a sponge for learning. With the unending excitement of discovery, I hardly noticed the weather.

As Christmas approached, airplane tickets were difficult to obtain, so I had a three-day wait before my KLM flight back home. Rather than stay around the skeleton staff at the university, I decided to drive up to Spakenburg and try to dig into my ancestry. I had avoided doing that so far, worrying that the pain of Maaijke would return. But the best way to put that episode behind me was to prove to myself the imaginary nature of it. Or so I thought. And the best place—the only place—to do that was Spakenburg.

On the way, I stopped in Utrecht and had lunch at Le Bibelot on the Oudegracht. The chive omelet went well with the sauvignon blanc, and I watched the still water in the canal, imagining how much nicer it would be in warm weather. And imagining how much nicer it would be with Lisa. And trying not to imagine what it would be like to share the meal with Maaijke.

The drive to Spakenburg took about four hours, even with the leisurely lunch. I again checked into the Hotel Sint Nicolaas, and when they gave me the same room I had the summer before medical school, I hoped it was not an ill omen. I naturally thought back to what I heard so many times (and with such humiliation) from Dad—that the best cure for falling off a horse was to get right back on, as Great-Grandpa would have done. And here I was, perhaps near Great-Grandpa Pieter's home.

My genealogy inquiries could not begin until the next day; the genealogy institute was closing when I arrived. So, back in the hotel, after a shower, I had a drink across the street, then wandered the familiar streets without any plan. I ended up in front of the Visrestaurant de Pieterman again. I was at first a bit leery of the smoked eel but found it very nice as an appetizer before my dinner of *plaice* arrived. It was cooked very much like I might have cooked trout back home, with almond slivers topping the light white meat sitting on its crisply fried skin. By the time I left, three hours and 750 ml of wine later, I enjoyed a contented stroll back to the hotel. Three times, I was alarmed to see girls who at first glance might have been Maaijke. With each, to my relief, I was mistaken.

In the morning, after breakfast, I walked down to the harbor. Looking at the botters, I was startled to find the *Het Houten Paard* appearing exactly as she had five and a half years before. Jacob was aboard, also unchanged to my eye.

"Peter, Peter. I remember you. The sailor who didn't know how to sail. Come aboard. Can you sail any better?"

Shaking hands, we embraced with left arms, and I laughed. "Actually, Jacob, I can."

"Then come with us. Show us. We are racing today."

"Jacob, it's winter."

"Ja, Peter. No matter: we still sail. The water; it's our life."

The single-cylinder engine slowly putt-putted through the packed harbor and out through the harbor entrance canal before we—they embraced me as a trusted crew member—raised the sails.

From sailing friends in medical school, I had picked up some skills. Jacob gave me the helm, and for two legs, I steered. I was much better than before. I kept the wake nearly straight and lost no distance on the other boats. I didn't ask about Maaijke; Jacob didn't mention her. At first uneasy that Jacob might talk about her, I became more relaxed in the absence of her name, and more convinced that she existed only in my mind.

As we slowly made our way up the harbor, the same women in period costume could be seen guiding tours. I was relieved not to spot Maaijke among them. But also, a little disappointed. After Jacob's crew secured the boat for the night, they left. Jacob opened two beers.

He asked about medical school, about my career, my research, residency, and my planned career path. Surprisingly sophisticated questions from the grizzled old sailor. I told him about Lisa, our plans to marry, and her research.

Jacob had a concerned, puzzled look and said, "Why didn't you marry her?"

"I just said, we are going to at the end of this year."

Jacob ignored me. "She loved you, you know. Totally. Completely. Like I have never seen. Why, Peter?"

Breathing became difficult. The world closed in. I was in a dark tunnel rapidly squeezing in on me. My head felt weighted down. I began sweating. As my breathing quickened, my hands and lips cramped. I could not see out of the blackness of the tunnel. Tears dripped down my cheeks and onto my shirt.

"No, Jacob, no. Stop. Lisa and I are getting married."

"Do you love Lisa?"

"Of course I do."

Jacob's bushy white eyebrows arched up. "Really? Really? Are you sure? *Lieg je niet?*"

"What?" I asked.

"Maybe you are lying?"

"No. Of course I am sure, Jacob." I realized he was right. I was lying to Jacob, trying to convince myself.

"Yesterday," Jacob said, "she went sailing with us."

I jumped from the boat and ran up the quay. It was dark when I reached the Sint Nicolaas, and dinner time. But I felt sick, uprooted from my life. I could not eat, couldn't even contemplate eating. With clothes still on, I pulled back the covers and slid into bed in turmoil. I cried, sobbed, and finally fell into a troubled sleep, awakening a bit after midnight, still sick. I vomited in the toilet, then took a long, hot shower, and in pajamas, went back to bed. I awoke several times until, at six the next morning, I awoke for good. Although exhausted, I resolved to see this through—to try to find Maaijke.

After a breakfast I could neither taste nor recall, I went back to the harbor. Jacob was on the *Het Houten Paard*. He stared. "You don't look very good," he said.

"That's because I'm not.

"Jacob, do you think she will come back? Maaijke?"

Jacob shrugged his shoulders and motioned for me to sit with him in the cockpit. We sat silently, sometimes with his hand on my shoulder. After an hour, I left, walked up to the top of Spuistratt and sat on a bench, looking down toward my hotel, thinking what to do next.

CHAPTER 45

Maaijke

— 1836 and 1976 —

I CONTINUED GOING TO SPAKENBURG, ALWAYS ADVANCING THE TIME TO which I traveled by how much older I thought Peter would be, hoping to see him again. Finally, it worked. But I noticed, again, something strange about time. My time with Pieter at home appeared to move at a different rate than did Peter's time, because I could jump ahead. So, when my little Pieter was two and a half, I went to Spakenburg about three years after I saw Peter, but by Peter's time, it was five and a half years later. As I walked down toward the quay with its never-changing botters, I saw a man standing at the foot of Spuistraat. Though visible only in outline, not moving to reveal a clue as to identity, I knew it had to be Peter.

CHAPTER 46

Peter

— 1976 —

L ONG BEFORE I COULD DISCERN ANY OF HER FEATURES, I RECOGNIZED the bouncy, vibrant, energetic walk. Shoulders back, a long stride from high on the toes, head high. As she drew nearer, I saw navy blue slacks, tightly fitting around her hips, and a loose, brick-red, heavy sweater. Her calf-length navy wool coat was open. She ran straight to me, cried "Peter"— nothing else—and raised her arms to encircle my neck. Her coat pulled open, and I slipped my arms inside and around her sweater. We were back five years earlier. Nothing had changed.

I ran one hand up her back to cradle her head. The kiss went on and on. People began to stare. At last, she pulled her head away. "I was going to go sailing."

"No."

"Yes, I think no, too," she said. "Come."

We walked as one, holding hands, stopping every block to embrace.

Arriving at the same boxwood shrub and cutting through its tunnel, we came to the same old brick house. Outside, and inside, it was unchanged. The bedroom was the same. The bedclothes were freshly cleaned and pressed, as before.

We frantically undressed each other, and then I stood to look at her. I had maintained an image of her, my conception of perfection. She was still that, as beautiful as before. Her body seemed unchanged. But it was the embrace of minds, the realization that we were irrevocably intertwined that spoke to me most powerfully.

In bed, we made love as before, resting in an embrace between times. As the sun began its descent in the west, I watched her, marveled at her. In fact, she had changed slightly. Her nipples were browner than the pink I remembered, and she had a small gold chain on her neck with a heart-shaped locket. She was still my idea of perfection. She was sleeping but seemed to be smiling. Her lips periodically scrunched together as if she were trying not to laugh. Barely touching her, I ran my hand across her belly, upon her breasts, and up to her neck and face. She smiled more, still clearly sleeping. After a while—as her shadow began to ascend the wall—she rolled on her side, opened her eyes, and pulled me in with her smile. Her eyes smiled, her nose smiled, her mouth smiled.

CHAPTER 47

Maaijke

—— 1836 and 1976 ——

I LAY STILL AFTERWARD, COMPLETELY CONTENT, WARMED BY HIS STARE enveloping my face and body as we lay next to one another. I thought back to Dr. Comfort's book, De Breugde van Seks, and how he talked about post-coital (that was his doctor talk for after doing sex) contentment. That I had. But it was more, much more than that. Lying next to Peter, I felt as if I were forever protected, and safe, forever happy. Even though I knew better, I couldn't help feeling that way. Looking at him looking at me gave me total confidence about the future. Even lying there, not touching him, simply watching his face, I was completely enfolded into him.

CHAPTER 48

Peter

—— 1976 ——

AS WE LAY THERE, EYES PROBING EYES, SHE SAID, "I AM SORRY, PETER, so sorry that I left you before. Since then, I have wandered the city and gone down to the harbor many, many times, and never did I see you. But I am happy now. Happy and fulfilled. You make my life."

"Maaijke…me too. What happened? I spent two weeks looking for you. It was so odd—this house was gone; it was only a ruin. The boxwood hedge was gone. The neighbors said there was no house here. What happened?"

She put her finger across my lips and said, "Hush. Later, maybe I can explain. I am beginning to have hunger. We missed lunch. What a wonderful way to miss lunch." She kissed me, her tongue probing. "I do not have food here. Can we go to a restaurant?"

I nodded. We got up from bed; I felt weak. Weak from lack of sleep, weak from no food, but mostly weak from Maaijke. She went down the stairs and brought back a bottle of wine and two glasses. We began to dress, but it was a very slow process with many steps backward. By the time the sun was down, and the wine was gone, we finished the process.

"Do you have a hotel room, Peter?"

"Yes, same as before."

"Good, we can stay there tonight. Let's drop my clothes there before dinner."

As we walked to the hotel, I thought of Lisa. I knew, now, that our relationship was a shell of mine with Maaijke, and that I needed to talk to Lisa, to tell her we could not marry. Perhaps tomorrow.

Arms around each other, Maaijke and I headed to a restaurant that was new to me. We sat at a table near the fireplace with its glowing embers, which the staff refreshed every hour or so with new logs. Four loads of wood nourished the fire as we slowly drank and ate. The food was wonderful; neither of us could remember any of it. Holding hands, legs entwined, we talked and talked, cocooned together. Nothing could intrude.

Finally, I said, "Your English is much better."

"Yes. You taught me. I have practiced."

"And you have a locket. It's new?"

"Yes, Peter, new since we were together three years ago."

I let it pass but thought her sense of time was warped. It had been over five years since I had seen her.

"What's in it?"

"A lock of hair."

"Yours?"

"No. Pieter's. P-I-E-T-E-R."

"Who is Pieter?"

"I told you before. In the letter I wrote to you when I left. He is the son I hoped to have. Your son."

I stared at her. I could feel blood draining from my face. I felt sick. The walls, the tables, the plates and silverware and glasses, all faded to black. I laid my head down on the table and clenched my eyes, trying not to pass out, tensing my entire body as I had learned to do in the Navy flying high G turns. Later…I was not sure how much later…I awakened to find my head in Maaijke's lap. She stroked my hair as her tears dripped into my hair.

CHAPTER 49

Maaijke

—— 1836 and 1976 ——

WHEN WE GOT BACK TO THE HOTEL, WE GOT INTO BED, AND HE FACED away from me and slept until the sun awakened us. The first thing he did was ask about the locket, about Pieter. "After, I will explain it all." He knew what I meant by "after," for he shared my hunger. Every time, it seemed better than the last. He made me feel that everything was perfect. I wanted to be with him always; I know it is impossible.

We fell asleep again, and when we awoke, it was too late for breakfast; it was even too late for lunch, so I pulled him into me again. This time, it was very lazy. Languid. But the outcome was better, and so much better than anything Gerta described with Johannus—but maybe it was only that she wasn't so good at the description of making love, or maybe she was too private to tell me everything she felt.

CHAPTER 50

Peter

— 1976 —

I T WAS EARLY AFTERNOON BEFORE WE FINALLY MANAGED TO GET DRESSED. The café was mostly deserted. We had sandwiches and coffee, and then shared a bottle of wine. I talked less and less, then watched her.

"Peter, hold my hand." I did, leaning across the small table. "What? You stopped talking," she said.

"Maaijke, how could you have a child, our child, and not tell me?"

"I tried. I came back here many times. I talked to people on the harbor. I talked to Jacob. I went to the hotel. No one knew where you were. No one knew how I could see you."

"You could have found me. You knew where I came from. You knew I was in the navy. You knew my name. You could have gone to the US Embassy. You could have found me. When I stayed in the hotel, they recorded my passport number and sent it to someone in the government, didn't they?"

Her eyes misted. A tear ran down one cheek. "Peter, I tried. Really. I tried hard. Are you trying to make me cry?"

"*Pieter*. Tell me about Pieter. How do you know he is my son?"

"Peter, you are the only man I have ever been with. He is yours. Yours and mine together."

"How old is he?"

"He will be three next May."

After a long pause, years and pregnancy duration spinning together as I tried to calculate, I said, "That's not possible. We were together in 1971, almost five years ago. How could we have a child who's less than three? He should be at least four. How can it be my child?"

"Do you think time always goes at the same rate everywhere? When you are having fun, doesn't time speed up? And slow down when you aren't?"

I went silent, thinking about what she said. Trying to confirm a birth date nine months after early summer of 1971. Unable to understand it, knowing the impossibility of a child not yet three. Five long minutes passed.

"What is he like?" I finally asked.

"He is like a small you. His hair is the same as mine—maybe slightly darker. He climbs everything he can. He scares me. He is more curious than anyone I have seen."

"Where is he now? Can I see him?"

"No. He is home with my sister now."

"Where is home?"

"Spakenburg."

"Good. Let's go see him."

"I can't."

"Why? Why, Maaijke?"

"He can't travel like that. Like I can."

"But he's here, in Spakenburg. We can walk to him."

"No, Peter. Not this Spakenburg."

"How many Spakenburgs are there?"

"Only one."

"You aren't making any sense."

"You would not be able to understand."

"Try me."

"Later."

"Maaijke, I tell you everything about me. I feel…I feel inside me that I know you better than anyone in the world, but at the same time, I know nothing about you. I don't know your family. You tell me we have a son. I don't know him. Why don't you tell me? We want to be together always, but you don't tell me anything about you. Why?"

"Peter, I promise to tell you everything, but later."

"No, Maaijke. No, dammit. You say you love me. Last time, when we were together less than a week, you said the same thing. But you refused to tell me anything about you. I told you all about me. Everything. But you, nothing. Why? Something's wrong."

She smiled at me, light sparkling off the moisture clouding her eyes, and reached up, gently holding my face, and saying nothing, but her lips formed the words, "I love you. Forever."

And my anger fled. She had sucked me into her little nebula again.

CHAPTER 51

Maaijke

—— 1836 and 1976 ——

BACK IN THE HOTEL, HE WAS DISTANT. I TRIED TO ENTICE HIM BY SLOWLY removing my clothes; he showed no interest. In bed, he turned from me and was quiet. I asked him why he was treating me as if he wanted me to be gone. He said he could not understand how I could love him, and I very much did, and not tell him anything about me. Finally, spooned together, we slept but not well. We both awoke tired.

I removed my locket with Pieter's hair and made a present of it to him. He said nothing but went to his pants and took out a knife. For a moment, I was frightened, especially when he brought it up to my head. Before he could move, when I thought he was going to cut some of my hair, I pulled out a small tuft, or maybe he pulled out a small tuft. I think out of anger. Then he opened the locket, placing some of my hair there, too.

And we were back to normal. I touched his hair, his face, and moved my hand down slowly until he started to smile. It took no time at all to have him back inside me, and when we were done, I started to laugh in happiness.

"Oh, Peter, thank you, thank you."

Then he laughed too.

"Why are you laughing at me? Was that not good?" I said.

"Wonderful. Even better. But you don't say, 'thank you.' You say, 'oh, Peter, that was wonderful.' Or you moan or something."

"No Peter, I mean thank you. You have given me the greatest gift I could ever have. So, thank you."

We had finally had enough, at least for the moment, and went for lunch. After dinner, we played in bed together. But I could feel the difficulty in staying much longer. It took a lot of concentration to stay in Peter's time.

I also worried that he was becoming more impatient, more frustrated, and more intolerant of my answers to his many questions.

"So, if Pieter is nearby," he said, "why can't I see him? If I am really his father."

"Peter, you don't understand. In one way, he is nearby, but in another, it would take you a long time to go to see him. And besides, I want to spend all my time with you, holding you. Don't you see how important that is to me?"

"Maaijke, we have the rest of our lives to be with each other. And don't you want help raising Pieter?"

"Of course. But it might not work out."

"Holy Christ!"

"Peter, you have never yelled like that. Never used the Lord's name in vain with me. What is wrong with you?"

And with that, he was suddenly on the defensive and seemed to lose track of my not telling him about me. At least for now, but I knew he would come back to questioning me. How could I possibly explain to him the truth? He would surely think me crazy.

CHAPTER 52

Peter

—— 1976 ——

WE MUST HAVE GONE BACK TO SLEEP AND AWOKE IN TIME FOR LUNCH. Afterward, we got my rental car and Maaijke directed me south, then right on the A1, then right on the A27 and across the bridge at the end of the peninsula separating the Eemeer Lake from the Gooimeer Lake, and then we went left to Almere. She led us to a small restaurant on the harbor, the Restaurant Brasserie Bakboord. After a slow dinner and a liter of wine, we retraced our course back to Spakenburg and the hotel. On the way back, I repeated my request to see my son, and still she managed to evade answering.

I thought again of Lisa and promised myself that I would call her today but if not, then tomorrow.

Maaijke said, "Stop. Stop now."

I braked to a quick stop, pulling to the side of the road.

"Now, my turn to drive," she said.

I got out and switched places with her, after twisting the key to kill the engine. She sat in the driver's seat playing with the steering wheel, resembling a little child playing at driving her father's car.

"Now, what do I do first?" she said.

"Well, how about starting the car?"

"Tell me how."

"What do you mean? Just like always. Turn the key."

She did that, then said, "Now, what's next?"

"What do you mean? You just shift from park to drive."

She gave me a look of incomprehension and pleading. I suddenly realized she didn't know how to drive. "You don't know how to drive?"

"No, Peter. So, teach me. You are such a good teacher."

"You must be twenty-two or twenty-three—and you don't know how to drive?"

She was silent, thinking.

I'd seen other girls her age driving here. How could she not know?

Finally, she said, almost as if it were a question rather than a statement, "No, twenty-one. And because my parents are very strict and never let me learn. They said it was too dangerous." She ended the statement with a rise in inflection and pitch as if she were testing the statement for plausibility.

"Well, that's weird," I said. "Let's switch places again and find a big parking lot before you drive on the roads, especially at night."

We found an Albert Heijn supermarket, and she again got in the driver's seat. I explained the brake and accelerator, the gear shift lever, and the automatic transmission. She started up with the car jerking erratically, and I almost hit the dashboard as she jumped on the brake pedal.

"Why did you stop?"

"We were going so fast, I was scared."

"But Maaijke, the speedometer needle hardly moved. We weren't going fast. Try again."

Gradually, she smoothed out. Fortunately, she was going slowly when she ran into the light pole among the empty parking spaces, and the front bumper suffered so little that I didn't think the rental agency would even notice.

She flew from the car. I leaned over and turned off the key and got out on my side, only to be almost knocked over as she ran into me, leaping up with her arms around my neck and her legs wrapped around my waist.

"See," she said, laughing. "You are such a good teacher, so I love you even more. Your turn to drive. Quick, drive me back to the hotel."

I did.

Back in our room, back in bed, Maaijke placed me inside of her. Forgotten, at least for now, was our contretemps over her son, and perhaps my son.

"What we do now," she said, "is see who can go the longest without moving."

"*Ooh*. No."

She shushed me with her finger.

"Oh, yes. Whoever can be still the longest wins the prize."

"What prize?"

"Shhh. Don't move."

She closed around me, squeezing.

"You moved, Maaijke."

"No, I didn't."

She squeezed again and within a minute of the start, we had both conceded.

"So, what's the prize?"

"What prize?" she said, and smiled an almost maternal smile before falling asleep.

The sun looked around the window jamb and chased us out of bed. We dressed, and, holding her hand, I pulled her across to the café. During onbijtkoek and coffee, Maaijke was quiet. Not her usually happiness. She also looked sick: red skin and sweating.

"Why are you so subdued? Are you sick?" I pushed away my fear.

"I'm not. I remembered that I need to go back to the house to get something."

"I'll go with you."

"No, I only be a minute. You wait. I be back before you finish your cake."

She sprang up, left the café, and heavy coat flowing out behind her, ran up the street and disappeared. I wondered if I had time to go to the post office and call Lisa. No, probably not.

The thought gripped me that Maaijke was gone again, like before. I went to the café door but couldn't see her. Forcing myself to believe she would be right back, I ordered two more coffees, one for each of us, and thought rationally that after the last couple days and hours, she could not leave me again, so much did we obviously mean to each other, so much did we, or at least I, plan our lives together. I drank my coffee. Hers went from hot to cold. I paid the bill and started off to her house.

As had happened when she disappeared the last time, I found the location but no house. It was again a pile of rubble. The hedge was gone. I pushed my hand against my chest but couldn't slow the allegro tempo. My shirt stuck to the middle of my back. I ran back to the Hotel Sint Nicolaas, climbed the stairs, and unlocked the room door. The letter was there. On the floor. I fell on the bed, dreading to pick it up, trying to deny what I knew it would say.

But I did, I picked it up, tore open the envelope, shivering and crying even before I read.

Peter,

I could not tell you. That I love you, I hope you know. That I want to be always with you, I hope you know. But I did not know how to tell you this with your trusting face staring at me: I have gone. I cannot see you again. One reason is that I have less than a year to live.

I know you love me as I do you. I am not being cruel; I am not toying with you or trying to torment you. But I am unable to explain all of this to you; you would not understand.

I am carrying your son again. I am sure of this. His name will be Martijn.

I have left you a letter. It will explain everything to you when you are able to understand it. You do not need to look for the letter. It will find you during your research.

I love you, Peter. I always will. I always have. Do not be angry. Pray for me.

Maaijke

I lay down, numb, again the victim of a cruel hoax. Finally, I went down to the dock and found the *Het Houten Paard*. Jacob, his right hand covered with a leather sailmaker's palm against which he was applying force to a large needle, was mending a sail.

"Have you seen her, Jacob?"

"Ja, Peter, I have. She was here this morning after breakfast. She seemed sad. She didn't say much. Did you have a fight?"

"No, Jacob. She just left. She put a letter under my door. She said she is not coming back."

"She said the same to me. I almost wanted to cry. She didn't say why. She kissed me and said 'vaarwel' and left. She was sobbing, tears dripped on her coat. She walked straight up the Spuistraat and turned off to the right. I have not seen her since. Have you?"

I couldn't answer. I turned and went up the street, avoiding the gaze of those who stared at my tear-spattered face.

CHAPTER 53

Maaijke

—— 1836 and 1976 ——

Tears blurring my vision, I walked to aunt Jenny's and was immediately back in Bertus's house, still crying. I managed to stop before my husband returned from the fields. He probably wouldn't have noticed. Would he ever understand? Was he capable of understanding? Would he continue to live his life in his sterile isolation?

CHAPTER 54

Peter

—— 1976 ——

I WENT TO THE SINT NICOLAAS, PACKED MY BAG, AND CHECKED OUT. I remembered nothing of the drive to Schiphol Airport, where I left the rental car. I caught my scheduled flight back to Boston and canceled the next leg to Wyoming.

It was afternoon when I arrived at Lisa's apartment. There was no answer to my knock. I waited on the front steps of the dingy apartment building off Huntington Avenue and spied her nearly a block away, with her dignified, somewhat stiff walk.

She looked at me and said, "Peter, what is wrong? You look like hell."

I kissed her. Like I would kiss my sister Anna. We climbed up to her apartment.

"Lisa. We can't get married."

"Okay," she said. Not very disturbed by the news. "Why?" Almost relieved.

"Another girl. In the Netherlands. I love her."

"You are going to marry her, instead?"

"No, I can't."

"Why not?"

"She went away."

"Do you love her?"

"Yes, as I said."

"And does she love you?"

"Yes, of course."

"Where did she go?"

"Don't know."

She hugged me. "You're not making much sense," she said. "How could you not know where she went?"

"Didn't tell me."

"And she loves you? Do you want to talk about it?"

"It's hard to explain. It's almost as if we are the same person. We think the same thoughts. We can finish each other's sentences."

"So, why did she leave you?"

"She had to, I think."

"Had to? Why?"

"She wouldn't tell me. Said I wouldn't understand."

"What do you know about her?"

"All I need to," I said.

"Like what? Have you met her family?"

"No."

"Have you been to her house?"

"Yes, I think so."

"You think so?"

"Well, it's not there now."

"What's that mean?" Lisa grew more and more confused.

"Well, do you know her name?"

"Sure."

"That's at least something. Then you can look her up, can't you? In the phone book? In some records office?"

"I tried. I can't find her name anywhere."

"Peter, either you are putting me on, or she was putting you on. When did you meet her?"

"Before medical school," I said. "Before I met you."

"You never said anything to me about her."

"That's because she went away then."

"She's left you twice?"

"Yeah. It's worse. When I just saw her, she told me she has—we have—a son who is not yet three. And, when we were together, it was in June, just before I started medical school."

"And?"

"And now it's almost Christmas, four and a half years later. Do the math."

"Forget the math. How could you not tell me this?"

"I am."

"I mean sooner. When we started dating and everything."

"Because I didn't know. I didn't know any of this. We spent about a week together, a perfect week. Then she disappeared, leaving only a letter saying goodbye and that I wouldn't be able to understand why she left. But she hoped she was pregnant. That is the last I heard from her, until last week when she showed up again, claiming to have our child. But I couldn't see him. And after another few days together—I was supposed to be on the way home from Brussels but stopped in Spakenburg. And there, I met her again and after a few days, she was gone again. All she left behind was another letter."

"Show me the letters."

"I can't find them. Either of them."

"Peter, is this some sort of scam? Is she trying to get money from you? Are you imagining all this? Do you need some help?"

"No, no, I don't know, I don't think so. The first time she left, it took me two years before I was even interested in any other women. You were the first. And I loved you. Still do. But it's not the same as with her. And I don't know if I will ever see her again."

"Peter, I think you need to go. I think I am grateful you told me. *Sort of.* I must say, I am not surprised there was someone else; you always seemed to withhold something of yourself from me. But an imaginary person?"

And I left.

CHAPTER 55

Maaijke

—— 1836-1837 ——

I WAS AGAIN CARRYING PETER'S BABY.

Of course, I knew I was before going to find Peter because I had traveled forward about one year past my present time. I went to our church first, and in the records found a notation of Martijn's birth. So happy I was: first I knew I would be finding Peter again, for Martijn could never be fathered by anyone else, and second, I would again have the comfort and joy (and to be truthful, the occasional frustration) of raising another boy of his.

Now that I was back home, and pregnant again, I returned to the church records, going forward in time, a month after the date of Martijn's birth. There, I continued to browse the records, and about a week after the time of Martijn's birth, I found my own name. The words made no sense. My breathing became rapid, shallow, difficult. The world seemed to condense around me and blacken. I don't know how I got onto the floor but as I lay there, I saw the church secretary walk toward me, to help. But naturally, she could not see me and walked on past, through me it seemed, without noticing me at all. When I was able to stand, it was dark outside, the church was quiet, and I was alone. The doors were locked, and I had to crawl out a window, but I was not thinking of any of this. Only of what I read: "Maaijke Maasen, died 10 August 1837, age 22 years."

I was back home, sobbing in my bed, when Bertus came in from the fields. He must have heard me, because he came upstairs. For the first time, he came into my bedroom. The bed shook with my convulsing cries. My pillow was wet with tears. I was bleeding where I had bitten my lip, and blood, mixing with the wet of the tears, inked a large pink blot. This he saw. For the first time, he was kind and empathetic. He sat beside me, and held me, his hands kneading my tense back. So miserable did I feel, I permitted this act of charity.

It was dark when I awoke, and going downstairs into the kitchen, I found he had made dinner. Or he at least had tried to. I was grateful and ate with him. It was vile, and I had difficulty in not throwing up. I made it through, but barely.

"Why were you crying?" Bertus asked.

"Because I think I am having another baby."

His visage darkened briefly before he recovered and said, "That's wonderful. When? So why are you sad?"

"Bertus, I am afraid of dying. That is why."

"Don't be silly, Maaijke. You will do perfectly fine, like you did after Pieter was born. I am so happy. I will be a very proud papa."

Again, he seemed to have no understanding of how babies are made.

That gradually changed over the next few months. He started asking me, as he had with Pieter, if I were sure he was the father.

"Of course, Bertus. We discussed this when I was carrying Pieter. You know I am always at home, and we have had no men visiting us alone. Stop talking silly." He would not look directly at me when he asked me these questions. But I could not look him in the eyes either. I didn't lie, at least not exactly, but I could not tell him the whole truth.

He began to go to bed earlier and earlier. He spoke to me less and less. Sometimes, I listened at his bedroom door and heard him crying, and I heard muffled "no's." He worked longer in the fields and began skipping lunch. He looked thinner, tired. When I made him breakfast and dinner, he ate only a portion, and the portion seemed to get smaller each day. His eyes were red when he came down in the morning.

"What's wrong with you, Bertus?"

He shook his head.

One day, he came down in the morning and said, "Maaijke have you lied to me?"

"What do you mean, Bertus?"

"About the baby, the babies," he said. "About the father."

"Bertus, what a horrible thing to accuse me of. Have I ever been out of the house, or out of your sight except when you are in the fields?"

He did not seem convinced. He became more withdrawn.

One morning, he did not come to breakfast. I knocked on his bedroom door, but there was no answer. I was afraid to open the door because of his anger when I had done so in the past. Later, he still did not come down. He still did not answer. I finally tried the door, but it was locked.

I ran to Gerta's house for help. She and Johannes came with me. He knocked hard at the bedroom door. Still no answer.

"Maybe he's sick or hurt," I said.

With that, Johannes left Gerta and me alone, staring at each other. After several minutes, Johannes returned with a large sledge. He stood toward the hinge side of the door and swung the weapon at the lock. Nothing happened. He did it again, and again. The noise was terrible. Other neighbors came running to our house.

Then, on about the tenth blow, the door splintered and flew open.

Bertus was there, motionless, hanging by his neck from a rope tied to the rafter. Next to him, an overturned chair.

I screamed in horror. But I could not cry. I could not even be sad. Well, maybe a little, because I was now alone—even though with Bertus here, it was worse than being alone.

The doctor came and pronounced Bertus dead. The funeral home director took him away. After the burial service in the church, several of the town's men said nice things about my husband, during which I tried to appear appropriately grieved. I even managed to shed some tears while I was mostly thinking whether I would ever be able to find Peter one more time.

After the funeral, my friends and family brought meals. They were good, I am sure, although to me, nothing tasted good. I had little interest in eating, but it was nice that they wanted to help me.

When they left that night, I lit a lamp and went to Bertus's bedroom, that hateful place. I had no clear plan. I needed some of his records to figure out what I could do with the farm, how much money we made from it, and how much we had to pay those who worked it with Bertus. But the desk was locked. Looking around for a key seemed futile until I picked up a small ceramic vase with a matching top. It had a clinking sound when I shook it. With the top off, I found a key, the key. And I opened the desk.

I lost all intention of finding the financial information on the farm, at least then, when I found a letter in the top drawer addressed to me. Bertus told me why he hanged himself.

He was not as ignorant as I appeared to think, he said, and he knew that Pieter and my unborn baby could not have been his. He wasn't sure how I became pregnant, but he accused me of somehow taking another person to my bed, even though I never left the house. He said that because I had deceived him and cheated him of having children, everyone in town would know he was a cuckold, and he was completely humiliated. Killing himself was to be my punishment, and his revenge.

On the contrary, it was my release from his captivity. In his dying, in his death, I thought, he was no more perceptive than during his life.

I burned the note and never spoke to anyone about it.

I found no will. Bertus, an only child, had no relatives. His parents were dead. I was suddenly the owner of a farm but had no idea how to manage it.

I went on a trip again the next day after the funeral, and went forward to June, the month after my death. This time, instead of looking at church records, I looked at civil records of the events in the month before. I found the certificate of my death. "Puerperal fever, complication of child-birth," it read.

Bilious fluid crawled into the back of my mouth, its acrid burning causing me to spit out the green liquid. Barely, did I avoid throwing up. What I had done would take my life. My love for Peter, my desire to have his child again would kill me. Was God angry with me?

I knew that in Peter's time, mothers rarely died from giving birth. If I could go there and have a baby, it would save my life. But I realized that was impossible. I could never maintain the concentration long enough to have a baby in 1978, and even if I could, how could I take the baby back to my time? I could go forward, but then would have to go back, and the baby could not make the trip.

Peter was a doctor! Maybe he could come back with me to my time. Peter could care for me; he could save me from dying. He would know how. But I knew that was impossible. I was never able to travel backward in time, only forward; I didn't think Peter could either. He certainly couldn't do so to help me, because it would require that he interact with and change the past, which would change everything that has happened already—it would change everything in the future too. Maybe the world would be destroyed. Whenever I visited a future time, it was always the same as it was on my previous visits to that same time in the future. How could the future have two different existences? It was as if the world's history and future were parts of a ruler—but it was a time ruler, and the numbers could not be changed. Everything lay on a linear track. If only I could find a way to change those numbers on the ruler. If only…

I thought about that for a while, until I realized I was going to die and nothing could help me. I had less than a year to live. But aside from realizing that fact, I felt wonderful. I felt as wonderful as I had with Pieter growing inside me before he was born. I wasn't dead yet; I would continue to live as much as I could while I could. Since I traveled forward by imagining it, maybe none of what I learned would happen. Maybe I was imagining all of it. That made me feel better. At least a little bit. But it was nearly impossible to believe that without ignoring the reality of little Pieter crawling all over me, jumping up and down, playing roughly with the other little four-year-old boys and the occasional girl.

My face and breasts began to swell, a now familiar and comfortable experience. I looked and felt healthy. My friends, especially Gerta, commented upon my radiance and my beauty and pronounced that I would thus be having a boy. I laughed with them—they because of invoking an old wives' tale, I because I knew them to be correct.

I was now about two months pregnant. I tried to keep at bay the thought that I was destined to die soon after Martijn was born, but I was not very successful. I desperately wanted to raise my two boys.

I also wanted to be with Peter again, even if for only one more night. And that led me to dream of another plan, maybe one that would save my life.

CHAPTER 56

Peter

— 1976 —

Back in Wyoming, I told Anna everything. She didn't believe me. Which made me feel worse. My bitter smile was evoked by the painful irony of hearing, "We Wish You a Merry Christmas" on the radio. I wondered if I did need help. Therapy, maybe. But with vacation ending, I flew back to Belgium to finish my research year.

I found difficulty focusing on the work, but nevertheless was able to have my name on three publications based on the transplant research. I probably didn't deserve it; Professor Alexandre did much of my work. For the entire remaining five months there, I was crippled by the memory of Maaijke. And then the research year was over; I headed back to Boston to restart my residency. On the way, I stopped again in Spakenburg. Jacob had not seen Maaijke since I had. I was of a mixed mind: on the one hand, deeply disappointed, but on the other, relieved that no one else was able to see her either.

CHAPTER 57

Maaijke

— 1837 —

Gerta came to see me a lot after Bertus died. My childhood friend was even closer to me now, and very comforting. She too was carrying a baby, her third. After several visits, she talked about Bertus.

"Maaijke, remember before you got married and I told you I had heard rumors about Bertus?"

"Sure. But you never told me more."

"Well, that's because the rumors were obviously false."

"Then you should be able to tell me."

"Did he talk about his mom much?"

"Almost never. Only that she died alone, after Bertus's father died."

"The way I heard it from my parents, Bertus's father and mother fought, and once he beat her when Bertus was about twelve. She grabbed a kitchen knife for protection, and he beat her even more. I'm not sure what happened exactly, but he ended up dead with that knife plunged into his heart. And she went to jail, where she died. When she was sent to jail, Bertus went to live with his aunt, his mom's much-younger sister. She never married, and I heard my parents criticizing the arrangement; she was only about ten years older than Bertus. Everyone said that he developed into a strange boy after this, and then into a strange man. Johannes told me that he heard his parents saying that the reason Bertus married so late was that he was afraid of women and thought that sex with a woman was dangerous. That he was unable to have sex. That's why I seemed shocked when you told me you were going to marry him. But now, with Pieter growing up, and your next baby inside you, I guess that story was wrong. So, I'm sorry if I worried you before you even got married."

I sat silent, stunned. Finally, I held one of her hands and said, "Thank you, Gerta. You are the best friend anyone could ever have. I guess none of that matters now that he is gone."

"I wonder why he did that? Hanged himself," she said. "Was he sad about something? If he never talked about his mother, maybe he was too ashamed. Could that have had anything to do with what he did?"

"No. He never seemed to be sad or upset about his mother." Now, with her story about Bertus's childhood, I understood him, finally. At least better than I had before. But I never said that to Gerta. And I could never have told her about falling in love with someone in the future. Not then, not ever, could I do that.

CHAPTER 58

Peter

—— 1979 ——

"TAXING, DEBILITATING, EXHILARATING, EXHAUSTING, STIMULATING, depressing, joyous," I thought, after finishing the first two years of my resumed residency in 1979 at the age of 33. This, during a rare period of reflection—rare because I almost never had the time for it. The rapid building of responsibility, the continued need to do the "scut" work, all of it almost too much to grasp. My coterie of residents didn't spend much time in reflection; like me, they had no time for such luxury. Indeed, we had no time for anything except the residency, with an occasional few minutes or hours to eat and sleep.

It was identical to our internship schedule but with progressively more responsibility. Arriving at the hospital at 5 a.m. for rounds on a Monday, repeating rounds at 7 with the attending surgeon, work all day sometimes in the OR, sometimes caring for patients, and rarely getting any sleep that night, whether operating or not, to begin again at 5 Tuesday morning for a new day as measured by a clock and calendar, but not by any change of my schedule or work, and with no sleep and none available until I went home that second night at 9 p.m. And then up again to be in the hospital by 5 a.m. Wednesday to repeat the two-day cycle. Mercifully, I would then be off duty for the nights only of Thursday and Friday until Saturday morning. Cruelly, we all thought, home would then be in the hospital from Saturday morning until Monday evening, with only a few hours of sleep during that sixty-hour marathon. Then, the pattern was reversed for the next week with continuous duty from Thursday morning until Saturday noon to pay for the partial weekend off.

On superficial assessment, there might have seemed no time to learn. But never had I learned so much, so quickly, and each day brought an increase of confidence with the newly won knowledge and abilities, and sometimes, horrible humiliation with the minor failures. In some ways, it was like the navy again; surgical residents developed a confident swagger that distinguished us from all other trainees.

At the beginning of the final two years, the pace eased slightly with the junior residents bearing the brunt of the drudge work, and the more senior residents taking it easy with hundred-hour workweeks. More operations. More responsibility during the operations. More often, I became the surgeon with the attending surgeon needing less and less to guide my hands.

My social life was marked only by its complete absence until one day during a hemigastrectomy for a bleeding ulcer, gloved hands smeared in blood, I handed the specimen off into a plastic bag and looked up into Lisa's lively, familiar eyes. Even in scrubs, her lissome shape was clearly retained. She spoke only, "Thank you," and left.

After the operation, I went to the pathology specimen lab and found that she had taken part of the tissue back to the transplantation laboratory where she worked. The reunion with her was delightful, an old-acquaintance type of meeting. That night we had dinner; much of the talk was about work. Her deep commitment to the field of transplantation had carried her far beyond me in sophistication, but I was fascinated. Held so tightly in thrall by what she was doing, I found her overflowing enthusiasm contagious.

Two nights later, we met again and spent the night in her apartment. A strange, curious pattern developed. We each satisfied a need for the other, but never again did a romantic attachment return; just two good friends having a good time together.

The relationship was defined by an event one night. She was on top, riding up and down, clearly aroused, when she suddenly stopped. "So," she said, "you know how toxic the anti-rejection drugs are in the transplant patients? Well, what do you think about the idea of creating an animal from birth that has both human genetics along with the native ones? A chimera if you will. Then, we could use that animal as a donor in the future, and maybe thwart the rejection phenomenon."

I burst out laughing. She fell on top of me, laughing too. "Oh, I am sorry. I know we were supposed to be in the throes of passion, but what if that works? Think how that would change medicine. Now, if we transplant an organ from one species into another, the organ is rejected within seconds or minutes. But if by changing the genetic material so that it looks human, maybe we could transplant a pig organ into a human. Immediately, there would no longer be organ shortages." We were both quiet for a few minutes, and she jumped up. "I have to jot these notes and ideas down before I forget them," she said.

"I guess," I said, "that is what is meant by casual sex." She laughed in agreement and was clearly elated, but by her intellectual breakthrough, certainly not by what we had done together.

I knew Lisa to be far smarter than me. After she voiced her proposal, I asked several of my active transplant colleagues across the country about it. All thought it an intriguing idea but an entirely unworkable one. I also thought her idea to be impossible, at least in our lifetimes. And I was also sufficiently savvy not to tell her that.

While no one, certainly not us, could call our relationship passionate, neither did it diminish our friendship in any way. Sex seemed to heighten her creative and inventive ideas; she always kept note cards and a pen near her bed so she would not lose any of her arousal-induced research thoughts.

If I knew then what I later learned, my assessment of our nights together might have been very different.

CHAPTER 59

Maaijke

—— 1837 and 1991 ——

S HORTLY BEFORE CHRISTMAS THAT WINTER, I BEGAN TO HAVE SOME BLEED-
ing and cramping. Not much, just a little. I worried, but I tried to ignore it. When I visited Mama and told her, she seemed even more worried
than I, and would not allow me to go back home. She made me stay in bed
in our old house and brought me all my meals. I was suddenly her baby
again. I am not sure who was a bigger burden for her, me or Pieter, who she
also had to care for even as he boisterously bounced all around her home
like a rubber ball.

"Mijn liefje," she now called me, as she had when I was a small child.

"Mama, you are so nice to me. I'm not a baby anymore."

"I know, I know, but I don't have any more babies at home. Humor me
and let me treat you as one for a little while."

But she said all of this with a frown of worry. I was frightened. I spent
Christmas there.

After a week in bed, the bleeding stopped. The cramps stopped. Mama
helped me out of bed, and I began walking a little bit. My fear abated; still,
Mama treated me as an invalid for another week before her usual happy,
placid face returned. As did mine. Before I left for home, she told me that

it might be too dangerous to have the baby on her kitchen table and that I should have it in the new hospital, where the doctor could supervise my labor and childbirth. I thought it might be too expensive. Mama reassured me that it would not be, and so I eagerly agreed.

Mama found a doctor for me. We went to visit Dr. Oosterhuis in February. He was so nice; I liked him. He examined me without having me take any of my clothes off; the midwife was also there and was a bit more intimate with her examination. Dr. Oosterhuis was very nicely dressed, completely unlike any of the farmers I knew, although his fine coat had dark stains on the front and sleeves. He made me feel confident, and I began to think my fears were unfounded. Everything, he told me, was perfect, and he expected no difficulties with my delivery. Mama thought him to be professional, and she had great confidence in him. We both found him rather handsome. He was so knowledgeable: he would clearly make sure Martijn's birth was safe.

But as soon as I left Dr. Oosterhuis, the confidence he imparted in the future waned. I returned to thinking of the entry I found in the church records when I read forward to the week after Martijn's birth. And I remembered that when I first met Peter, he was in Spakenburg to learn about his ancestral heritage, so I decided to be sure he understood who I was and what had happened to us—me, Pieter, and Martijn—in case the records about my death were correct.

I traveled forward systematically to the Spakenburg town hall, where the civil records were kept. My thinking was that if I went forward one month at a time, and searched for Peter, I could discover his tracks. In the town hall, there was a registry of who had accessed the records and when. So, each month I visited, I looked at the registry for the previous month. It was tedious, laborious, and boring—but I was determined to tell Peter about us. I started in 1978 and slowly worked my way ahead in time. I knew at some point he would look at the records. But if I left him a letter long before he visited the town hall, it was likely that someone else would find it and remove it.

Finally, I found his name. He had looked at the records on July 14, 1991. So I wrote him my letter and, traveling to that time, inserted it on

July 13, one day earlier. I stayed through the next day to see him take it. He did not see me; I did not want him to. Immediately, I was back in my time.

Part II

CHAPTER 60

Peter

—— 1978–1979 ——

ARLIER, DURING MY FIRST YEAR OF RESIDENCY, I HAD GRADUALLY COME to appreciate the conscientious work of my resident mate, Manny Rodriguez. He was the first college graduate in his family, who then went directly to Columbia Medical School, then on to his internship and residency. Thus, while in my resident class, he was five years younger because of my detours.

Manny was gay. The first night we were on call together, Manny, who displayed none of the mannerisms sometimes assumed by others of his group, sat down at my table at the free 9 p.m. dinner in the cafeteria.

We talked about patients. We complained about the amount of work, the lack of sleep, the crummy food. In other words, we did what all residents did every night.

Then, without a logical segue, Manny said, "In case you didn't know it, Peter, I have boyfriends, not girlfriends. I am gay. It has no bearing on my work; I hope you will judge me only by my performance as a resident and colleague."

"Of course, Manny, no problem. I couldn't care less," I said, as he finished his dinner and walked away with an indecipherable look. I wasn't certain I had reassured him. I wasn't even certain I meant what I said. I sat there for a long time, staring at the lemon I had added to my iced Coke. I was not sure that I had met anyone before who freely admitted to being gay—certainly never in the Wyoming ranch lands of my early years—and despite my assurances to Manny, I felt uncertain as to how to relate to him. But gradually, Manny's integrity, honesty, hard work, gifted surgical skills, and enormous intelligence and knowledge overcame my hesitation. Those qualities, plus his self-deprecating sense of humor, led to him becoming my best resident friend.

At the start of my third year of residency, Manny offered me the use of his house in Provincetown for my vacation. The house would be unused; Manny was on the transplant rotation. With some initial reluctance, I finally accepted. It proved to be a momentous, life-altering decision.

The two weeks began with a drive down I-93 to Route 3, on to Route 6 beyond the Sagamore Bridge, and then to P-town on the tip of the Cape. After unlocking the house on Carver Street, I found Manny's mountain bike. I changed into beach-appropriate clothes, and I took his bike east along Shore Road between East Harbor and Cape Cod Bay, crossed to Route 6 for a couple hundred feet, and then took High Head Road across the Cape to the ocean side. When High Head Road faded to nothing, I left the bike in the clumps of Cape beach grass and, now in bare feet, turned to the east to walk to the Atlantic shoreline, pushing my toes into the soft sand with each step.

I found some striae of different-sized pebbles, round and smooth. The bands of smaller pebbles were closer to the water, the bands with larger ones were higher on the beach. A green flash caught my eye; nestled among pebbles of a similar size was a piece of green, burnished, smooth glass. I soon found another, in satiny clear glass, then some of cobalt blue and a few of brown. Those few of clear glass were the most difficult to distinguish from the surrounding stones in which they hid.

I walked along, head bowed, bending to pick up the occasional piece of sea glass until I had a handful. I stood straight to shove them into my pants pocket and saw a figure approaching me with the same bent-over posture I had abandoned, walking slowly, head bowed. When closer, I saw it was a woman with strange coloring. She had tan arms and legs but was dead white from neck to upper thighs, and was wearing a dark, two-piece bathing suit. When she got closer, still oblivious to my presence, I realized my mistake. Her white beach cover-up was slit down the front for a few inches, and the bathing suit, obviously wet, had soaked the linen, making it transparent. She looked fragile, needing protection perhaps. Ten yards from me, she sensed my presence and looked up, startled, eyes wide.

She laughed, nervously. To soften her unexpected encounter with me, I reached into my pocket and withdrew a few pieces of the sea glass.

"Here, I brought you something," I said, walking to her and depositing the glass in her hand.

Color returning to her face, she laughed more genuinely. Her hair hung in damp, clumped tendrils with some dried salt near the top of her head. "You must have better eyes than I do. I only found three pieces."

"Maybe you haven't been looking in the bands of pebbles. That's where the sea glass rests. I think that the smaller pieces lie with the smaller pebbles, and the bigger pieces with the bigger rocks. But you are welcome to have those." I pointed to her hand.

She transferred the sea glass to her left hand, held out her right hand, and said, "I apologize for appearing frightened. I was so absorbed in my task that I had no idea you were there. I'm Celia." Her smile produced splendid, becoming dimples.

I shook her hand and said, "No, I apologize for startling you. I'm Peter. Also, you walk too fast."

She squinted at me, paused for a few uncomfortable seconds, then grunted a feeble laugh. "What do you mean, 'I walk too fast'? You have no idea how I walk."

My turn to feel awkward. "No, that didn't come out right. I meant that for hunting sea glass, I have found that it's better to take a step or two, then stare down in the pebbles and rocks at your feet, trying to focus on the distinction between the glass and surrounding pebbles. That's what I meant."

Then she gave a real, honest laugh. "Thank God, I thought you were criticizing me. You need to be careful. I may be very sensitive to such comments," she said, twitching her nose.

"Well, anyway, Peter, thanks for the sea glass." She dropped my hand and continued her walk, as did I. Nearly a mile down the beach, I turned around to walk back to my bike lying in the beach grass, but she was gone.

I ate dinner at Napi's, where I had a problem concentrating on the food because of the attention evidently and successfully sought by the other diners. With one exception, all tables were single-gender tables—mostly men. Many of the men were dressed as women: tall women with large Adam's apples and large shoulders. Those not cross-dressing often had tight, skimpy clothing that made me uncomfortable. The only mixed-gender table had two couples dressed, by my standards, more normally, and who had obviously come from a boat. With no immediately adjacent angry ocean, it was strange that one of the women wore her orange life preserver throughout dinner. Was she trying to compete with the outfits of the gay men?

I anticipated going to the same beach the next day, perhaps to run into Celia again, but it rained all day, and I entertained myself—wearing some old oilskins I found in the house—by looking into the often-bizarre storefront displays.

That night, stars shone brightly, correctly portending a sunny day to follow. I read in the morning, and by eleven o'clock was laying the bike down at the same spot on the outside of the Cape. As I began another search for sea glass, I kept looking ahead, hoping to find Celia. I saw no one else walking. But after a quarter hour, I saw a figure lying on the beach several hundred yards distant. As I approached, it was clearly a woman, and closer still, I noticed she wore only a green bathing suit bottom. Veering closer to the water so as not to embarrass her, I saw it was Celia. As I passed her, she recognized me, and sat up, covering her breasts with her hands. Medium brown hair hung wetly at mid-neck level. It was covered in sand where the back of her head must have extended beyond her towel edge.

"Oh, Peter," she said, and began giggling, then laughing. "I'm laughing at myself. Here I think I am a modern woman, but as soon as someone catches me playing that role, I revert to my upbringing and try to cover up. Although, there's not that much to cover."

"Celia! I am sorry I startled you again." While I didn't reply directly to her self-disparagement (her observation was indeed correct), after a pause, I said, with justifiable honesty, "No, you make the beach look very nice."

She blushed and lay down on her belly. As I reluctantly began walking on, she said, "Stop! Thank you, I guess. Stay. Talk with me."

I sat by her. We exchanged what-do-you-dos. So that I could find out more about her, I spent as little time as possible describing my surgery residency. She worked as an officer for the Fish and Game Department. To me, viewing her as timid and fragile, that seemed an inappropriate job.

"So, what do you do, exactly? I used to hunt upland birds a lot when I was younger."

"Mostly," she said, "I ride around and look for hunters, making sure they are hunting in season, that they have legal guns, and that they don't exceed the game limits."

"Do you wear a gun? What do you mean, 'legal guns'"?

"I have an issued sidearm, but I really don't like to carry it. And legal? For example, most waterfowl hunters use semi-automatic shotguns that can hold up to five shells. To be legal, they must be plugged so that they can hold no more than two in the magazine, plus one in the chamber. So, I have them unload the guns completely, then reload and check that they can't insert a third shell in the magazine. Stuff like that. I never saw a bird hunter even think of an illegal weapon; they don't want anything heavy to carry as they walk the woods and mostly use a double-barrel of some type."

"Yeah. Same for me. I always used an old Fox 20 for bird hunting, but I never did hunt ducks or geese. Did you ever have to shoot someone?"

She laughed. "No. Never. Never even close. But I do have two shotguns myself, and hunt as often as possible. Birds and waterfowl. Both."

"Really? Would you take me hunting sometime? I haven't had any chance since I left Wyoming. I don't know anyone around Boston to go with. I'm sure there are a number in the hospital who hunt, but I don't know who they are."

"Sure. I'll make you a deal. You take me to lunch; I'll take you hunting. And I guess I should stop being embarrassed." With her arms, she pushed off the ground and twisted to a sitting position. Sitting, her breasts and belly were partially covered by sand sticking to sunscreen. "There. How's that?"

"Ummh, ah, very nice," I said. It was my turn to blush.

"I need to get the sand off, first." Grabbing her bathing suit top, she jumped up and ran into the water, submerging herself before she put the top back on. Back ashore, she slipped on the same linen beach cover-up she wore two days earlier.

"How'd you get here?" I asked.

"Bike."

"Me too. Where's yours?"

"At the end of High Head Road," she said.

"Mine too. I didn't see yours."

"Well, you know where High Head Road turns left before going into the ocean, where you see some cars on the beach? That's what I meant. I left it off the road where it turns left and walked down this way."

"Okay, mine's at the end of the road after it turns left. Farther west. Over there," I said, pointing back to the west. "C'mon. We'll get my bike and walk back to yours." And we did.

"I have to change before I go to lunch. I hate sitting and eating in a wet bathing suit," Celia said. "So, we need to go to where I am staying, first."

Arriving at her apartment a few blocks from Manny's house, she invited me in. "I'll only be a few seconds." She emerged from her bedroom in sneakers, khaki Bermuda shorts, a yellow web belt, and a white men's shirt tucked into her pants, sleeves rolled up to her elbows.

We rode to Mojo's on the harbor. Two murals on adjacent cinderblock walls set the atmosphere. One was of tall ships; the other was of a sea dragon with a gaff-rigged cutter sailing by. We ordered and shared an awful meal: awful for our health but wonderful tasting, consisting of linguica sandwiches, fried mushrooms, and French fries, which we ate on the picnic tables outside. An overnight boat race from Marblehead had finished early that morning; several of the crew wandered and stumbled about, clearly having started drinking long before noon. One of them succeeded in sitting at our picnic table, where he stared at Celia (even drunk, he clearly had good taste) for about half a minute, saying nothing, before he rejoined his friends.

"Brilliant conversationalist," said Celia. She gave a wry smile, which I returned.

"I've never heard that name before, 'Celia.'"

"It's not really my name, it's a nick name. My real name is Cecelia. I have a sister two years older and when I was born, she had difficulty with four syllables and called me Celia. It stuck," she said.

We had arrived for lunch after one o'clock, so there was no pressure to vacate the table. Two hours escaped without me noticing. I thought back to another first lunch in Spakenburg many years ago. This was different: less urgent but still pleasant. Celia was easy, comfortable to talk with. I hoped to see her again.

Back at our bikes, she said, "Dinner?"

I interrupted before the second syllable with a quick "Yes," and we both grinned, a mutually communicative grin.

"Okay," she said. "Come by at seven."

"I have a car. Should I drive?"

"No. It's an easy walk."

I spent the remainder of the afternoon happy with the anticipation of dinner. And without any solid indication from her, I began to roll around the idea of Celia in my future.

CHAPTER 61

Peter

— 1979 —

A T SEVEN O'CLOCK, CELIA AND I WALKED TO THE MEWS RESTAURANT. She wore linen slacks of a faded red, blue flats, and a simple white cotton blouse, loosely fitted and open at the neck with the upper two buttons unfastened. She wore no bra. The sun, low in the west to her side, backlit the fabric, silhouetting her breasts. We arrived shortly after seven; she had made a reservation.

We forewent cocktails and instead ordered a bottle of Sauvignon Blanc; she did not like the oaky flavor of most chardonnays. We shared a seafood sampler—oysters and clams, shrimp and lobster, and fish ceviche—as an appetizer, followed by an Asian-inspired beef tenderloin for her and a pork vindaloo Indian dish for me.

"Are we on a date?" she asked before oysters arrived.

"I guess," I said. "Maybe you should tell me your last name."

"Rawlings."

"Maasen," I said, jabbing my chest with an index finger. "I had a baseball glove made by Rawlings."

"I know."

"How could you know that?"

"I don't mean I knew you had one," she said. "I meant that I know the company." She paused. "I wouldn't normally say this, but since I feel quite relaxed with you, I will. For being on a date, you're not paying much attention to me. You are looking all around the room at other tables."

I reddened and confessed to the sin.

"But I don't blame you, and I don't feel neglected. When I first came to Provincetown, I had the same need to look at the spectacle. For example, do you see the couple two tables over there? The guy with the very pretty woman? I saw the woman at the beach a couple weeks ago in a tight, small bikini that on top barely contained what were obviously artificial breasts. Way bigger than mine. And the bottom barely contained what he—yes, he—was naturally given at birth. You're getting red again! After a while, you get used to it."

"Okay, point taken. I have a very good friend at work who is gay. I'm staying in his house here. But he is…well, less theatrical," I said, drawing two quotation marks in the air with my fingers.

"Yes. These people are often acting a part. Putting on a show. But a lot of them are my friends and most are quite nice. Certainly not threatening."

"Bet not many of them hunt! How did you end up being a game warden?"

"I wanted to be a vet. But admission to veterinary school was tight, and I was deferred a year. So, I took this as a temp job but found I liked it, so I stayed."

"Where do you live when you are not here?"

"Westport."

"Massachusetts?"

"Yeah. It's nice. I hunt ducks on the river, and geese in fields around there. In the summer, I fly fish for striped bass and bluefish right in the river, or right off its mouth out in Buzzards Bay."

"Do you hunt upland birds there, too?"

"Not much around here. There is some pheasant stocking around there, but mostly we go up into New Hampshire or Maine for grouse and woodcock."

I was surprised to feel some jealousy. "We?" I spoke.

"Yes, we."

"Is the other part of 'we' a male or female?"

She must have seen where I was going, and appeared to conceal a flicker of smile. "Oh, very definitely female."

"Does that mean…? You know, being out here in Provincetown, and hunting with another woman…"

"Well, I can say I am very, very close to her."

Judging from her face, I must have looked crestfallen. I sure felt that.

"Well, that's nice, I guess. Do you live together? What's her name?"

"We've lived together for the past five years. She goes by Red."

"Oh. Red hair, I suppose. I feel sort of foolish. I confess that I was thinking we might get to know each other better," I said. "Are you sure you want to have dinner? I've sort of lost my appetite."

Finally, she began laughing. "Yes, we've lived together since she was eight weeks old, and I named her Red because of a reddish patch on her rump, in front of her tail. Otherwise, she is all black. A lab. And as far as getting to know you better, I think I might like that."

I had been holding my breath and let out a long sigh. Then a smile slid into a laugh. "Oh, man! You had me going. Okay, my appetite's back.

"Red! Are you kidding me? I had a great hunting dog, two actually, one named Rusty and the other Red. Both Irish setters. Hard to believe that our dogs were both named Red. A sign?"

"Maybe. Now it's your turn. When we were on the beach, you said you worked in a hospital as a resident. What do you do? Are you a doctor?"

"Yup. A surgical resident. At the Brigham. Peter Bent Brigham Hospital."

"How did you end up being a surgical resident?"

"To start with, I wanted to go to the Naval Academy but did not get in. All three of the Wyoming slots went to star football players. So, after I graduated…"

"From…?"

"Harvard. How about you? Before you became a game warden?"

"Wellesley."

"And did what?" I said.

"French major."

"Bet that comes in handy as a game warden!"

"Actually, it does. You can't imagine how many hunters speak only French in Massachusetts." I interrupted her with a laugh. She continued, "And I am a killer date in a French restaurant. But you were going to tell me how you ended up as a surgical resident."

"So, after I graduated, I went into the Navy, and they taught me to fly. Went to Vietnam."

"So, you asked me this question, it's my turn. Did you ever shoot anyone?"

I paused to allow a brief shudder pass through me as I thought of Willis.

"Not sure, really. I did shoot down five and a half planes, and I saw a couple pilots who bailed out and their chutes opened. But mostly, as soon as their plane was hit, I was headed back to the ship to avoid getting shot down myself by the surface-to-air missiles—SAMs, we called them. I sort of hope I never hurt any of the other pilots, but maybe. I liked shooting planes. It was a little bit like shooting birds. You have to shoot where they are going to be. Almost exactly like a proper lead with a shotgun. A major difference, however, is that the birds can't shoot back. But even more, we were dropping bombs…"

"And?"

"Nothing. They exploded," I said, looking away.

"What happened to the half of a plane you didn't shoot down?"

"No, the plane was totally shot down, but it wasn't clear from our gun cameras who got the credit, me or a squadron buddy of mine. So, we each got half credit."

"So why didn't you stay in the navy?"

"I almost did. I was offered a promotion and a job teaching in the Fighter Weapons School—you may have heard it as TOPGUN school—in California. I loved what I did, and I loved the navy. It's embarrassing to admit; I even loved the uniforms. But I realized that the only way up was to leave what I really did well, and really liked—flying planes—and become an administrator. That did not appeal much to me. And I didn't like war all that much, I guess. Plus, I wanted more challenge, and I thought medicine and especially surgery would be that. So far, it's far exceeded my expectations. Both physically and mentally challenging."

"Do you have a girlfriend? A wife?" she asked.

"That's some segue!" But I didn't answer. "Did you do any sports at Wellesley?"

"Ran cross-country for three years there."

"Any good? What happened the fourth year?"

She added, "I would say I neither dragged the team down, nor lifted it up. Middle-of-the-pack sort of runner. The fourth year? It was actually my junior year. I did a junior year abroad in Aix-en-Provence at the Aix-Marseille University."

Dinner was delicious and deliciously slow. We both knew the other well by the time it was over. How different, I thought, than with Maaijke, who told me almost nothing about herself, whose mystery caused me to doubt her existence. It was a couple minutes before eleven when we left, the last two remaining diners in the restaurant. For dessert, we had finished a second bottle of Sauvignon Blanc.

"With all that, glad we didn't drive," I said.

Celia leaned against me and placed her arm about my waist. "Me too."

We walked in comfortable silence to her apartment. We stopped. I felt a sudden awkwardness; she appeared to as well. She looked up at me, expectantly, but then suddenly stepped back.

"You didn't answer my question," she said.

"Which one?"

"Girlfriend or wife?"

"No, I guess I didn't. No, not really. I was engaged to a girl with whom I still work. We occasionally have dinner together, even spend the night. But mostly, we're simply good friends. It's partly because of another girl many years ago. Some time, some other time, I might tell you about it. You?"

"Only Red now. There have been a few guys in the past. Nothing very remarkable."

She turned to go inside, turned back to me with a warm smile and her deep dimples.

"Goodnight. Thanks. I had a wonderful time. Wanna go to the beach again tomorrow?" she said.

"Yes, very much."

"Come by on your bike around ten. Want me to bring a lunch?"

"Sure. G'night," I said, and began to walk away, unsure whether to be disappointed about the end of the evening or encouraged by Celia's invitation.

CHAPTER 62

Peter

— 1979 —

I WAS PROMPT THE NEXT MORNING. CELIA HAD TWO BAGS, ONE IN EACH pannier on her bike. We left our bikes at the very end of High Head Road, where I had left mine before. We each carried one of her sacks and walked down to the beach. No one was in sight, and we turned left.

"Down this way to the west, it's always deserted," she said.

After about a half mile, she turned left again, away from the water and up into the dunes. In a wind-protected hollow, surrounded by beach grass, we set down the bags and spread large towels.

"It's too early for lunch. Wanna go for a swim—so we deserve lunch?" she said.

"I didn't bring a suit. The last two times I was down here, I walked along the water. I didn't really think about swimming."

"Can you swim?"

"Sure."

"Guess what. I expected to swim, and did not bring my suit either. That's why I took us to this lonely section."

She wore knee-length shorts and a shirt. She pulled the shirt out from under the belted pants and reached up behind her back. She first withdrew one bra strap from under the shirt sleeve, drew it down her arm, and after withdrawing her hand from the opening under the strap, pulled the bra back up under the shirt, then out the other sleeve and dropped it on her towel. Then she looked up at me and smiled.

"Your turn. Or are you too modest?"

I could feel my face flushing, turned away from her and pulled my shirt off, and dropped my Bermuda shorts, kicking off my shoes. Behind me, I saw her shorts and the tiny silk bit of panties on the towel, and saw her walking to the water, shrugging off her shirt onto the sand. I dropped my underpants and self-consciously followed her.

I waded in until the surf came up to my belly, as she candidly appraised me.

"If you're trying to use the water as a modesty shield, assessing your condition," she said, laughing, "I would say maybe you need to wade a few inches deeper."

I blushed, again, then dove at her and pulled her underwater. We surfaced together. I was coughing from laughing underwater, and I drew her to me. She kissed me very slowly, writhing against me. I held her shoulders and pushed her away.

"You're right," I said, studiously observing her droplet-studded breasts, "there may not be a huge amount to cover up there." She lunged at me, but I grabbed her wrist before her blow landed. We were both laughing. "But they are perfect."

We walked from the water, holding hands, and at towels' edge, she lowered her gaze and said, "It doesn't look as if you are quite ready for lunch."

"No. Maybe later." I held her, stroking her wet hair, and lowered her to the towels.

Enfolded by her, we languorously made love. I felt no urgency. It seemed as if we had done this many times. It was totally different from the near frenzy I felt the first time with Maaijke, but it was the same in that I knew this was where I wanted to be as far as I could see in the future.

"So?" I asked, as we lay together on the disheveled towels.

"So? Do you mean, 'how was that sexually or emotionally?'"

"I guess the first is obvious for both of us. What about the second?"

"I'm too old to be coy with you. We belong together," she said, with a finality accepting no contradiction.

"Are you sure? So soon? You seem so different than when I first saw you. I thought you were timid, fragile, needing protection."

"Well yes," she said. "And I think I would like you to protect me the same way again after lunch."

We put only our shorts on. She now seemed totally unself-conscious with me. She opened one bag and pulled out two lobster salad sandwiches, and from the other, two plastic wine glasses and from a cooling sleeve, a bottle of Perrier-Jouët.

"Expensive taste!"

"Not really. It was a gift, and I was saving it for a special occasion. This qualifies," she said, her dimples showing prominently, salt crystals glistening in her hair.

"Perfect," I said, after my first sip.

"The wine?"

"Well, that too," I said.

After the lobster rolls, and the full bottle of champagne, we lay in the sun for what seemed a few minutes. Awakening, it was nearly two hours later, and we made love again, before reluctantly pulling on our clothes and riding back.

That afternoon, I moved into her apartment. By the end of the week, each of us thought we knew everything about the other.

On my last night of vacation, after a slowly eaten home-cooked dinner, we lay on her couch together, and she said, "Well, are you going to ask me? Or do you expect me to?"

"Ask you?"

"To marry you," she said, with her confident, dimpled smile.

"I guess my first impression was totally wrong. You don't need protection; you're not exactly frail. And anyway, didn't you just ask me?"

"So, is that a 'yes'?"

I grabbed her and between kisses, said, "It's more—it's when?"

I paused for a minute. "Maybe to be considerate, we should meet each other's parents. The problem is that I won't be able to get time to go home until I have another vacation. Might not be until Christmas."

"Try sooner. It's an easy drive up to Ipswich. We can meet my parents any time…and Peter? I want you to tell me about that other girl."

"Maybe later," I said.

She feigned displeasure with a pouting, sour face, then smiled. "Okay. But not too much later."

In the morning, Sunday morning, we drove in tandem to Westport, stopping for lunch at a diner off Route 6 in Bourne. We passed through the village and drove down to Westport Point between the two branches of the river and to her small house off Main Street. Red jumped out and ran in circles in the tiny yard when Celia opened the door.

"Cookie?" she said, and Red tore back into the house.

"Where do you hunt and fish?"

"We're on a point between the east and west branches of the Westport River. I have a little boat at a dock down on the water. I can hunt anywhere on the river that's far enough from houses and can fish anyplace. We get a lot of ducks in the fall, geese mostly on the east branch, and a lot of small striped bass and bluefish in the summer. Next weekend you have off, we can fish."

"Okay. Good."

We moved together, and after holding on each to the other as if it were the last time we could be close, I said I had to leave for the drive home.

"You know, I love you," I said.

Grinning, she said, "I love you more!"

"No, I more," to which she buried her face in my chest, laughing.

When I arrived back at my apartment, I realized that I remembered nothing of the drive home. All my thoughts were of Celia.

Back in the hospital on Monday, the vacation memory—but not that of Celia, which became sustenance for me—was pushed deep into my brain by the work and the hours and the learning compulsion. My residency continued uninterrupted. My friendship with Manny grew stronger. When I had first returned from his home in Provincetown, he apologized for not forewarning me about the social milieu. "I must confess that some of what I encountered there even made me feel a bit uncomfortable at first. But what you might think is for show is very serious to them. In the end, they're people, just people," he said.

"All that turned out to be only a distraction. For something else, I will be forever grateful to you, Manny. By the loan of your house, I met my wife to be. So, thanks—thanks for the most important week of my life." I gave him a big hug. A bit awkwardly, self-consciously, perhaps.

CHAPTER 63

Peter

— 1979 —

CELIA CAME UP TO BOSTON MANY NIGHTS, AND ALL WEEKENDS. SHE loved hearing me tell of the challenges of my surgical residency, and of the impossible hours we worked. She was at my apartment to greet me, awakening from her sleep when I returned late in the evening after working continuously the day and the night before. I was too tired to do more than to delight in being held by her before succumbing to a slumber that was cut short at five the next morning, first by the alarm clock and then by Red's wet licks on my cheek.

"Peter," she said one evening, "I want to meet Lisa."

"Why? You know we were once engaged."

"Because it will help me know you even better."

The next weekend, Lisa came for dinner. After meeting Celia, Lisa almost immediately confessed to her that she and I had been engaged. Celia assured her that was no reason to feel awkward. She, Celia, did not have any problem with it. After an easy, comfortable dinner, Lisa left.

"She's a lesbian, right?" said Celia.

"You're joking. We were engaged. We've had sex together. Lisa? Hardly."

The next weekend, Lisa asked us to her apartment for dinner and to meet her friend.

"Peter, Celia, please meet my very good friend Sandy, who works with me in the lab."

Celia, beaming as she looked first at me, then at the two women, bridged the distance between them and shook hands and hugged each. I mumbled a greeting. Most of the conversation at dinner was between the three women.

Afterward, as we went back to my apartment, Celia said, "See?"

"Man…am I stupid. I never would have guessed. I am trying to figure out if that should make me feel inadequate. Choosing a woman over me."

Celia laughed, then I joined in. She leaned into me and said, "Inadequate, you are not."

The next weekend, she took me to meet the Rawlings, her parents, in Ipswich on Labor-in-Vain Road. What a weird name for a road, but that was where they lived. They made me feel completely welcome in their warm home. I loved the handsome cedar shake house high on a hill overlooking the golden salt marshes, where, using their 40-power telescope, I could see many species of ducks. We arrived at her parents' home in the mid-morning of a crystalline-clear day. The water in the nature-carved canals was sapphire blue and the marsh grass a brilliant yellow, so brilliant that it reminded me of the rolling wheat fields of eastern Wyoming. Except that the marsh grass by comparison rendered those vast wheat fields to the horizon as pale, dusty fakes.

Sam Rawlings had a sizable collection of shotguns and promised to take me out on the marsh creeks in the fall in his sneak boat. He also had a trophy room full of baseball gloves, many of which were very old and with almost no padding.

"I used to have one of those when I was a kid. Probably still have it," I said.

Sam smiled.

On the drive back to my apartment, I said, "Your father sure has a lot of baseball gloves. Seems an unusual collection. How did he end up having so many?"

"It's a family collection going back many years. His great-grandfather was a leather-smith who started making baseball gloves, and he started the collection you saw."

"What an idiot. Are you that Rawlings?"

Celia nodded.

"Why didn't you tell me? I must have looked silly in your dad's eyes."

"First, no you didn't. He liked you a lot. And second, I wanted you to like me because of me, not who my family were. So there." She playfully stuck her tongue out at me. I grinned and reached out to grab her hand.

A few weeks later, driving back to Boston after our second visit to her parents, she said, "So, when should we go visit your parents?"

"I still don't think I can get any time off until Christmas."

"I would rather meet them before I am too fat," she said. Her voice trembled.

"Why would you get fat?"

"Well, not fat, but big." An awkward silence followed; I twisted up my face, trying to decode her statement.

"I don't…" I pulled off to the side of the road, left the car and went to the passenger door, opened it, and pulled her out. "Do you mean…"

"Yes, I do. In eight months, if you want to know."

I wrapped my arms around her, looking at her face. She was beaming. Smiling.

I buried my face in her neck, squeezing her. "Really?"

"Really."

I stroked her hair.

"Are you angry? Upset?"

"Are you crazy?" I said. "I'm ecstatic. You are serious, right? You're pregnant?"

"May, early May."

I danced her around. My smile transformed into a laugh as I enfolded her in my arms, holding her.

"Okay. Let's get married. Right now."

"Standing on the side of the road?" she said.

"Ha! Next weekend?"

"But your parents. Won't they want to know? Want to meet me?"

That night, I called them in Wyoming and told them I wanted them to meet the girl I was sure I would marry. Bring her out, they suggested. But I could not get the time off from the hospital. After a few minutes, they said they'd come to Boston. They wanted to meet Celia, and I put her on the phone with them. She was an immediate hit; they talked for a half hour, mostly my mom and Celia.

We met them at Logan Airport the next Friday. The connection between Celia and my parents was immediately forged. They loved her, they told me at dinner when she left for the bathroom.

"Good. We have some news for you."

"What?"

"Wait 'til she comes back."

Which shortly she did. With my arm around her, I said, "we are going to get married."

"Anything else?" my mom asked with arched eyebrows. I said nothing.

"Hon," she said to Celia, "when?"

"You mean when do we want to get married?"

"No, but I think you might want to do it soon. Congratulations."

"How did you know? Early May."

My Dad had a totally puzzled look. "Okay, you want to get married. Good. Are you talking about something else?

My mom started to laugh. "Bill, you can be dense sometimes. Peter and Celia are having a baby."

"Oh my God," Dad said, and he shook my hand and hugged Celia as familiarly as if she had been his daughter.

CHAPTER 64

Peter

— 1979 —

A MONTH LATER, MY PARENTS FLEW BACK AGAIN FOR THE SMALL WED-ding in Ipswich at the First Church, one of the early New England churches dating from the 1600s but recently completely rebuilt after a fire. Bill and Sam, both hunters, felt total compatibility notwithstanding their enormous differences in backgrounds—an industrialist and a rancher. Our mothers seemed to have known each other for centuries, so close did they immediately become.

After dinner one night, Dad pulled me aside.

"Go ahead, Bill, tell him," my Mom instructed.

"Well," Dad said, "I am not real good at this."

"Go ahead, Bill, tell him."

"Well," Dad said, extending his hand and shaking mine awkwardly, "well, I am proud of you."

"Because my girlfriend is pregnant?"

"Peter, stop that. Just listen to your father," Mom said.

"No, Peter. That is not what I meant. I mean, proud of you for what you have done. What you did in the Navy, where you are headed, your training, your accomplishment. As I said, I'm not much good at this sort of thing, but

I am. Proud of my son. And of my new daughter."

I bowed my head, then looked up and tentatively, hesitantly, put my arm around him. I guess I'm not so good at that sort of stuff either. "Thanks, Dad. Thank you very much. I have missed that for so many years."

I should not have, but could not prevent myself from saying, "As good as Great-Grandpa Pieter?"

Rather than bristling, Dad grabbed me, held me, and laughing, said, "Better, Peter, much better." My tears wet his shoulder.

CHAPTER 65

Peter

— 1979–1982 —

OVER THE NEXT FEW MONTHS, CELIA AND I FISHED ON THE WESTPORT River, catching stripers and bluefish, with Red, Celia's lab, barking at each fish coming into the boat.

The three of us went up into New Hampshire for grouse and woodcock hunting. Red stayed close so when he flushed, as he always did, we had a decent chance for a shot. But I longed for my own Red, and the wonderful pointing instincts she had.

Sam took me duck hunting in the Essex and Ipswich marshes, first for teal, and a bit later in the season, for mallards and black ducks. When a line of ten bluebills flew toward us, Sam cautioned me that because of their flight speed, I needed to give them a bigger lead than I might think appropriate. I followed his advice, leading the first bird in the string by several yards. I shot, and the last bird in the line fell. Sam laughed, and I looked sheepishly at him.

"Guess I have some to learn." MIG 17s and 21s were easier to bring down.

I did all this and still continued my total immersion in the residency. The information load thrown at me was both focused and broad, and always so intense that much bounced off, but as much stuck. I was always tired, always eager for more.

In what seemed like scant time, the baby came. At full term, she was six pounds, eight ounces. We named her Samantha, and called her Sam. After a couple days, as she began nursing, I was fascinated—fascinated by the whole process and by Sam, and I had to admit to a pang of jealousy toward Celia, whom I envied for the immediate, irrevocable closeness it brought between her and our new daughter. And watching, I found it impossible to suppress laughing because of Sam's behavior. She was ferocious. She allowed nothing to come between her and a breast. No amount of outside distraction deterred her from her goal. She was so single-minded: if she lost the breast, she screamed and struggled mightily to regain it. As she got a bit older and could see clearly, engage faces, smile, and play with toys hanging from her crib, nursing was still her primary focus. Nothing could interfere. I wondered at the time if even at this neonatal stage, her nursing behavior would predict her personality. Celia thought the idea silly. "There is nursing, and that's it. Period," she said.

Other than the joy of Sam and Celia, each day continued to be indistinguishable from the next for me, marked mostly by this unusual case or that. My residency unwound behind me as I got closer to the end.

In 1982, when Sam was two, another baby, Patsy, came.

At the end of Patsy's first week, Celia said, with a smile of defeat, "I concede."

"About what?"

"Watch her nurse. Not anything like Sam. She is so distracted, so casual about it, and sometimes even forgets to suck, especially if you are talking."

By three months, when Patsy was smiling in response to our faces, the differences between her and Sam were even more pronounced. Any movement in the room, especially if it was nearby, and Patsy followed with her eyes. She would spit out the nipple and smile as she watched motion or a face. Celia, supporting her head, would have to guide her back to the breast, but feeding went on interminably, so easily was she distracted. Other times, she would back away and seemed to use the operative breast as a toy, bouncing her chubby little hand off it.

On finishing the residency, I joined the staff at the Brigham Hospital, focusing on solid organ transplantation. I ended up working a lot with Lisa, who became a better and better friend, but always just a friend.

Peter

— 1983-1984 —

AFTER TWO YEARS ON THE STAFF, IN 1983, WE LOOKED AT A HOUSE IN Dedham, Massachusetts—my first toe-dip into the real estate water, and a frightening experience because of all the money involved. Still, it was thrilling for Celia and me. The house, built in 1820, was brick with a gambrel (Dutch design, appropriately) roof, on about a half acre of intimidatingly mowable, and in the fall, oppressively leaf-rakeable lawn. The third-floor center dormer was pushed out from the house to align with a similar prow on the second-floor bay, which in turn stood atop the porch over the front door. On the left of the center hall was the dining room with kitchen behind it, and on the right, the living room with a den in back.

Upstairs, there were four bedrooms, three of which had fireplaces. As we were shown the house, Celia, apparently intoxicated with the thought of our own home, leaned into me and whispered, "How romantic. We can fuck by the fire." She mostly suppressed her laughter at her own uncharacteristic outburst. I blushed, and the realtor said, "What?" thinking, I presume, that she did not hear what she heard.

The asking price was more than I thought we could afford, but when I called Dad, he said go for it. He thought land and property was always a good investment. Of course, a rancher would say that. But I appreciated his fatherly advice.

We bought it, and almost immediately we realized that we did not over-buy: another baby was on the way, perhaps one conceived by the fire. This time a boy, and as the birth approached, we searched for a name. Celia wanted to name him after her grandfather and father, but we had already used the name Sam, so she suggested someone in my family. My grandfathers were a Peter on dad's side, but I did not want a junior; and on mom's side, William, the same as my dad's name. I thought Bill a bit boring; and Celia asked about my great-grandparents.

"Well, on Mom's side, they were Jeremiah and Benjamin. And on my dad's side, they were Martijn, and…" I stopped talking and began sweating, and Celia saw my sudden pallor.

"What's wrong? Are you sick?"

I sat down. "No. Just, I dunno…"

"Peter. You were about to tell me your great-grandfather's name and you stopped and looked sick. What is it?"

"Well, his name was Pieter, spelled with an "i" as in "P-I-E-T-E-R. But we can't use it."

"Why not?

"It's too old-fashioned. Maybe Martijn," I said. Celia's look of skepticism turned to annoyance.

"No. He'll be Marty. I don't like that name. How about Benjamin?"

"Sure, Ben's okay," I said. I didn't care, as long as it was not Pieter.

We spoke no more about the name. But there was a tension between us, an unresolved conflict. A week later, I took Celia to the hospital. She and Benjamin came home the next day. Both were healthy.

"So," with Benjamin on her chest noisily sucking two days later, Celia said, "why the big cloud that came over you when we talked about names? What is it about Pieter?"

"I can't say. Can't tell you."

We didn't speak again until after dinner.

"Okay, Peter. Enough. You've never acted this way since I have known you. What is it? Tell me. Don't put me off."

I walked out the door and came back an hour later.

"Peter, sit. Tell me what it is. Tell me now. Right now." She poured two glasses of wine.

"Well." I sighed, resigned to what had been inevitable since I met Celia out on the Cape.

"Well, what?"

"Remember that week we met, and I told you I had been engaged? I said it did not work partly because of another girl. You asked about her, but I brushed you off. And since you did not ask again, I did not tell you."

"Yeah?"

"I met her in the Netherlands between the navy and medical school. Maaijke. She meant a lot to me, almost as much as you. And then she disappeared. It took me several years to get over it. And then, during my fellowship year, I went back to the same village. Spakenburg. I was engaged to Lisa at the time. I was down on the dock, talking to an old sailor I met through her, through Maaijke, and I see her. Walking down to the docks, looking the same as she had earlier. More than five years earlier. Almost five had years disappeared," I snapped my fingers, "just like that. I still loved her."

Celia dropped her hands to the table, the glass of wine in her right one hitting and jostling ruby red onto the white tablecloth. Her mouth twitched. Her face contorted as in pain. Her eyes glistened in advance of tears darkening the cloth next to the spreading wine stain. I had never seen her look like this.

"I knew I would have to tell Lisa. How could I marry her when it was Maaijke, only Maaijke? And that night, Maaijke told me she had a son. *We* had a son. *Pieter.* He was not yet three, which made no sense: it had been four and a half years earlier when I had seen her. I told her he could not be my son. She said I was the only man she had ever been with, and he was my son. When I asked about the time discrepancy, she said I wouldn't understand now, but maybe later. I was angry and sad that she had a son and did not tell me. She had tried, she said. I asked where he was, and she said he was in Spakenburg. But when I asked, she said I couldn't see him because he was in a different place, or something like that. It was all so irrational. I guess I was able to suppress all the inconsistencies and ignore her not telling me because I needed her at the time. She felt the same. I thought I would be with her forever. And then, a few days later, she was gone. Again. She left a note saying she was pregnant—how would she know so soon?—and what was worse, wrote that she had less than a year to live and that she would never see me again."

"That makes no sense, Peter."

"You're right. I couldn't explain any of it. But she was correct. I never saw her again. Eventually, after a couple years of confusion, emotionally anyway, and sorrow, I began to believe that I had imagined it. I was so immersed in my work, returning to residency—it saved me. And then I met you. You know the rest. But that story, whether imaginary or not, is why I did not want to use the name Pieter. The story continually recedes, for which I am grateful. 'Cause when I dwell on it, it makes me wonder if I *was* crazy."

"Oh, Peter. That story is so hurtful. Not for me. For you. I am sorry you have borne that burden. You should have told me earlier," she said.

"You wouldn't have thought me crazy?"

"Peter, you are the least crazy man or woman I have ever known."

She threw her arms around my waist, her head buried in my chest. She held me until Ben's crying started and she broke away to feed him. Ben ravenously attacked her breasts; he too had his unique nursing style. It wasn't that he was distracted like his sister, Patsy. Instead, he would begin avidly and then fall asleep even before he had exhausted the first breast. Celia would then jostle him, and he awoke crying, to be pacified when he found a nipple, but then would again fall asleep. As with Patsy, nursing took a lot of time.

CHAPTER 67

Peter

— 1984 —

THE CONVERSATION ABOUT MAAIJKE MUST HAVE STIRRED UP SOME OTHER repressed, old memories, because one morning a week later, lying in bed, Celia asked, "Were you dreaming?"

"Why?"

"You were thrashing around, and I thought even crying. You said, 'Willis,' several times, and 'Willis, I'm sorry.' Who is Willis?"

"Don't know anyone named that."

She locked me in her eyes with an expression I had seen before, but fortunately, not often. She knew I was lying.

"Well, maybe a long time ago. When I was a kid, there was a neighbor named that," I said.

"Go on. Tell me the rest." It was not spoken as a suggestion but as a stern demand.

"Well, Willis was about my age, lived on the next ranch. He was bigger than me, better at most stuff, except he wasn't much of a student. He had a mean streak. Took my first girlfriend away. I think he even got her pregnant. In ninth grade! I grew to dislike him, a lot. But he was an aggressive and very good football player, and I always thought he took my place at Annapolis where I wanted to go. Wyoming only sent three to the Naval Academy; I wasn't one of them. I resented him. No, more than resented him. He was a bully growing up and often focused his bullying on me."

"And?"

"And then I went to officer candidate school after college—we called it OCS. After that, I ended up in flight school with him. He was a pretty good pilot, and we were on the same carrier, and in the same squadron in Viet Nam. We weren't exactly friendly but got along okay."

With a bemused expression, she said, "So? That's hardly remarkable. Lots of kids have spats and outgrow them. It sure doesn't sound like a foundation for nightmares."

"There was a Korean War story, a true story, about Jesse Brown, the first black navy pilot who grew up as a poor sharecropper's son. Another navy pilot, Thomas Hudner, a preppy product of Phillips Academy in Andover and the Naval Academy at Annapolis, served in the same unit and the two pilots became close friends overcoming the vast differences in background. Brown was shot down by small arms fire while flying cover for the Marines near the Chosin Reservoir. He crashed in the mountains and was trapped in the cockpit. Despite all pilots having been warned against doing so, Hudner crash-landed his plane next to the first one to save his friend, Jesse Brown, the trapped pilot. He was unable to extricate Brown from his plane, even with the help of the helicopter rescue pilot who landed, and the trapped pilot died as they tried to save him. Rather than being disciplined, Hudner, the pilot who tried to help, was given the Congressional Medal."

"Peter, what are you are talking about? I thought you were talking about yourself, and a guy named Willis."

"Yeah. I was. I am."

"Korean War? You were only a little kid then."

"Wait. They're related. One day, I was flying a mission over North Vietnam. So was Willis. A distress signal came over the radio indicating a pilot had ejected. I saw an explosion on the ground as his plane crashed, and a towering smoke column rose. Then I saw the parachute. Only one, even though Phantoms had a crew of two. I'm not sure if I knew who it was. He landed in a rice paddy, and was surrounded by Vietnamese with pitchforks, and machetes, attacking the pilot. They held him down. Beat him. I flew low, too low, but got away with it. I tried to strafe around the pilot but after every pass, the throng kept coming back. I was low enough to see blood all over the pilot as they continued to attack him. And then, I saw them tie him to a pole, and light the wood they had stacked around the pole.

"All I could think of was the story about those two Korean War pilots. But I could not bring myself to land next to the pilot. I would have been killed. I felt helpless. So, I gained altitude, rolled inverted and dove from about 10,000 feet, releasing a bomb and pulling out into a high G turn. Despite my G suit squeezing my legs and abdomen, I started to gray out—lose vision. When I recovered in a minute or so, as far as I could tell, there were no survivors. Not the pilot either, who was at the center of the blast. I saved him from the certain torture before death. At least that is what I convinced myself."

We got out of opposite sides of the bed, and Celia walked around and wrapped her arms around me, comforting me.

I continued recounting what had happened. "When I landed back on the Ranger, I confirmed that it had been Willis. After the debriefing, I was exonerated, even praised for doing the right thing. Maybe I did…but with my background with him—which no one else knew about—it was hard to convince myself that some resentment didn't play a role in what I did. Killing him. And even though I didn't find out who it was until I landed back on the ship, I think at the primitive base of my brain, I knew all along. Dishonor…that's what I felt. Still feel.

"There's more. No one in the squadron knew any of this and remembering it made me feel worse. You're the first person I have ever told. When I was about ten, I rode over to Willis's ranch. It was early spring, and we were up in the hay loft above one of the barns. He said he had just started a secret club and wanted me to be the second member. The initiation consisted of both of us shutting our eyes and simultaneously, tightly squeezing a rock. He had several of these gray rocks on a plate. He placed one in his own hand with some tongs, and as he squeezed it, told me to close my eyes as he placed another in my hand, again using the tongs. I dropped it immediately. My "rock" wasn't a rock at all but a piece of burning charcoal, completely covered with gray ash so that it looked like the rock he had. Stray pieces of hay on the floor caught fire where I had dropped it. Willis jumped up, stamping out the flames, laughing at the joke. I climbed down from the loft and cried during the entire ride home. The humiliation hurt more than my hand. Willis was a cruel boy, a bully. And as I recalled that episode and then others, I felt more guilty about his death.

"That's part of the reason I left the navy. Not all—but part. I thought I didn't deserve to stay."

Celia said only, "Peter." She held me as the spasms of tears flowed. The release from the guilt seemed to be as much hers as mine.

CHAPTER 68

Peter

─ 1984-1990 ─

WITH RAPIDLY SPROUTING CHILDREN, WITH CELIA, AND WITH MY RE-search and clinical work, during the rare interludes I had the time to be contemplative, I thought that I had been captured by a maelstrom, going deeper and faster. A maelstrom of life. I loved it. With several papers published on transplantation research, I gained a modicum of recognition in those circles. I was asked to give lectures. A few times, I was even honored as a visiting professor. All during this time, Celia was my strength. I leaned on her for difficult decisions. We grew ever closer. Still, after she forced me to tell the story of Maaijke, I sometimes thought of Maaijke, sometimes visualized her.

From the start, Celia insisted we visit Wyoming to give our kids more exposure to my family and to ranch life. So, every summer for a couple weeks, we vacationed on the ranch. One day, with thunderstorms scuttling our plan to fish, Celia leafed through the old family bible. There, she found inscriptions commemorating births, deaths, marriages in my family.

"Look what I found," Celia said.

"Oh, yeah. I know."

"Okay, then, I'll quiz you. Peter—no 'i'—was your grandfather. You told me Pieter with an 'i' was his father. Where was Peter—no 'i'—born?"

"Michigan."

"City?"

"Not sure. Where?"

"Zeeland, Peter. Your grandfather was born in Zeeland. Sounds like a good Dutch name. Where the hell is that?"

We got out an atlas and found it, not too far from Lake Michigan and near Holland, Michigan.

"Let's go," Celia said.

"Maybe sometime. We don't have time now. I'm too busy. You're too busy. Our kids are too busy. Besides, I have to prepare the talk for Chicago."

"But that's not until next year."

"No, hon. It's this fall, 1990. Not next year."

After dinner that night, and after we had tucked the kids into their beds, and even after my parents had retired for the night, Celia and I were sitting on the couch. She reached out, touching my shoulder.

"Peter, there's something we need to discuss."

"Uhh, Okay," I said with apprehension. "What have I done now?"

"No, Peter, you have the wrong idea. It's *me*. I am missing something. Not you, not us, me. I've been thinking about it a lot. Remember when we first met, and I had taken the job with the Fish and Game Department while waiting for vet school? Which I never did attend. Well, I want to go. I need to go. Our children are all in school and doing well. So, I can do it without affecting them. The classes are during the day; you will hardly know I am away. Really, it's not about you. I couldn't live without you making me so much more complete, but I so need to feel that I'm doing good. I'm pretty sure I'm a good mom, that we're good parents, but this would be so important to me. Please, please."

I grabbed her and hugged her. "Hon, that would be great! Do it."

"Oh, I was so afraid you'd be against it. Thank you, thank you, thank you."

"But what if the school you get into is far away? How many vet schools are around home?"

"There's only one in all of New England. Tufts. In Grafton. It's only a thirty-five- or forty-minute drive."

"Well," I said, "if there's only the one, you'd better start applying. Soon."

"A little confession. I already did, and I'm accepted for September. You're not angry, are you?"

I tried unsuccessfully to suppress a laugh. "Of course you did. I should have guessed that from the start. You are too much for me. Too good, too. That's fantastic. Maybe you can teach me a few things."

"Well, I doubt that. But I can try. Up in bed. Now."

I followed her up the stairs.

CHAPTER 69

Peter

— 1990–1991 —

BACK AT HOME, WE HAD CONVERTED ONE OF THE FOUR BEDROOMS TO an office with a desk for Celia and one for me, separated by the fireplace. There, next to the flickering of the burning oak and maple, I worked on the talk for the transplantation section of the American College of Surgeons meeting in Chicago later in the fall while Celia studied her vet books prior to the start of school.

On the flight to O'Hare Airport from Boston, I searched Michigan through a cloudless sky, trying to guess Zeeland's location. I saw the large lake pinched to a narrows where it drained west into Lake Michigan and remembered Holland to be on that lake, with Zeeland to the east.

The talk at the ACS, I thought, went well, and generated a vigorous discussion. The next day, I skipped the meeting and took the ferry to Muskegon, where I rented a car and drove down to Zeeland. In the little town hall, a clerk told me I "talked funny, like you're from Boston," which I took as an indictment of my Wyoming loyalty and revealed an abandonment of my heritage. But then she helped me look up my grandfather in an index that led to a copy of a birth certificate. My namesake, my grandfather, was born in Zeeland in 1868. This allowed us to go a generation back to his father, my great-grandfather, Pieter. He arrived in Zeeland in 1858 from Spakenburg, in the Netherlands, married Mary Elizabeth Brunjes in 1866, and moved to Wyoming in 1871. On reading the name of Pieter's town of origin, Spakenburg, a cold dread settled on me, as if a sea fog enveloped me. Still, I recorded the salient facts in a small notebook, then drove back to the ferry terminal, returned the car, and took the return ferry to Chicago.

Upon the return to Massachusetts after the meeting, Celia met my plane. I told her about the meeting, about my talk, and about the trip to Zeeland. All her questions were about the side trip, none about the meeting or my talk. She wanted to go to Spakenburg and find my relatives.

I was reluctant, scared because of my association of Maaijke and Spakenburg. But Celia's persistence won, and in late May of the next spring, after Celia's classes were over, we loaned the kids to friends with children in the same grades. We were both slightly disappointed that our kids were not only not sad to see their parents leave, but excited.

"Growing up, they're growing up," Celia said, consoling both of us.

The time in the plane collapsed to seemingly nothing as Celia launched into an almost five-hour soliloquy, bubbling over with enthusiasm about school. "Did you know," she once interjected, "that pets, dogs especially, fake injuries? Usually means their owner is not paying enough attention to them. If I start to limp, you'd better remember that," she said, as she hit me on my shoulder. It was fun to see her so happy, so animated.

We rented a car at Schiphol Airport but lengthened the couple-hour drive to Spakenburg by taking a detour to Utrecht. We had a leisurely lunch on the Oudegracht Canal at Los Argentinos, feeling, in our freedom from kids and responsibilities, as we did at our first dinner together in Provincetown. After these many years, I marveled at the closeness and mutual support and love we still shared. Which lent a slightly guilty feeling to me for the juxtaposition with my time with Maaijke. But it was Celia's idea to be here.

In Spakenburg, I refused to stay in the nicest hotel in town; I had too many emotional connections to it. We did, however, have a savory meal in the Visrestaurant de Pieterman. As at lunch, the freedom was liberating. We seldom traveled without Sam, Patsy, and Ben, so that freedom was tinged with a slight (very slight) sense of parental irresponsibility. In bed, we held each other until sleep came.

The next morning, after breakfast, we both felt wonderful, unrestrained, eager for the day. The genealogy center opened at nine. We were waiting when the doors were unlocked. As I explained what I sought to one of the curators, Celia took the opportunity to tour the town. With my great-grandfather's name, Pieter Maasen, and the arrival date in Zeeland of 1858, we found a copy of a church record, "Pieter and Martijn Maasen, age 22 and 18, left for America, September, 1856." The curator translated from the Dutch for me.

"So, is that all? Can we go further back?"

"Of course. It is a slow process, but possible. If we look up Pieter's name in the index, we will probably find several entries. By looking at the likely ones, we might be able to find his birth record. There, we would find his parents, and then we could go back with their names and find a wedding certificate. From that, we might be able to find the towns where they were born and go back to find their birth records, and so on."

"These are copies, right?"

"Yes," the curator said. "Copies of both church records and civil records. Before Napoleon—we drove him out in 1813—there were only church records.

"Let's start with Pieter to demonstrate how this works. He must have been your great-grandfather, right? So we use the index, and there are multiple entries for him—the last is in 1856, when he went to your country." She went to the date.

With another hour of work, we found the birth records of both Martijn and Pieter, born in 1837 and 1834, about three and a half years apart. Their parents were *Maaijke De Jongh* and Bertus Maasen.

After very little more effort, she said, "Oh, no! This is the last entry for Bertus, in 1837. It is the last entry because he died then. Maybe you won't want to hear this. It says, 'died of his own hand.'"

"Would you like to go back further?" the curator asked.

"Uh, yeah. I guess." Already, we had found enough, too much. How could that Maaijke and my Maaijke be…? Even formulating the question was impossible. The coincidence was strange, at best. That my Maaijke had the same name as my great-great-grandmother's maiden name—De Jongh—and that my great-grandfather and his brother had the same names as the two boys Maaijke—my Maaijke—had was much more than merely strange. The implications hideous, unthinkable. The big difference—and thank God for it—was that my Maaijke was not married. That and, of course, the fact that my Maaijke was only a few years younger than me, whereas my great-great grandmother Maaijke lived in the nineteenth century.

From the marriage certificate in 1832, we had the ages of Maaijke De Jongh and Bertus Maasen, and from those, found Maaijke's date of birth in 1815 in both the church and civil records, and from the church records, found that Bertus had been born in 1788. He was twenty-seven years senior to Maaijke.

Looking up, the curator saw me heading for the bathroom. I returned about ten minutes later, sweating, pale, and with eyebrows pulled together. A look of fear. My hair was mussed, damp.

"What's wrong? You look sick."

I felt sick.

"No, I'll be okay. Must have been something I ate for breakfast."

"Are you sure?"

I did not answer directly. "Where are the originals of these?"

"Well, Bertus's birth will be in church records only, but the other records—those after about 1813—will be both in the church and in the civil records."

"And where are those? The civil records?"

"They should be in the town hall."

"Can I see them?"

"I believe so. Would you like me to introduce you to the town clerk who may be able to direct you?"

"Please."

Betje Bunschoten spoke excellent English and was gracious and eager to help me. I had to wait a while as she descended into the archives and lugged the records up to a reading room, where she gave me a chair and large table on which she spread out the volumes. The books looked heavily used. Betje first helped me wade through the handwritten Dutch, where we found the birth certificate, in 1815, of Maaijke De Jongh. I was not as interested in Bertus's records but instead asked to see the birth certificates of the two sons. As Betje got the 1834 records, someone came into the town hall, and Betje excused herself, leaving me alone.

As I leafed through the entries in the civil record and came to the date of Pieter's birth, a letter fell out. Its envelope was addressed to Peter Maasen. I had to wade through a period of spatial and time disconnectedness to realize that that was me. Looking around and finding I was still alone, I slipped the envelope into my pocket. The entry record confirmed Pieter's birth date and his birth parents, Maaijke and Bertus Maasen.

Betje returned and translated the entry for me and found the birth record for Martijn in 1837.

"Oh, my," she said, as she leafed through the dates. "Poor woman. Look, here. Seven days after Martijn was born, she died of infection. Puerperal sepsis. And with her husband dead, the poor boys grew up as orphans."

CHAPTER 70

Peter

— 1991 —

I MET CELIA AT OUR BREAKFAST CAFÉ. SHE WAS NURSING A CUP OF COFFEE and reading about the local history. I sat across from her and at first, said nothing.

"Peter, I'm tired. You look tired. Let's take a nap and then find a nice place for dinner."

Rested, we wandered Spakenburg and ended up in the Restaurant de Mandemaaker.

"Okay," she said. "You are still quiet, uncharacteristically so. You also are trying to figure out something, I would guess. I know that look. What's up?"

"Well, remember when I told you about the girl I met here? Maaijke?"

"Sure."

"Well, help me with this puzzle—a family puzzle."

For a few seconds, I saw a flash of anger flash in her eyes. She quickly doused it, and said, "Yeah… Go on."

"When I met her, she said she was eighteen. When I met her several years later—four and a half years later—and still distractingly in love with her, she told me she had a child, my child, named Pieter, who was three years old, but I could not see him. I told you this when we were searching for a name for Ben. Lots of stuff Maaijke told me made no sense. Such as the fact that this child, my child, could be younger than three when he was conceived four and a half years earlier. But I was so smitten, I overlooked what she said. In fact, she told me very little about herself and her family. That seemed strange then, and stranger now.

"Then today, in the town clerk's office, I found the record of a woman— my great-great-grandmother—and her husband. She had the same maiden name as my girlfriend—I only knew her for about a week at two different times—Maaijke De Jongh. That Maaijke—my great-great-grandmother— married my great-great-grandfather when she was seventeen, so when she was eighteen, her last name—her married name—was Maasen. My Maaijke also had the last name De Jongh—same as the maiden name of my great-great-grandmother before she married. But when I first asked my Maaijke for her last name, she hesitated, as if she were making up a name. I thought about that, but it didn't matter to me. I was too much in love. Does this bother you? Make you jealous?"

"No. I love you. You love me. That's all that matters."

"So, quite a coincidence that my girlfriend had the same name as my great-great-grandmother before she was married. And that the names of the two children she told me she had were identical to the two names of the sons of my great-great-grandmother."

"Not really. Family names often repeat," Celia said.

"Sure. But my Maaijke, as far as I know, was not related to my family, not related to my great-great-grandmother, Maaijke. Right? But the coincidence of everything about them being the same? That doesn't strike you as odd?"

"Oh, I am beginning to see," she said. "Is this some sort of scam or hoax?"

"Don't know. But when I opened the records book today, a letter fell out, addressed to me. Read it and you will see why I have been so quiet. I'm confused, Celia. Maybe it is a hoax." I handed my wife the envelope; she shook out the letter.

Dear, dear Peter,

From the minute I saw you on the street in Spakenburg, the very first time I saw you, I wanted to be with you forever. As you will see, it was not and will never be possible. You will find this difficult to understand; you may not believe what I tell you. Much of what you will read is the consequence of my imagination, but please understand that nothing in this is imaginary, if that makes sense. I imagined traveling to different times and places, and in so imagining, I actually did it.

I was born in 1815. I met you and fell in love when I was 18, in 1833 by my time. I had our baby boys in 1834 and 1837, a little more than three years apart. Unfortunately, I developed an infection after the birth of Martijn and died a week later, when I was 25 years old.

I know the time is hard for you to understand. Pieter was born in 1834, and I visited you next in 1836, when Pieter was 2½, even though I jumped ahead 4½ years of your time to find you. And now, as I write this, it has been less than three months since I saw you, but you are 16 years older now. My time doesn't go any faster or slower than yours, but in my travels, I can jump forward many years in a minute or two.

It was obvious, soon after my birth in 1815, that I had a heightened curiosity and imagination. As I grew into early childhood, when I was alone, I imagined what it would be like to be in other places. These thoughts gradually became more and more vivid. They seemed real. In fact, they were real. The first time I realized that I had this ability was when I "saw" my father buy a birthday present for Mama days before he actually bought it. I had a sense of freedom, being able to escape the present if I was bored. The more I concentrated on being someplace else, the better it worked. I began traveling to other countries, and in other times. But I always was invisible to others in those countries and times because it was all in my imagination. That changed the first time I traveled in the future to Spakenburg. I was suddenly an actual person in the time where I traveled. Because I was already dressed like the ladies giving tours there, they assumed I was another tour guide and brought me into their group. That is when I met you.

But staying in another place or time was very difficult. It depended on me maintaining the vividness of imagination. As soon as my concentration sagged, I was transported back to my own time. I found that I could only go forward from my own time, never backward. I think that was because if I could go to a time before, history of what came later would change, but because that history had already occurred, it could not change, and thus I could not go back.

When I was pregnant with Martijn, Pieter was almost three. I went forward to see what my new baby would be like and, to my horror, found records of my death from what they called puerperal sepsis one week after Martijn was born. I have read about this. I know this rarely happened in your time, but it happened a lot in our time. How could I prevent this? If I went forward in time to live with you, I would have to leave Pieter behind (remember you asking why you could not see him?). If I gave birth to Martijn in your time, he would not be able to travel back in time to my time. And I would have the usual difficulty of staying with you because my imagination would occasionally lapse. While going to you would almost certainly have saved me from dying, it would have meant forever separating our children. In the end, the only way they could grow up together was for me to stay in my time and accept that I would not be able to raise them, and never be able to spend my life with you. That is what I had to do; that is what I did.

When I discovered my fate, I began going forward in time until I found you in the genealogy center in 1991. The day before you visited, I placed this letter in the records where I knew you would find it: where Pieter's birth was recorded.

Do you remember our first lunch together? I asked your name and you told me. I became confused and very concerned; my last name was the same, Maasen. You might think I lied when I recovered from my anxiety and returned from the bathroom. I told you my last name was De Jongh. That was my maiden name, but I could hardly tell you that I was married, and my married name was Maasen. I had been married less than a year when I met you, married to Bertus Maasen. But it was not a good marriage. He was older, very respected and for our town, quite wealthy. I did not find him attractive; I did not love him. My parents arranged the marriage, and finally I became resigned to my fate. I dreaded my wedding night initially: I did not know how I could make love to a man almost three times my age. But I came to accept what I would experience that night, even to savor the thought of it. I had long been fascinated by sex (you may have noticed) and looked forward to doing it, so came to believe that Bertus was better than no one. But in fact, it was as if he were no one. He called me a whore on our wedding night because I had a sexy nightgown Mama gave me. He sent me from his (not our) bedroom and forever kept me out. I was a virgin (do you remember how I mispronounced the word and you laughed?) when you and I met. Bertus looked upon sex as something unclean, of which one should not speak. I am sure he died without ever experiencing it. He was also ignorant of it. Until I became pregnant with Martijn, Bertus seemed to believe that he was the actual father and to harbor great pride in Pieter, as if he were his own accomplishment. No one except me—and maybe my mama—knew better.

Bertus died a month ago. He hanged himself after he discovered that a second child was coming. I shed no real tears.

The coincidence that you and I had the same last names did startle me during our first lunch. Wouldn't it be strange if we were somehow related?

I do not know if you can believe this or understand it. I don't even think I can ask you to. But know that I love you more than I ever imagined possible.

My lovely Peter. Please remember me with love.
Maaijke

My face was red. I resisted crying. Celia, face ashen and serious, said nothing, then stood and walked around the table, enfolded me in her arms. I stood to soak up her love.

She pushed away from me a small bit.

"Look," she said, "you traced your family back to your great-great-grand-mother through your father, then his father, and then to your great-grandfather, Pieter. And then to his mom, Maaijke, your great-great-grandmother. All that I believe. And you fell in love with a young woman with your great-great-grandmother's name before you went to medical school. I'm sure that is true. And she told you she had a child named Pieter, and another named Martijn, both from you. That could be true. But to have her claim that she traveled from the 1800s to meet you is not possible. And the implication that she could be that same great-great-grandmother—your great-great-grandmother—unthinkable. It's impossible. Think of the ramifications. That you could be the father of your great-grandfather? Not only is it phys-ically impossible but is logically disprovable. If it were true, it would mean that your great-grandfather could not be born until you fathered him, but since you descended from him, he had to come before you."

She paused, drew in a deep breath, took a sip of wine, and a large gulp of water before continuing.

"So, it is all some sort of hoax? Why, I don't know. Is someone trying to get money from you? Child support?"

"Nope. Nothing," I said.

"So, then let's call it a huge coincidence of names, plus someone—may-be this Maaijke girlfriend of yours—playing a sick joke for some unknown reason," Celia said.

"Yeah. I s'pose. But what about this letter?"

"What about it? Another part of the hoax."

"But how would anyone know that I was going to access these public records today?"

"Well, she could have guessed that you would look for your heritage based on something you said or did in the past with this Maaijke, and then left the letter where you would find it."

"No," I said. "That doesn't make sense either. If this letter were placed there sometime in the past, why wouldn't it have fallen out or been discov-ered a long time ago? These are public records. Do you think they could have sat there, unused by anybody, in the last 140 years or so? Anyone could be looking through them. Lots of people. The letter almost had to be placed there very recently just to be sure that I would find it. Doesn't that mean somebody had to know I would be going there? Today? But no one knew."

"Okay," said Celia. "So the appearance of this letter, that's difficult to explain, except with your logic. But it doesn't override the impossible explanation of travel through time."

"So, what do we do?"

"Do? We don't need to *do* anything, except live our normal lives, raise our kids, do our jobs. You are a surgeon, not some ancestry conspiracy theorist. And I am going to be a very important vet," she said with a huge grin.

I sighed, my shoulders slumped, I sat down again.

"You're right. You must be. I was a slave to my emotions about her back then. Not thinking straight, I guess. Let's go back to the hotel and sleep. Sleep with you holding me."

But I still had profound doubts. I kept running through possibilities and explanations, even as she held me that night in bed.

CHAPTER 71

Peter

—— 1991–1994 ——

B ACK IN BOSTON, MY USUAL DAILY RHYTHM RETURNED, AND I DWELLED less and less on what must obviously have been some joke or hoax. I worked on a few manuscripts. The journals returned all to me requiring only minor revisions before being accepted. I operated, better and better, I thought. My patients did very well.

And Celia? She continued to have an unshakeable enthusiasm for vet school.

One evening after a two-case day, driving home from the hospital in the rain, my windshield wiper stopped wiping. At the car dealer the next day, the problem was easily diagnosed: the wiper motor had burned out. It was then that I realized my old car—ten years old—was tired, and I eventually bowed to the inescapable conclusion that I needed a new one and could afford it. The dealer was not reluctant to help. The sale consummated, it only required me to dredge up the old title to complete the transaction. I found it in my safety deposit box at the bank. The safety deposit box use record showed that this was the first opening of the box since I deposited the automobile title for the then-new car, ten years earlier.

Extracting the old title, an envelope caught my attention. One word on the front: Maaijke. Puzzled, I felt something irregular in it. Slitting it open, I found a locket, the locket Maaijke had given me many years ago, my second time with her when I was a research fellow. The locket with her son's hair and some of hers. I pocketed the locket and envelope.

Driving my new car back home, I dwelled upon that old locket. Driving into our garage, I thought about the hair samples.

Sitting in my office after my case that next morning, I shut my eyes and leaned back in the chair. What Celia said, I knew, was correct: she, our children, were too important to perseverate on what might have happened many years before, and more recently, on what I found in the clerk's office in Spakenburg. But what would it hurt to test the hair samples I had in the locket, samples of both a putative son, and Maaijke? It might help explain the mystery.

I could find no scissors in my desk, so with a brief wince, I pulled out a small tuft of my hair. I added the new sample to the locket.

Harald Dahlen had been my classmate in medical school and was now a geneticist at the school. As I walked through the med school quadrangle after checking on my case from the morning, I wondered how I would ex-plain my request.

"Hey, cowboy," Harald greeted me. "Long time, no see. Where's your boots, your big belt buckle? What brings you here? Don't have many sur-geons wander in here. Never had a transplanter."

"Yeah, strange. I know. But I have a couple genetics questions and a favor to ask."

"Okay," Harald said. "Shoot."

"So…when you are looking at genetic samples, how do you assess famil-ial relations?"

"Do you want the simple answer, or the more complicated one?"

"I'm a surgeon."

"Okay, simple it is." Harald gave a brief, unconvincing chuckle.

"Well, after analyzing DNA, it's basically mathematical. For example, you have half of your father's DNA and half your mother's. So, you would have a quarter of your grandparents', an eighth of your great-grandparents', and so forth. But it is not so straightforward. Mutations are always occurring, and even whole chromosomes are not inherited unchanged, because there is often breaking apart of chromosomes, and recombination of them. So, statistically, you would have half of each parent's DNA, but it would be a little less predictable." He paused, assessing my comprehension. "And the favor?"

"If I gave you three hair samples, could you estimate the level of relatedness of the three people?" Peter said.

"You may have seen this done on detective shows, but cut hair samples are very difficult to assess unless you are looking only at the female lines."

"Why?"

"The only substantial amount of DNA in a piece of hair is called mitochondrial DNA. And all mitochondrial DNA is passed down from the mother to the child—none comes from the father. So, if you want to follow the male line in a family, it cannot be done with hair cuttings. You need nuclear DNA, and there is very little in the ends of hair. On the other hand, hair follicles contain nuclear DNA and are easier to work with. But that is a fairly involved analysis and technique. Maybe it will be easy in another ten or twenty years, but it takes a lot of time now. Time and money."

I said, "I think we might be lucky; these might be pulled hair samples, not cut hair. And I would be happy to pay to have it done."

"Someone in your family? Illegitimate son? Paternity suit?"

"Ha! Neither of those two. Maybe from my family. Not sure. But maybe," I said, feeling the flush of my face.

I gave the locket to Harald, who opened it and dumped the sample on a white piece of paper. He slid it under a microscope.

"First, without any fancy analysis, I can tell you that you probably have three people here. Three colors of hair. Yellow or blond, light brunette, and an in-between. Also, one sample is thinner and probably a woman. Also, two look dried out and are probably old. The third is quite fresh and close to your hair color. It's not yours, is it? But if you want anything more, it will take several weeks. If I can sneak it in with another run, it won't cost you anything except a bottle of Dom Perignon."

Peter

— 1994 —

Y OPERATIVE SCHEDULE SEEMED TO EXPAND; INCREASINGLY, PATIENTS were referred to me. I often arrived home late—late and tired. Between cases, I worked with Lisa on a speculative manuscript on ways to induce tolerance to transplanted organs. Celia and the kids soaked up a lot of my time and also rendered great emotional support to me. Thoughts about a DNA analysis were pushed from my mind.

So, it was with a bit of surprise when, returning to my office after a case a month later, there was a pink message note on my desk: "Call Dr. Dahlen."

"Hey, boots," he said on the phone, "come on over when you have chance. The DNA hair analysis is back." I could feel my heart accelerate, sense the sweat on my forehead.

My next patient was already in the induction room with the donor kidney on the way to the hospital by helicopter. The case was long; I got out of the operating room after seven. After a late dinner, Celia and I were in bed by nine.

"What's wrong, Peter?" Celia asked in the morning. "You kept me awake most of the night rumpling the covers, jousting with something in your sleep. Willis again? Another bad dream?"

"No, not Willis this time. Actually, I didn't sleep much. I guess I must be worried about my case."

"But you said you weren't operating today," said Celia.

"I meant worried about yesterday's case."

"You told me both of yesterday's cases went well."

"Yeah, I guess."

"Peter, you are not making sense. Something's on your mind. What?"

"Just tired, I guess. It's nothing."

After a quick breakfast, back at work, I made rounds on my patients, made some suggestions to the resident staff, then walked over to the medical school. My heart pounded.

"Morning, Harald. I got your message. What'd you find?"

"Peter, good morning yourself. Well, this is sort of interesting. Those three hair samples were all analyzable, and are indeed related, but in a funny way.

"Let's call the three hair samples 'a' for the dark, fresher, male hair, 'b' for the woman's hair, and 'c' for the other hair of in-between color, also male.

"First, c appears to be the son of a and b. If we had only hair from a and c, then each would have about half of the other's DNA and without knowing the age, either could be the father of the other. But since we have the mother, we know that c is the son because he also has about half his DNA from b. If c mated with b, with a as the offspring, then a would have half the DNA of b and c but that is not the case. Instead, c has about half the DNA of a and half from b. So, a and b are father and mother of c."

"But then it gets a bit strange, because hair from the father, $a,$ seems quite fresh and that from the son, $c,$ seems older. But forgetting that for the moment, there's something else that's strange. The mother and father seem related. The father has about five percent of the mother's DNA.

"Now let's go to an illustration for a minute. On average, a child has 50% of the DNA of each parent. The grandchild then has about 25% of the DNA of the grandparents. And the great-grandchild has about 12.5% of the great-grandparents, and of the great-great-grandchild, about 6.25%. Using the same analysis, two cousins would share about an eighth of their DNA, second cousins would share 1/32, or 3.12% of their chromosomes.

"As I am sure you remember from genetics class in med school,"

"Not much. Don't remember much," I said.

"Hush. I was about to say that none of these numbers is correct for any single relationship for a number of reasons, one of which is that the chromosomes are often passed down with changes between parent and child. Still, we can start with the averages I just told you about.

"So, back to your three sets of hair. In your case, the father - we call him "a" - shares about 5% of the DNA with the mother – called "b." Since there is a range of possible sharing percentages for any relative, the most likely relationship is 1/16 or 6.25%, which would occur with first cousins once removed. So, if your father is a cousin of a woman, you would have about 6.25% of her DNA. The next step away in family relationships would be a second cousin. They would have about 3.12% shared DNA, but the range would be from about a little less than 3%, up to just over 5%."

"So *a*," I said, "and *b*, who share about five percent of their DNA, are likely to be related by being first cousins once removed?"

"Yeah, that's about right."

"Any other possibilities?"

"Well, we talked about a second cousin. Could also be first cousin twice removed."

"And that's it?" I asked.

"Probably. Mathematically of course, *a* and *b* could be great-great-grandmother and great-great-grandson, or great-grand aunt and great-grandnephew. But that is silly. Although mathematically possible, it's biologically impossible. No great-great-grandmother could be young enough to mate with her great-great-grandson. She'd be way past fertility stage. Hell, Peter, she'd be way past life and long dead, most likely. Besides, who'd want to fuck someone that old?"

"Yeah, right. Thanks much, Harald. I owe you one."

"One bottle of Dom. Remember?"

"Okay. It'll be on your desk tomorrow."

CHAPTER 73

Peter

— 1994 —

T HAT NIGHT, CELIA ASKED ME ABOUT THE EXPENSIVE BOTTLE OF CHAM-pagne. "New girlfriend?"

"Nope." I crossed my arms, protectively. "I owe a guy at the medical school—I don't think you've met him—and this is my thanks. In fact, he negotiated this gift before he did the favor."

"What favor?"

"He's a geneticist, and a med school classmate. He helped with a case," I said. I looked away from her.

"For real? You look like you're struggling for an explanation," she said. "When you cross your arms like that, you are withholding some part of the story."

"No, really. This case is complicated. He's helping with a genetic analysis."

"That's not what you usually do, is it? I thought you checked blood types and cross-matched them and did some HLA thing between donor and re-cipient." She stared at me in an inquisitional way.

I hesitated, again averting her glance. "You're right, human leucocyte an-tigen. But we are starting a new trial. Trying to see if we can improve organ and recipient compatibility."

Celia didn't say anything, but skepticism etched her face.

In bed that night, she moved close and put her arms around me. "Peter, something's wrong. You're not acting normally. Last time you acted like this, it was about Maaijke, and then about Willis. Tell me."

"In the morning. Let's discuss it in the morning."

"Okay." She turned away from me in what? Scorn? Disappointment? As she had infrequently done before. I hated not feeling the warmth of her closeness. I reached out, touching her exposed shoulder. It was cold. She gave me both an actual and virtual cold shoulder.

CHAPTER 74

Peter

— 1994 —

I N THE MORNING, I AWOKE FEELING STRANGE. I LAY IN BED FOR A MINUTE, turned to Celia, who seemed to have forgiven me, and held her. "Something is in my head," I told her.

"Well, tell me about it. What are you thinking?"

"No, I mean something is in my head. Some *thing* that doesn't belong there."

"Well, everyone has thoughts they feel guilty about. Tell me."

"No, no. Something. Not a thought. A *thing* in there. I can feel it."

"Do you have a headache?"

"No."

"Pressure?"

"No."

"Peter, you make no sense. How can you feel something in your head if you have no symptoms? Do you mean like a tumor?"

"I don't know. I feel something is wrong in there."

"Well, let's see how you feel tonight. Come on. I'll make breakfast."

I had no case that morning. Instead, I visited one of my old medical school professors in the neurology division, Dr. Adam Reynolds.

"Thank you for seeing me, sir. I don't know if you remember me—I was a student back in the—" I was interrupted.

"Of course I remember you, Peter. Cowboy boots, big belt buckle, a bit older than the other students—navy pilot, right? And I tried to talk you into being a neurologist. Not much of a salesman, I guess."

I laughed. "Still the same infallible memory, though."

"So, Peter, what can I do for you?"

"Well, this is a bit strange; I'm even embarrassed to be here for what is probably nothing."

"Okay, tell me your symptoms."

"None."

"None? So why are you here?"

"Because I awoke feeling as if there is something in my head. Not a thought. Something foreign."

"Well, Peter, I must admit that to be a new one. Tell me about it."

"Well, Dr. Reynolds, that's it. I've never had this before; I've never seen a patient with this before. I...I guess I'm scared."

"Peter, I have seen everything there is to see in neurology. At least I think I have. And what you describe, I've never heard of. But let me look at you for a bit."

After he conducted a very thorough neurologic exam, he said, "Peter, I don't know if this will reassure you or not, but I find no evidence of anything wrong. To anticipate your next question, I do not recommend any further tests. No CT scan or anything like that. You are fine."

"As I said, I am embarrassed to have wasted your time. I never thought of myself as a hypochondriac, but I guess I must be."

It was Dr. Reynolds's turn to laugh. "No, Peter. Neither a hypochondriac nor sick. But why don't I leave you with an open invitation to return at any time. No prejudgment. Okay?"

"Okay. Thank you very much, sir."

That night, with no sick patients, and no cases that day, I had the rare good fortune to get home early.

At dinner, Celia asked about the thing in my head.

"I went to see Dr. Reynolds, one of my idols in medical school. He is still working, still brilliant as ever, and, as a neurologist, he was able to reassure me that I am okay. He even reassured me that I am not a hypochondriac!"

"I might have to change his mind about that," Celia said.

I smiled sheepishly and walked around the table to hug her.

The next day, it was work as usual. Two cases, work on a manuscript, resident evaluations.

CHAPTER 75

Peter

— 1994 —

A COUPLE WEEKS LATER, ON A SUNDAY, AS WE LAY IN BED SLOWLY COMing from sleep, Celia rolled toward me, took my head in both of her hands, and gave me a warm, full-dimpled, inviting smile.

"Okay with me, but what about the kids? You don't think they will be bouncing in the room any minute?" I said, quickly discovering she had something else in mind.

She laughed. "Sorry, Dr. One Track Mind, but that will have to wait. I only wanted to remind you of the omelets you promised.

So, omelets it was. In unison, Sam, Patsy, and Ben turned up their noses to the idea, so after juice and cereal they escaped the house to play outside.

"Spinach or asparagus, Celia?"

"Mmm, I think...asparagus. But that's not all, is it?"

"You need more?" I said with arched eyebrows.

"Of course," she said. "Always."

"Okay, Celia. Team approach. You do the asparagus; I'll do the mushrooms."

I washed the latter, blotted them dry, cut them, and threw them in the frying pan with a bit of olive oil, while Celia sprinkled the asparagus with oil, and broiled them. When she finished, I cut the tips into small bits, whisked the eggs with some water and cayenne pepper, then poured them into the omelet pan, already lined with sizzling butter. The asparagus tips and mushroom slices were distributed about the surface, followed by a handful of shredded Mexican cheese. After folding the omelet onto a warmed platter, we split it onto plates.

Celia wore an extreme grin.

"What?" I said. "You're thinking how lucky you married me."

"Yes, I am. And thinking how lucky for you, too. And how lucky we both are to have three such nice kids," she said.

"Remember breastfeeding them?"

"Sure. I remember how jealous you looked, too."

"No, I meant, remember what I said about their differences in their nursing tactics? Do you think what I said was true? That their future personalities could be predicted?"

"I thought it a silly idea then. But I think you might have been correct. Sam, the determined, focused nurser; Patsy, the distracted, take-forever nurser; and Ben, the laid back one. Now, with their developing personalities, they haven't changed that much. Sam is still determined, focused, and with enormous capacity to concentrate on whatever task she tackles. Patsy is the most social, talkative, gadabout of the three. And Ben, he drives me crazy with his casual approach to even the most trivial task. He daydreams his way through every project," Celia said.

"Yeah. They seem a lot more nature than nurture." And I thought, but would never say to Celia, how frightfully Sam reminded me of Maaijke. Same blond hair, same athletic inclination, same stature, vivid imagination, immense curiosity, overwhelming charisma. But, as much as Celia gave me understanding, the improbability, the contradictions about Maaijke had rendered discussing her a forbidden topic.

CHAPTER 76

Peter

— 1994–1996 —

THE NEXT COUPLE YEARS WHIZZED BY, ROUTINELY, ALMOST MONOTO-nously filled with daily excitement and new experiences for both of us, and for that matter, for Ben, Patsy, and Sam, too. Transplantation techniques and knowledge grew in an explosion, as did progress in rejection treatment. I was in demand as a speaker and was twice a visiting professor at other medical schools.

Each new grade brought thriving success to the kids. Sam was at right wing on the varsity soccer team from her freshman year. She didn't run with the ball; she danced with it, eluding the defense, pirouetting around them with the ball seemingly attached to her feet with bungee cords. Patsy managed to discipline her distraction and got consistently good grades, but she was still a social magnet. She was surrounded by other kids, like bait fish driven to the surface by predators are surrounded by swirling gulls and terns. And Ben continued with his casual academic approach, surprising us and even himself with effortlessly superior school performance.

Celia graduated, and now we had two Dr. Maasens in the family. I was so proud of her. She began working in a small animal clinic in Dedham, where she was allowed to follow her passion of a pure dog practice, which nicely balanced the practice of a veterinarian cat lover at the clinic.

CHAPTER 77

Peter

— 1996 —

B Y THE TIME THE EMTS ARRIVED, I WAS AWAKE, THE SEIZURE OVER.
"No, I certainly will not get into that ambulance. Anyway, I'm only tired and want to sleep a bit more before my case today," I said.

Finally, with my total intransigence, Celia apologized to the ambulance crew and dismissed them.

Then, my wife screamed at me for the first time since we were married. "Peter, you had a fucking seizure. You are not doing a fucking operation. Ambulance or not, we are going to the hospital. You and I. What was the brain doctor's name? We will see him."

"I don't know. What brain doctor?"

"Peter! Neurologist. Your teacher in med school. Name? Think!"

"Oh, yeah. Adams? No, Reynolds? Reynolds."

An hour later, Celia described my seizure to Dr. Reynolds. He examined me. I was still a bit sleepy.

"Mrs. Maasen…"

"Celia, please."

"Celia, Peter." His face was ominously serious. "We'll begin with an MRI. A seizure could be a one-off occurrence, or it could be serious. The MRI should tell us."

"Serious? In what way?" she said.

"Let's wait for the test, okay?" Reynolds said.

"Fine, if you will tell me what 'serious' might be."

"Well, possibly a tumor. But many other things far less serious."

The MRI was squeezed in late that afternoon.

The following morning, Celia answered the phone before the first ring finished and pressed the phone's speaker button so I too could listen.

"Mrs. Maasen—Celia, this is Dr. Reynolds. I am afraid that this is something potentially serious. A type of tumor. Could you both come into my office this morning?"

After no sleep, Celia and I, who felt much better rested, were back in the neurologist's office. Neither of us asked any questions, so Dr. Reynolds began. I felt as if I were about to hear a jury verdict, in which I was the guilty defendant.

"So, as you can see from these scan images, there is what appears to be a tumor. In fact, there appear to be several."

"Signifying what?" she said.

"Well, there is a chance that this is malignant, and we need to biopsy it to plan treatment."

"You have to cut his head open?" Celia asked.

"Well, no, not exactly. What we plan to do—it has already been scheduled for tomorrow morning by our chief of neurosurgery—is a needle biopsy. He will have Peter's head stabilized in what is called a stereotactic device. Based on the images from yesterday, it will guide a needle into one of the tumors, and that's it."

"You are going to stick a needle through his skull?"

"Well, first, he will be asleep. Anesthetized. Then, using a rounded drill bit—a burr, it's called—we create a small hole in the skull and the needle is inserted through the hole. It's quick. It's painless."

"And then? What are you expecting to find?" she asked.

After a long pause, and a sigh, he said, "Celia, we don't know, obviously. But I am afraid this could be a glioblastoma. We will know more—"

"No, Dr. Reynolds," I said. "I feel fine. I do. Really." But I was thinking, *Guilty as charged.*

CHAPTER 78

Peter

—— 1996 ——

ON THE DAY OF THE BRAIN BIOPSY, WE ARRIVED IN THE PREOPERATIVE clinic at 6:00 a.m. Afterward, I awoke in the late morning with Celia sitting on my hospital bed.

Dr. Reynolds and the neurosurgeon walked somberly into the room.

Celia began to cry. I tried to comfort her.

"Well," said Dr. Reynolds, "it is what I feared, a glioblastoma. And we need to talk about treatment."

I was more alert, more myself, than any time in the previous three days.

"No, no we don't."

"Of course we do, Peter," Celia said. The two doctors nodded.

"No. I repeat, no! I have seen too many of these. You can operate and won't get it all out. You can use radiation therapy. You can even do some types of immunologic treatment, trying to convince my body to reject the tumors. I've seen all. In exchange for a few extra months of survival, you would wipe out all my functioning humanity and working brain. Am I right?"

"Well, not exactly," the neurosurgeon said.

"Actually, Peter, you are at least partly correct," Reynolds said. "There are no good options. Please, go home, talk about it, call me."

Our kids were staying with a neighbor, so Celia stopped for take-out food on the way home. We ate in silence. Every few minutes, she jumped up, wrapped me in her arms, and started to cry. That night, Celia's tears soaked my pajamas so much that I had to change into a dry pair.

In the morning, Celia was finally able to talk.

"Even if there is a slight chance of curing this, shouldn't we take the chance?" she asked.

"Celia, you really do not understand. There is a slight chance of prolonging my life a few months. But there is no chance of cure. And the price to pay for the extra two months is that you would have a live body that was your husband, but perhaps no husband left. I cannot do that. I want to be as normal as possible for the short time I have."

"Peter, you can't die."

"Hon," I said, grabbing her and burying my head in her fragrant hair. "I am so sorry to put you through this. All of this. We can only hope; we can't change what is. So, we should both enjoy each other, enjoy our children, as long as we can. You know I love you."

"But I love you more."

"No, I more," I said.

CHAPTER 79

Peter

—— 1996 ——

W E BOTH CRIED—AND DID SO FOR MANY DAYS AFTER. EVERY DAY, I tried to help Celia, to support her, to comfort her. And we both tried to do the same for our three kids. I stopped my practice and every day tried to bring joy to our family. No longer incessantly busy and harried, the time seemed to drag with a lugubrious inevitability. Despite the underlying dread shared but now unspoken by all, I succeeded in lifting my family. During that summer, Celia and I returned to Provincetown, where we met. We returned to the secluded portion of the beach to recreate our early encounters and intimacy. We didn't have precisely the same type of experience as the first time, but it was emotionally healing.

Maybe because of the warmth and comfort from our time in Provincetown, I thought it might be a propitious time to talk with her about Maaijke. I broached the subject with Celia, thinking, knowing that it would cause her distress. But I had concluded that, armed with Harald's explanation of my possible (yet physically impossible) genealogy, I needed to make one last trip back to the Netherlands and to Spakenburg to look more carefully at the records of births, deaths, and marriages in the town office. It was more than a conclusion; obsession would be more like it. And with not much time left for me, I needed to get on with it.

"Celia," I said, digging my fingernails into my palms, hoping for a serene response.

"*What?*" she replied, clearly sensing from the way I said her name that something bad was coming.

"I need to go back to Spakenburg. I need to find out finally about my family before I die. Our kids deserve it. Please don't get angry." It was partly a lie. I was not doing it for our children, but for me. Would I see Maaijke again? I doubted it, and also feared that I might.

Celia looked at me for a long time, maybe five minutes, without saying anything. I was unable to hold her gaze. Then, she said very carefully and with a tinge of sadness, "Peter, I think I understand, and I won't stand in your way. I am against the idea. Nothing good can come from it. But with your health, I am going with you. No argument, please."

I gathered her into my arms, thanking her, both of us crying.

Part III

CHAPTER 80

Maaijke

— 1837 and 1996 —

I CONTINUED TO WORRY. IT WAS UNACCEPTABLE THAT I WOULD NEVER RAISE my children, that I would never see Peter again. I traveled to Amsterdam and went directly to the old university, the Athenaeum Illustre of Amsterdam, but did it in my own time, not Peter's time. Maybe I should have gone further in the future; I would have learned more. In the medical library there, I taught myself everything that was known—which was very little—about women dying after childbirth, from what was called puerperal sepsis. It was so difficult to study. Although what I read frightened me, the writing was so dense and required looking up so many words that it made me sleepy. I remembered when I read the book in England about the rabbit named Peter, and how the chamomile tea acted as a soporific for him. That's what those medical books were, soporifics. And every time my head fell to the book in sleep, I was back in my own home and had to start the journey over.

And then I went forward in time to watch over myself as I was birthing Martijn. It was dismaying, it was disgusting what I saw happen to me, to a Maaijke of several months in the future. I saw that Dr. Oosterhuis was right in predicting a smooth birth. Martijn's birth was easier than Pieter's for me. The midwife, backed up by Dr. Oosterhuis, delivered the baby. He, wearing the very nice coat he wore on the day I met him, helped with the afterbirth and I felt wonderful, almost as if I had been drinking an alcoholic drink.

Because I was now quite experienced, I did not worry when Martijn, frustrated at his unsuccessful nursing efforts, bruised my nipples and cried. Two days later, the milk came as it did with Pieter, and Martijn proved to be a hungry, sturdy suckler.

Later that night, I got very sweaty, and shivered. Something malodorous crawled through the air from between my legs. Mama came in with worry on her face. I would be better in the morning, she assured me.

What happened next, I could only observe from the past, because as it happened, I was in no shape to remember or report it. It was as if it were all happening to a different person, a Maaijke, but not me. Johanna, my mother, stayed with that Maaijke as she slid downhill. She applied cold, wet washcloths repeatedly to Maaijke's forehead when she was very hot; Maaijke felt better, but minimally, and only briefly. The fluctuations between shaking chills and hot sweats continued with greater swings: more severe chills, more drenching sweats. Maaijke's lower belly began to hurt. Any movement brought severe pain. Walking became impossible and she lay in bed, motionless, to avoid more pain.

Shortly, after she had severe lower abdominal pain, high fevers, and after bloody pus emanated from that Maaijke's vagina, she became delirious, then unconscious. The next morning, Dr. Oosterhuis pronounced her dead. Dead, despite all he had done for her. Dead on August 10, 1837.

Pieter and Martijn, my two beautiful boys, one needing a nourishing breast, neither with a parent. My parents suddenly becoming parents again. Mama finding a wet nurse for Martijn. For me and my two boys, that's what lay ahead, unless…

Because I had gone forward to see Martijn's birth, I knew that back in my real time, I was two months into my pregnancy. I knew I could not, would not allow that—my death—to happen. I had to find a way to change those numbers on the ruler of time.

I thought how to prevent my premature death. I spent nearly every awake minute scheming. After three days of almost no sleep, a plan grew.

While having Martijn in Peter's time might save me, leaving Pieter behind was not something I could do. But, if, if I could somehow bring Peter back to my time, he could save me. And that would have the added benefit of Peter being with me and being a father to Pieter and Martijn. I knew that I could not travel back in time before my actual life. I thought that would be true for Peter too. But I also knew that Pieter, and now Martijn, both conceived in the 1970s, did travel back to my time by being inside my belly. If there were a way to travel back with Peter inside me, would he come with me? And he could be there. Inside of me, that is. He has been there, gloriously he has been. One problem is that I go back to my own time when my concentration ebbs. But would it be possible for my concentration to ebb when Peter was inside me, making love to me? That is when my concentration is most fierce. Maybe right at the end, with him still inside, I could try to think of being home instead of thinking only of Peter, and we could travel together.

And maybe he would be there—here in my time—forever. He could run the farm with me, raise Pieter and Martijn with me. I became so happy thinking of our life together.

In that false glow, I did something I had never tried. I traveled to an old city in America in one of the early areas settled by people from Europe. Boston, I discovered, had an enormous, intricate, and rich history. It didn't occur to me that a country so young could have much history. Boston was only about 200 years old but already had a rich history by the time I was born. Much of that history seemed strange to me. For example, even before I was born, they had what they called a tea party, which sounds like anything but. For some reason, at the party, they threw a lot of tea into the harbor, apparently trying to complain about taxes. But I tried to ignore all of that. I was completely focused on finding Peter, on saving my life.

The first time I went, I found Peter in his office in a hospital next to the Harvard Medical School. Peter couldn't see me. He couldn't hear me, so there was no way to convince him to return with me. And worse, he seemed to be married to another woman, standing by him at his desk, even as I carried his next son inside me. Trying to think how to get him back, I lost my focus on being there and was suddenly back in my farmhouse with Pieter.

A few days later, I went back there, arriving almost a year later in Peter's time. I went directly to his office. He wasn't there. On a pink note on his desk, I read the words, "Remember appt. with Dr. Reynolds. Mass General. 2 pm." So, I went to this other hospital. I was able to find Peter in a white brick building at an old hospital. For some reason, they named the building after its color, which seemed strange. Or maybe they built it white because of its name. Inside, I found Peter in a doctor's office with his doctor. And with that same woman, his wife, named Celia.

I screamed and cried. I beat my feet on the floor until they hurt but failed to get his attention. Of course, no one could hear me. They definitely could not see me. I was, as usual when I travelled, invisible. I have never felt so bereft of hope. It was worse, I think, than when I saw myself dying from giving birth to Martijn. Worse, in part, because it might mean I would not be able to convince him to come back with me, which would be my death sentence. All this time, I was hoping that in some way, Peter and I could be united, could be married, could raise our family as we should. It is the way of things in the world, or should be, I think. But to find that he had given himself to another! I had a sudden, severe pain that seemed to cascade through every part of my body. My head felt as if it were preparing to explode. *Betrayed.* How could he? I gave him everything. Never would I have considered being with another. I wanted to hurt that woman. What could he see in her? I was younger and prettier, and I am sure I could satisfy him better. She was old. I hated to admit it…but she did seem nice.

But it got worse. The doctor—not Doctor Peter, but Peter's doctor—said that Peter had some terrible tumor in his brain. A tumor that would inescapably kill him, and soon. One for which there was no effective treatment.

Abruptly, I was back home and still dwelling on what I had seen and heard. Maybe I am hopelessly optimistic, but I realized that there was still a chance, and that my plan could be doubly happy: I might be able to save my life and save Peter's life too.

CHAPTER 81

Peter

— 1996 —

T HE NEXT DAY, CELIA AND I HAD SECURED FLIGHT RESERVATIONS, AND the day after that, we were on the way with a brief stopover in Reykjavik. As before, we rented a car when we arrived at Schiphol. The only rooms we could get were in the Hotel Sint Nicolaas, which I worried might be portentous. Worse, we were in the same room I had been in with Maaijke. I did not share that information with Celia.

After dinner and early to bed, we arose with the sunrise and had breakfast across the street. I stood from the table at nine o'clock to go to the town hall. Celia stood too, wanting to come with me. I started to object.

"Oh, no, Peter. Against my better judgement, I agreed to your coming here. But we are doing this together. I am going to see the records with you."

"Okay," I shrugged. That turned out to be a grievous error.

At the town hall, Betje, the same, very helpful clerk was there. She remembered me. When I told her that I would like to review the records again, and detailed for her which ones and which years, she went straight to her index file and then told me that some of them had already been pulled and were in use. She cautioned me that this person was also looking at records in the room, and we would need to be quiet.

I walked through the doorway, Celia on my heels, and came to an abrupt stop. Celia ran into me. Sitting with her back to me was a young woman with shoulder-length blond hair and an athletic-looking back, wearing a yellow sweater with short sleeves. A blue wool winter coat lay over the chair next to her. I could barely breathe.

Before she turned her head, she said, "Peter." Then, standing and turning in one smooth motion, she fixed on my eyes, while Celia stood behind me. Maaijke took two long strides and threw her arms around my neck. "Oh, Peter, it's been so long. I need you, need you badly."

I turned my head in time to see Celia's befuddled, angry countenance as she turned and stalked from the room. I yelled after her, to no avail. I tried to run after her, but I was held tightly by Maaijke and by the time I wrestled free, I could not find Celia. I returned to the room, back to Maaijke, who was still standing but crying, her sweater darkened where the tears had fallen.

"Peter," she said, sobbing. "Help me. I don't want to die. And I want to be with you always. And I know how it can be done, at least I think so."

I held her. "Maaijke, you have not changed." But she had, slightly. Her face was fuller and maybe I could even feel the swelling of early pregnancy pushing against me. And completely against my will, I was swelling against her.

"Peter, you have. You look older. I understand. It has been many years in your time but for me, only months. It doesn't matter. I love you more than ever. You still look younger than my husband when I married him. He is dead. By his own hand. And you can come back with me, and we can live to old age together and raise our children. I have it figured out. And from what is pushing into me, I know you want to be back with me, in me.

"Who was that woman?"

"My wife. We have three children."

"Oh," she said. "But what about us? I love you. I thought you loved me."

"I did. I still do, but Celia and our children…"

"No Peter, I am dying and you can save me, must save me. I want to raise our children. Pieter, I have told you about, and Martijn is in here now," she said, placing my hand on her lower belly.

"Maaijke, that's impossible. It has been many years since we were together. You can't be pregnant now from me."

"You read my letter the last time you were here. I explained it. Do I look any older than when we were together before Christmas in 1976? By my time, I am only a few months older. I know that by your time, the time I traveled to, it's fifteen years later. I came forward all these years because I need you to save my life, so I can raise my two children, *our* two children. You are a doctor. You can spare my life. Come with me and help with Pieter and Martijn. I didn't think I could take you back to my time, but I think I can. I think I know how."

"That's crazy. Anyway, I must stay with Celia, to raise my children, even if it is only for a few more months."

She said nothing at first and stared at me. Then she said, "What do you mean, 'a few more months?'" Strangely, she did not really seem surprised; she seemed as if she already knew.

"Maaijke, I am dying too, and there is nothing to save me. I have a brain tumor. A malignant brain tumor."

Another silence followed. Her crying resumed. Then her face brightened, she even started to laugh. "Oh, it's perfect, then. You can save my life. And I can save yours."

"No—"

"Oh, yes. When I am in a future time, as I am now, I have to keep concentrating to stay there. As soon as my concentration lapses, I am taken back to my time. And I always go back alone. But, if I allow my concentration to recede when you are inside me, then I think you will go back to my time with me. And then, you will no longer have your tumor, and you can save me from the infection—it is called puerperal sepsis—that kills me after Martijn is born."

She grabbed my hand, picked up her long coat, and began dragging me out of the building. I wanted to resist. I also wanted to go with her. And with my internal conflict subordinated to Maaijke's pleading and her appeal, I let myself be pulled by her. Of course, what I was doing was wrong, but perhaps I was doing it for partly altruistic reasons. If leaving would allow me to live, then even though I would never see Celia again, it would mean she and our children would never have to mourn my dying. And Maaijke could be saved. Our children would not be orphans. On the way, as I walked with Maaijke, I tried to convince myself that I was doing the right thing, that having sex with Maaijke was merely the means to a life-saving, salubrious end. Almost like when I tried to convince myself that dropping a bomb on Willis was an act of kindness.

We came to the long-ago familiar boxwood hedge. It hadn't grown. Through the tunnel we went, Maaijke looking back at me with her radiant face. And into the old gambrel-roofed brick house. Nothing had changed.

Up the stairs. I was no longer thinking of Celia, could no longer think of her. In the bedroom, Maaijke threw her coat over a chair. She kicked off her tailored leather shoes, the same ones I had seen before. Her skirt slipped to the floor, and with a practiced but slowly seductive move, she pulled her sweater up over her breasts and off. The scant cloth of her bra and panties were discarded. With the hinted fullness of early pregnancy, she was more lovely than ever. I felt as if I were suffocating. As protection, and almost as a mantra, I kept repeating to myself, "this is in everyone's best interest."

Except it wasn't, as I knew. I couldn't continue. Celia, ever and truly loyal to me. My children, my twentieth-century children. And what if what Maaijke said would happen did? Could I live in the 1830s? What if I couldn't come back? Maaijke had suggested as much. Anguish strangled me. In a few short minutes, I had to weigh my entire life, or maybe lives. Could I rationalize leaving Celia and my family for Maaijke and another family, if it even existed? Could I betray them? And who would I be betraying, Celia or Maaijke? And which children? Would saving my life and Maaijke's life be adequate justification? How could I be sure this wasn't some contrived story Maaijke told me? What would be in it for her? And if this was some sort of delusion of hers, or even mine, would it be—could it be—worth the betrayal of Celia, Sam, Patsy, and Ben?

And overlying this, clouding my reasoning was my undeniable and extreme arousal, the remembrance of which Maaijke made so excruciatingly vivid.

I placed my hands on her shoulders and pushed her away. Her expression suddenly changed from the joy I associated with her to a rapid transformation into sadness and horror.

"Peter, what's wrong?"

"Maaijke, I can't. I need my family; they need me. I can't desert them."

"But I love you. You love me. We have a family."

"No, I can't do it. I can't be that disloyal to my wife. And, also, I am afraid. What if I could not get back to my time?"

"But don't you care if I die as soon as Martijn is born?"

I gathered her back to me, squeezing her in my agony, and hers. "Of course, I care. But I think I can save your life without going back with you.

"First, tell me what happens to you," I said.

"After Martijn is born, a couple days after, I started to feel sick, and have a fever. Mom was with me, sponging my forehead to keep me cool. I got worse and within a week, I died. In the records, it was listed as puerperal fever."

"Do you have a doctor to deliver your baby? And did you for Pieter?"

"Not for Pieter. Mama delivered him at our house, with the help of my older sister and some neighbor ladies. It was difficult, and it hurt a lot, but everything seemed to go alright, and both I and Pieter were fine. But for Martijn, I have a wonderful doctor. Educated, so smart."

"And for your new pregnancy, does your doctor plan to deliver him in the hospital?"

"Oh, yes. Of course. It is the modern thing to do and is much better. He is at the university and travels to Spakenburg to teach. At the university, he takes care of pregnant women and teaches students by doing autopsies. He is widely respected."

"Maaijke. Listen to me very carefully, and I will save your life. Okay?"

She nodded yes. With dread written all over her expression, I could not be sure if she were listening or understanding.

"When you go back, dismiss your doctor. Do not give birth in the hospital. Tell your mother. Either find a midwife to deliver the baby or have your mother do it as before. And make sure everyone washes their hands really well before they help you deliver the baby. Wash all the way up to their el-bows. Make sure none of them is wearing long sleeves. Can you remember all of that? Can you do it?"

She cried convulsively, clinging to me. "But that makes no sense. The doctor knows the very latest techniques and has the most up-to-date knowl-edge."

"Maaijke, that doctor will cause you to die. I will tell you why, and why you must avoid him if you want to raise your children…our children.

"If you really come from the early 1800s, you would never have heard of Dr. Ignaz Semmelweis. In the middle of that century, he studied puerperal fever, and found that the chance of dying from this fever after childbirth was two to three times higher in the hospital, where doctors delivered ba-bies, than in the clinic, where only the midwives delivered babies. He con-cluded that the disease was spread from doctors and medical students who went from doing autopsies to delivering babies. This offended other doctors since it suggested that they were to blame for the maternal deaths, and they were. He was not believed in Austria and Hungary even though he achieved very low death rates by insisting that the doctors wash their hands with a chlorinated wash before delivering babies. Still, he was ostracized and died prematurely. He was forced into an insane asylum, where he died from ne-glect. Only later did doctors realize he had been correct. The deaths, we now know, were caused by tiny living cells called bacteria. They make infections. Have you ever seen pus in an abscess?"

She nodded.

"That is what bacteria do. They cause the body to fight them with white cells, cells that fight infection, and that causes the pus, the mixture of dead infection cells and the white cells.

So, when you go back, do what I said. Okay?"

Her crying had slowed. She nodded again. But she held me all the tight-er. Forcing myself to deny what I wanted, what we both wanted, I pushed away again and pulled her hands off me. I had become soft, and suddenly I was standing next to the tumbled-down foundation rocks of a house no longer there. Maaijke was gone. I had never been so exhausted, so depleted.

But now I felt as if I had finished a marathon. I knew I would never see her again.

As I walked toward the village center, these confrontations—with Maaijke, with my imminent death, with my sense of duty and integrity—whirled through my head like snakes writhing in a pile.

CHAPTER 82

Maaijke

—— 1837 and 1996 ——

MY LIFE ENDED. NO, OF COURSE IT DIDN'T, BUT THAT'S HOW I FELT. So inevitable did it seem that somehow Peter and I would be together forever that the final, inescapable outcome left me feeling desolate. Eventually, I decided that I could at least try to have Martijn and be with my two boys, the one not yet arrived. And that would require that I not die after giving birth. I wasn't sure that Peter was correct. How could the most modern, most respected doctors be causing mothers to die? But since I knew from the future records that I did die after Martijn's birth, any different course could not be worse.

It was enormously difficult to undo my relationship with my doctor. How could I tell Dr. Oosterhuis without hurting his feelings, without making him angry? How could I get Mama to deliver my baby when she was convinced the best way forward was with a highly respected doctor, one from the university?

I was afraid to tell Dr. Oosterhuis. So I started with Mama.

When I got to her house, she was in her favorite rocking chair, working with yarn of a light blue wool.

"Mama, what are you knitting?"

"Booties for the two new little feet on the new baby you are bringing to us."

"But how do you know it will be a boy?" I said, pretending that I did not already know.

"My baby, my grown-up baby, you are so pretty, it has to be a boy."

"Mama, you can't be sure." And then I burst into convulsive sobbing.

"What? What is it, Maaijke? You should be so happy now."

"Mama, I am afraid. Afraid I will die."

"Why? With Pieter, everything went fine. It will be the same. I promise."

"No, Mama. I don't like my doctor. I want my baby at home like almost everyone else."

"But you can have the best care. Bertus? Is that what is making you so sad? I know with him gone, it is hard for you, but you will be taking his memory forward with your new little one."

I looked at her as tears dripped on my dress.

"That's not it, is it?"

"No, Mama. No."

"Baby, I am so sorry. We forced you into marrying him." And she stepped into me, hugging me, and crying with me.

"But Mama, that's over. He's dead. I am crying because now I am going to die."

"Why? Why do you think that, Maaijke?" she asked.

"I don't know why. But I have a terrible feeling. Like I can see the future."

She started to get angry with me. "That is stupid. Maaijke, you have one of the best doctors. Don't be so stubborn."

"Okay, Mama. I admit I am stubborn. But if you want to make me go to Dr. Oosterhuis, when the time comes, I am going to tell no one and go out in the forest to have my baby alone."

I slammed the door behind me as I ran from her house. I fully expected her to run after me and give in to my demands. She proved me wrong, but only in the timing. After I had been home for two hours, she came to see me.

"I don't know why, my baby, but if you feel that strongly, your sister and I can deliver your baby at home. Antje will be happy to help. But together, you and I have to go and tell Dr. Oosterhuis."

Which we did. It was a most painful conversation. He took it as a grave insult, as if it were a personal criticism. I guess in a way, it was.

The next few months passed quickly. I was in good spirits, especially after I went forward in time a month after Martijn came and looked from then, backward until his birth. Nowhere in the records was my death recorded. And with my usual happy state back again, the darkness that I caused with Mama was wiped out by the dawn of my approaching new son.

Mama was good to her promise. She and Antje delivered my new baby boy on her kitchen table, after they both took off their over shirts and washed their hands and arms. They gave me a terrible tasting clear drink called jenever when my pains got bad. Our neighbor makes it from juniper berries, and the men—mostly the men—drink it at the tavern and then have trouble walking home. But it made me feel much better. Most of the pain was over, and I think I must have bled quite a bit, but that seemed to stop when Mama pushed up a thin towel soaked in very hot water after Martijn came out, followed by my afterbirth, and she also placed a hot towel on my belly and pushed the two towels together.

And although I was very weak for a few days, I had a glorious sense of good health, and I was alive and fine a week later.

Thank you, Peter, thank you for my life. And thank you for Martijn.

CHAPTER 83

Peter

—— 1996 ——

I FOUND MY WAY BACK TO THE CENTER OF TOWN AND IN THE TOWN HALL, talked to Betje again.

"Of course, you can look at the records. I have not even put them away. What do you want to see?"

"Can you first show me an index of the documents?" I said. "Show me Maaijke Maasen's children's births."

She found the names of Pieter and Martijn and followed the references to the documents where we found the birth of Pieter on May 13, 1834, and of Martijn on August 4, 1837.

"Now, can you find the date of Maaijke's death?"

"I thought you already looked at that with me. A week after Martijn was born."

"Yes," I said, "but once more. Please."

So, she went back to her master index and said, "Hmm, that is strange. I am sure I saw that she died about a week after Martijn was born."

"And?"

"But this shows that she died in 1876 at age 61. Remember, her sons went to America in 1854."

Then she showed me the records. Missing was what I had previously seen, the death of Maaijke in 1837, and instead, her death was recorded thirty-nine years later!

She had taken my advice!

I ran back to the hotel.

"You are too late," the clerk said, as I rushed past him and ran up the stairs.

"Peter," the note lying on the bed started. "I have gone home." It was unsigned but in Celia's unmistakable bold hand.

I swore and hurt my fist against the unyielding wall. And I cried. I had now lost the only two important women in my life, and all through my own stupidity.

I scooped all my clothes and toiletries into my suitcase and, stopping at the front desk barely long enough to submit my credit card, drove back to Schiphol, turned in the car, and went to the ticket desk. The clerk was kind enough to tell me that the flight Celia took had departed a half hour earlier. I was able to exchange my ticket for another flight, but it didn't leave until later that day. And it was to New York, not Boston, landing shortly after midnight. I took it.

I got the first shuttle from Kennedy Airport to Boston at 7:00 am. I didn't know how Celia had made it from the airport; I still had the parking ticket for our car. Exchanging ticket for car, I drove back to Dedham, first south on I-93, then west on 128, and then up to Dedham. At least that is how I would normally go, but I remember none of the trip. I was sweaty, alternating with chilly. I was filled with dread that Celia would not be there. I parked in the driveway, walked up to the garage, looked through the window, and saw her car. And a new dread replaced the old one: what would I say to her? What could I say?

I went into the house through the kitchen door, desperately trying to think of an appropriate story to tell her without outright lying. As soon as I entered, and looked up, Celia was leaning with her lower back against the kitchen counter, her arms folded across her chest, a face without expression, and she said nothing. She was surrounded by a keep-your-distance aura.

I moved toward her and threw my arms around her. She did not move; she did not respond. It was like hugging a statue, but a warm one. I pulled away from her. She stared at me. Finally, she said, "well?"

So sudden was my encounter with her that I completely abandoned any plan to mollify her, and blurted out what happened. I told no lies. But I was unable to tell the entire truth.

"I saved her life, Celia. That was Maaijke, the one I told you about. She wanted me to go back with her, back to 1837, back to prevent her death right after her child was born. Instead, I told her how to avoid the postpartum sepsis from which she would die. Then I went back to the town hall and looked in the records again. There was no entry for her death in 1837, but we found that she died in 1876. So she followed my advice, avoided the infection, and died much later. Then I ran back to the hotel, but I was too late. All I found was your note."

"Wait, stop," Celia interrupted. "So, you want me to believe this girl is from 1837? That this Maaijke was the one with whom you had a short affair in 1971 when she was eighteen, and then again five and a half years later in 1976, when she would have been twenty-three or so, and you now see her in 1996 and she looks no older? And it's been almost two decades since you have seen her, and she throws her arms around you as if it's been a week since she saw you? And she looks at you as if she wants to rip your clothes off?"

Celia started to beat upon my chest with anger, but she was crying, too.

"She *wanted* you, and not only for a medical opinion. And I also know how poorly you lie. You have had too little practice doing it. So, do you want to tell me the story? Or leave?"

I sighed, and sank down into a kitchen chair, defeated. "Celia, I didn't lie, and nothing happened between us."

"Peter…?" Her voice was tremulous with threat and disbelief.

I didn't try very hard to conceal how miserable I felt. Celia grabbed a dishtowel and dabbed my eyes. "She wanted to take me back. Both to save her and to be her husband. I told you about her first son, and she is now pregnant again, with my baby. I think I believe her. I know she believes it. She imagines herself into different times but can only interact with people when in Spackenburg. With me. She thought she could take me back to 1837 but only if she made the trip with me inside her. I admit, I considered it. Were it possible, I might no longer have my tumor. Yes, she tried to seduce me, but I was too afraid I might end up stuck in the last century, and besides, I couldn't betray you and our kids. I told her no and told her how to avoid getting puerperal sepsis—and suddenly she was gone, and I was no longer standing in her house but by the ruins of an old cellar."

"I can't believe it. If she is two months pregnant now, it's from someone else, not from you. And how old is this first child you claim to be yours? The one born 25 years ago, the one named Pieter?"

"She told me he is going on four."

"Peter," she said, as I searched vainly for some sympathy in her demeanor. "It is not possible or believable."

"Celia, remember I told you about my classmate, Harald Dahlen? You thought I was not telling you the whole story. You were right. I said he was helping with better matching for transplant patients and donors. Well, instead, I gave him samples of hair from a locket Maaijke had when I met her for the second time, after the birth of Pieter. The locket had samples of her hair, of Pieter's, her son, and I gave him some from mine. One genetic, mathematical possibility—not a mathematical certainty, but possibility—is that Maaijke and I are Pieter's parents, even though I know that seems biologically impossible."

"But you already traced your ancestry directly back to Pieter and then to Maaijke, who you say are your great-grandfather and great-great-grandmother. You expect me to believe you are the father of your great-grandfather? And Peter, in the time left, please, please do not ever mention that girl again."

And with that, she turned from me and ran up the stairs. I stood there numbly in the kitchen for maybe an hour, then followed her. I climbed into bed, facing her back, which she implacably presented to me while feigning sleep.

When I awoke, she was desperately holding me in a tight embrace, my face wet with her tears.

"Peter, you had another seizure. I didn't call the ambulance. It was about four hours ago, and now you are finally waking up. It's your tumor, isn't it?"

"Yes. Don't let me go. Not ever. Please."

That afternoon, Dr. Reynolds saw us in his office.

I said very little; I knew.

Celia said, "How much time do we have?"

"I can't tell you," he said. "It could be any day. It could be a month. But not long."

We both thanked him, both dry eyed, until we got in our car. As we cried together, Celia held me for a long time.

"I love you, Celia."

"I love you more."

"No, I more."

We smiled at the worn mantra, smiled while crying. Celia drove us home.

She made a wonderful dinner for us, for all five of us. The kids were somber, reflecting our mood.

Celia and I went to bed late.

"Thank you, my love. You have been, you are a wonderful wife." She held me fiercely.

Ever since the diagnosis, I tried to be a bulwark for her, and maybe I was the strength on which Celia survived. My facade was very convincing, I thought. Or maybe it was Celia who had the convincing facade of bravery. But one night, she was awakened by our bed shuddering. Facing her, I was crying, again. I couldn't find the peace to accept this.

"Celia, I'm afraid."

"I know, Peter."

"I don't think you do, not fully. It is not the dying; it is leaving you behind. Never to hold you, to be held by you. It is never seeing our kids grow up. Never able to play with them, teach them, watch their graduations. Never anything. All my life, I have had fears and have overcome them, given the appearance of strength, but it's false. I can't do this. Dying is hard. Help me. Please."

Celia, crying even harder, said, "Hon, hon, I…" Holding each other, we finally fell off to a sleep of no rest with Celia spooned into my back, arms around my chest.

Afterword

Celia

— 1996 —

T HE NEXT DAY, WHEN CELIA AWOKE, SHE FOUND PETER VERY STILL. HE didn't move when she prodded him. Not breathing. Cold to her touch. She barely cried; she had already grieved his loss. She got up, gathered the three kids around her, and they knelt by the bedside, praying but composed, and then she called the funeral home.

The crowd overflowed the Harvard Memorial Church. The eulogies were warm and often funny. The warmest, most sincere, and humorous was from his old resident colleague, Manny. A young, pregnant, blond woman, unnoticed, unseen, watched from the back of the church.

The private burial was two days later. The four of them each laid a lily on the casket before it was lowered into the earth. First Celia, grief etched into her face. Then Sam, grim, jaws clenched tightly together, oblivious of anything other than the flower and the casket. Then Patsy, crying and striking out with her hand to chase away a bee. And finally Ben, eyes closed, scowling as he held the stem with two hands before placing the lily on the casket and, eyes still shut, allowing a glimmer of a serene smile as he stepped back.

Maaijke

—— 1837 and 1996 ——

I SAT NEAR THE BACK OF THE CHAPEL. THE ORGAN MUSIC WASHED OVER me in cleansing, calming waves. I could not escape the finality of it all. He had been everything to me. Now, seeing Peter lying there, my life was also altered, a large part of it ended. I could never be with another. I had Pieter, and would soon have Martijn too. But the irreversible conclusion that I would never lie with Peter, share our children with him, leaves me empty. In my time, I am officially Bertus's widow, which is of no personal relevance to me. But with Peter's death, I am emotionally, grievously, irrevocably an actual one. At least Peter has saved my life, for which I should be grateful. Grateful for my desolation.

I went to the burial, watched his three other children place lilies on his coffin, stared at his oldest daughter. She could have been me when I was her age, not only in appearance but in demeanor.

I left a note on his tombstone.

Celia

— 1996 —

THE NEXT DAY, CELIA RETURNED TO THE GRAVE. LYING AT THE BASE OF the tombstone was a folded note. She opened it and read the words written in flowing cursive: *"I loved him too. M"*

ACKNOWLEDGEMENTS

There are so many to thank for the advice, suggestions for revisions, and overall encouragement (and occasionally discouragement), but I know exactly where to start: with the late Mildred McConkey. She was my high school senior English teacher in Kalamazoo who demanded that every student in her class write an essay to present every day. No prescribed topic. No limitations except that it had to be at least a full page. Fiction or nonfiction. She read and critically, expertly commented on each essay. Her literary seeding, at least in my case, landed on fallow ground, only to germinate much later. She was terribly demanding; we all loved her.

The author Kathryn Lasky headed me in the proper editorial direction with her referral to David Groff of New York who read an early version of Maaijke and said he liked it, but…. That "but" caused me so much work as I completely rewrote the book, resulting in it being so much better. The book was originally told from the viewpoints of Peter in the third person, and Maaijke in the first person. David cajoled / badgered me into rewriting it as two first person accounts. I am grateful that he stuck with me for several versions.

He subsequently introduced me to Alice Peck who seamlessly picked up the editorial responsibilities. She too caused me a lot of work, and further rewriting, all of which proved immensely beneficial to the final product.

Except that it was not the final product since Alice handed me to Crystal Sershen who billed herself a copy editor but was much more. She so far exceeded her remit that she became a third editor, much to my benefit and to that of the final product.

Duane Stapp turned what was an unprofessional book into a sleek, print-ready book with his expert cover and interior design. He also guided me into the foreign (to me) realm of book publishing.

I was lucky to have a coterie of talented readers of my many versions of the Maaijke manuscript. Tim and Julie Lutts spent an entire evening with me giving invaluable suggestions, plus Julie corrected my staid nomenclature for women's underwear.

Georgia Davis, longtime friend, and colleague, read one of the early versions of the book. Her early enthusiasm helped sustain me when plowing through subsequent versions would occasionally seem too tedious to continue.

Donna Thorland, the widely read author, pushed me ahead with encouragement after she read an early version. Later, when I was foundering with the process of publication, she sat with me in our dining room for two hours and then exchanged numerous emails with me as she donated too much of her own time in allowing me to profit from her immense knowledge of the book industry.

Another of our neighbors, Michael Selbst. Michael offered valued advice and the most entertaining comments of any of my readers.

My sailing friend, Chris Knight was an enthusiastic early reader who will certainly be disappointed that I did not follow his request to include more about the Navy experiences of Peter.

Bruce Cutler, my fellow intern, and subsequent colleague for decades, had cogent observations, and contributed to maintaining my humility.

Edna Kaplan and Barbara Ferro proved most helpful with astute assessments and suggestions for avenues to pursue in the complex, difficult field of getting a book published.

Debra McGuire spent hours with me and the book, working with me towards a publication goal. I am indebted to her devoting time to me and Maaijke amongst her movie costuming commitments, and to her reading fervor.

To the late Stephanie Baas I have great gratitude. This wonderful lady and dear friend read the book with critical, perceptive comments despite the progressive nature of her own difficulties.

Brother and sister, Charlie and Holly Whitin were early, savvy and perceptive readers with astute comments. Their enthusiasm buoyed me.

Rachel Day was a thoughtful, thorough reader with kind, helpful thoughts about the book.

In the 1970's, Sarah Ribeiro caught her finger in a closing car door and she has been my friend ever since I sewed her laceration. She read Maaijke late in its evolution and sent me encouraging assessments and suggestions.

Neighbors Jann Crespo and Lynda Pifrin refrained from letting friendship stand in the way of honest and valuable critiques, while at the same time gave me impetus to persist with the development of the manuscript.

Barbara Mack asked me for some information and photos for a Newport Bermuda race article she wrote. I turned the table on her, and she graciously read and then gave me valued feedback on Maaijke.

Rick Smith and I had several sessions discussing the book over coffee and pastries. His knowledge and unique views made these meetings almost lessons in philosophy. I appreciate his help greatly.

With his keenly enthusiastic remarks, Mark Kridler was the ultimate cheerleader of my efforts.

How could I subject anyone to reading and rereading nearly every one of the versions and rewrites of this book? Well, my wife Addie did and in addition to her support in all of my life, I am especially indebted to her for her helpful criticisms, and extreme patience with me as I became a writing recluse, cooped up in my office. She was a superb sounding board.

As a puppy, our dog used to romp until exhausted with Racket Shreve's puppy, bringing happy entertainment to all four of us. Racket, a friend, and neighbor is also a great and prolific artist so when I needed a cover, it was Racket to whom I turned with the result being the evocative watercolor cover gracing this book. Thank you, Racket!